Clock Watchers

2016

The Collected Works of Seaholm High School's
Creative Writing Students

Edited by Diana Kathryn Plopa

Grey Wolfe Publishing, LLC
PO Box 1088
Birmingham, Michigan 48009
www.GreyWolfePublishing.com

© 2016 Grey Wolfe Publishing, LLC
Published by Grey Wolfe Publishing, LLC
www.GreyWolfePublishing.com
All Rights Reserved

ISBN: 978-1628281729
Library of Congress Control Number: 2016959940

Clock Watchers 2016

The Collected Works of Seaholm High School's Creative Writing Students

Edited by Diana Kathryn Plopa

Forward

Rachel Guinn; Seaholm High School Principal

Seaholm Creative Writing classes and Grey Wolfe Publishing have joined forces to create *Clock Watchers*, an anthology of writing.

With a goal of reaching beyond the walls of the traditional classroom, our writers were compelled to edit, revise and meet deadlines following the established protocols of Grey Wolfe Publishing. In short, our students had to live the life of a writer, creating literature and working in a writing environment.

The genesis of this idea came from Diana Kathryn Plopa, associate publisher, editor, and a member of NEXT Writers, a 50+ Community group, who came to Seaholm for a two-week workshop. The goal of this project was twofold: collaboration between the senior and student communities and leading our students through the creative writing and publishing process.

The publication of *Clock Watchers* was celebrated the evening of December 5, 2016, in the NEXT headquarters near Seaholm.

Introduction

Peter L. Shaheen; Creative Writing Instructor

We live and breathe words. We assign names to everything—events, images, emotions, places, and even people. Language is how we translate the world. We hunt for perfect verbs and for delicious adjectives to express our ideas. We only fail when we fail to conjure the magic in words to express ourselves appropriately. The act of writing is not only an attempt to ascribe words that describe the wonder around us it is also an attempt employ the power of language to make sense out of an often confusing and irrational world.

There are those who write to discover what they think, and there are those who write to construct a point of view that they wish others to embrace. Words are also the material we use to reveal our minds and spirit. For this reason, writing is also a dangerous activity. Both are risky business because the writer displays himself or herself to the world. The writer is never certain of the response. Yet in the act of writing, the writer reveals something of him or herself and opens him or herself to the world's embrace or the slings and arrows of the reader.

The creative writing classes of Seaholm High School have taken a small, courageous step into the world of writing. There is much to admire in the courage of these young writers in their effort to reveal something about their minds and their souls.

Since we are novices, we have not fully honed our craft, but we are announcing ourselves as writers. We build worlds with words and tear them down too. We invent characters and endeavor to create insights into our lives and times. While we are works in progress, there is much that is rich and literate in our voices.

In short, over the course of this class, we have done our best to live and breathe words—to discover the magic inherent in language.

Acknowledgements

Diana Kathryn Plopa; Associate Publisher, Editor

One of my favorite roles, working with Grey Wolfe Publishing, is as a facilitator of writing workshops. I love sharing with people of all ages the wonderment of becoming a published author. There is no greater joy, for me at least, than watching the face of a new writer as they learn their craft and revel in the moment of first publication. Whether mentoring a youngster or a seasoned adult, nurturing the creative process never grows tiring.

Teenagers are masters of the Universe. They have a gentle wisdom that is far beyond their years, and they can easily express that knowledge through their writing practice. To work in a creative space with teenagers is to understand a new way of thinking and seeing the world, and its myriad motifs. Teens have an abundant sense of powerful energy which allows them to seek out new solutions for challenges ranging from the simple and mundane to grandiose issues that affect people the world over.

In this two-week creative writing workshop, we dove deep into craft, investigating the twenty major plots and forty-five major character foundations. We reviewed a version of Joseph Campbell's *Hero's/Mythic Journey* and investigated emotional motivations in story and essay. The students explored the importance of dialogue and dialect as it affects character, scene, and setting. An emphasis was placed on the technique of "show vs. tell" and students were encouraged to let their imaginations run wild... or tackle whatever social mores intrigue them. The program ended with a brief introduction to the editorial process and constructive peer review.

Grey Wolfe Publishing offered this workshop as a community service project for Seaholm High School. The result of our work together is the anthology, *Clock Watchers 2016*, which you now hold in your hands. On December 5, 2016, we held a Book Launch Event to give the students a true understanding of the "full-circle" experience of being an author. Some students were selected to read their work to an audience, and we sold books and held a "Signing Party" afterward. Proceeds from the sales of this book are returned to the school to enhance their literacy programming.

I am extremely grateful to Ms. Rachel Guinn, principal and Mr. Peter Shaheen, instructor, for giving me the opportunity to mentor their students and help them to produce this extraordinary collection.

I am very proud of these students and the tremendous amount of creativity and effort they put forth toward creating this book. They are an amazing collection of young writers!

Contents

1.
A Day In My Life
Grace; Senior

5:15 AM. That's what my alarm reads in a bright and loud red. 5:17 AM is usually when I roll out of bed and hit the floor. Then I slowly put on my suit, sometimes also on the floor. Then I exit my house, sitting in my car for a good two minutes, just trying to work up the courage to actually leave. Then when I finally do, I always have to put music on, it can range from really emotional songs to hardcore rap. What music I pick just depends on whatever mood I'm in. My drive to school is actually the most relaxing part of my day. There is no one ever on the road, and everything is just really quiet, and it always relieves some of my stress. When I arrive at school, everything changes.

Getting out of the car takes me at least another two to three minutes, and when I finally get out, it takes another two minutes to enter the school because I walk at a pace slower than a snail. When I finally make it to the locker room, I make the most of the time I get to sit on the bench until everyone starts getting up and moving to the pool. Finally, I make it out of the locker room. Getting into the pool has got to be the hardest part of my day. I'm always the last one in, and I have to either get pushed in by someone or have to get a running start into the water. Once I actually get into the water, it's not so bad. I zone out during the whole hour, get yelled at a few times, but it's not too horrible.

Getting out of the water is one of the best feelings in the world. I leave the pool and take a shower for at least ten minutes, and it's one of the best parts of my day. Depending on the day it will take me either five minutes to get ready, or it can take me thirty minutes to get ready. Another huge highlight of my day is when I leave the locker room and see pile and piles of food made by the parents for the swimmers. The cheesy potatoes they make is the main reason why I keep swimming. I love getting to sit down in the pool hall and eat breakfast with my team; it is for sure another great part, but then all of this is gone when I hear the ringing of the warning bell for school and everyone begins to get up and leave.

I slowly begin my walk to class. Never once have I made it on time to this day, but it's my goal to do it at least once this term. 1st hour passes, then so does 2nd, and by the time 3rd rolls along I am completely drained. The walk to 3rd hour is the hardest walk of my day, I go from opposites ends of the school, and there are way too many stairs involved. I finally get to the top of the stairs and file into class. 3rd hour is also usually a blur, and I don't really retain anything. My eyes are always on the clock just waiting and praying it will ring so that I can go to lunch. When it finally does, all of my energy comes back to me, and I rush out the door. I will either go out with my friends for lunch, go to the library, or sometimes I will just pass out in my car for forty minutes. Whenever me and my friends have a rough day, are go-to lunch spot is always Burger King. Usually, all of us order the chicken fries and some kind of shake, and it always brightens up our day a little bit.

But then, lunch is over and my energy level plummets. This is always the point of the day when I feel like I'm gonna just give up and call it quits. My eyes begin to droop, my head begins to ache, and my body begins to shake. Walking back into the school just tears me apart, and there are some days when I don't even make it in. On the days I find the courage to make it in. I get into my class and try my best. However, ten minutes in, my face hits my desk and doesn't leave until that next bell rings. Then off to my final class of the day, AP Calculus. By this point, I'm awake and ready to go, but still, I'm not able to retain anything throughout that period. I always leave there more confused than when I entered it.

Then the final bell rings, and it's off to swim practice, or in today's case, a swim meet. I don't have to be back to school for an hour, so I race out of the parking lot and go crash into my bed for however long. I get, some days it's a full hour and some days it's five to ten minutes. I take whatever I can get. Then after the very wonderful nap, I head back to school.

When I walk back into the pool, it sucks all of the energy I had left. We all set up the pool, and usually, no one wants to help, so it takes a lot more time than it should. When it is finally done, we all go stretch for warm-up which mostly consists of no stretching and just talking. Then warm-up begins, which is also usually a blur but is over very quickly. After the warm-up, we all go to the hallway and my coach tells us what we are swimming. Whenever he tells me I'm in the one hundred butterfly, I usually cry for a few minutes, but then I have to pull myself together. One fun part about the meet is when we get to do the cheers before it starts. I get to lead them, and it always gives me the extra energy I need to make it through the meet. Then the meet begins.

Diving is first, and this is when I try to get a quick nap in, but it doesn't go very long before I am screamed at by my fellow teammates and coaches. Then diving is shortly over and its time for me to swim. The first relay is never that bad, its two lengths in the pool and then I'm done. I'm done, for like five minutes until I have to get in again. The worst event of the night is the one hundred butterfly. It gives me so much anxiety and always makes my stomach go in knots. I step up to the block to do this horrendous event and take off. The first three lengths go okay, but then I hit the third and final turn, and everything goes downhill from there. My legs give out, and I close my eyes, and I put my head down and just go. Once I touch the wall I look up at the board, realize that gained two seconds, cry for a few seconds, but then I get out and go warm down, completely avoiding my coach. The rest of the meet is a total blur, but finally, it ends, and all that's left is to take down the pool.

This takes two times longer than setting it up. By that point, everyone is exhausted and just wants to go home. Eventually, I'm not sure how, it gets done, and everyone files out. Another plus during the meet is the food that is provided for us after, it's what gets me through the meet. But, because the pool take-down always takes four hours, I never ending up getting much. At that point, I just storm out and book it to my car. The car ride home usually just consists of emotional songs and a lot of tears.

When I finally get home from my meet, at approximately nine to ten, I am so tired and depending on how I'm feeling, I will either do all of my homework or not even take my backpack out of the car. When I finally give up on it, I put it all away and jump into my bed. Then I always wonder why I keep doing this to myself if it's going to make me this miserable. Then I remember how good I feel after I finished it and how much faster of a swimmer it makes me. I also try to think about how many amazing friends I have made because of it. Then I realize that it is all worth it and that's the reason that I am able to continue this cycle day in and day out. This is the last year of my 13th and final year of swimming, and I am going to miss it like crazy when it's gone, so I always try to make the best of it even at five o'clock in the morning

2.
A Sonnet For Abby
Emma Goodman; Junior

I remember when you were a puppy like me
You would run around happy, and blissful
Ever since the little girl you were graduated
I feel that I'm unneeded and purposeless

I miss the way you used to greet me when you got home from school
I no longer see your backpack at the door
I miss the way you would hold me when you needed me
I no longer get hugs the way you used to

Today when I was taking my daily nap I thought I heard you
My canine instincts kicked in, and I knew your scent
I rushed to the door to find you, college apparel in hand
And all that sadness rushed away

Although our time together is space
The thought of you is forever in my heart

3.
Abducted
Sydney Schulte; Senior

Jamie's head slumped against the window of the speeding train as she started to doze off about fifteen minutes after the train's departure. She woke suddenly from the sound of her cabin's door being slid open. Jamie looked up to see who was bothering her spare few minutes of rest and saw a handsome stranger gazing back at her. He smiled kindly at her, his hazel eyes glistening with a mischievous look, and showed off his unrealistically white teeth. His seemingly flawless appearance gave Jamie a suspicion that something about him had to be tragically imperfect.

"Is this seat taken?" The man flashed another artificial smile her way.

"No." Her response was short and concise, hoping she would give him the impression that she was in no mood to hold a polite and pointless conversation that neither of them would remember a few years down the road.

"Alright then." He sat on the plush padded bench across from Jamie and brought his small pack next to him. He extended his hand to her.

"My name is Nate."

"Jamie." She shook his hand quickly and returned back to the book she was reading before she began to fall asleep. As Nate sat, he took in the details of the frail-looking woman that sat across from him.

He had noticed how her fingernails were completely rigid from being bitten off. Along with that, big purple circles had formed under her eyes. Her short brown hair appeared to not have been brushed in an unusual amount of time, and her clothing appeared to be wrinkled and tattered as if she had worn them for days in a row. Jamie's suitcase was paralleled with her appearance, which was splayed wide open on her seat with the articles of clothing inside of it crumpled as much—if not more than the dress and wool pea coat she was wearing. Jamie's presentation surely made her appear years beyond her actual age, looking more like forty years old than a mere twenty-five.

"Are you going to do anything, or just sit there and stare at me for the entirety of the three-hour ride?" She snapped at him, her voice as cold as the crisp autumn air that was outside of the warm comfort of the train.

He seemed to be shocked at how blunt she seemed to be, the reason being a complete stranger should show a bit of politeness at the least. Nate shrugged this off and unfolded a newspaper he had gotten from his bag and began reading.

Jamie read her book as well, but still had an uneasy feeling regarding the suspicious man sitting across from her. The crisp pages of the novel she had read many times over and over again didn't hold the answers to who the man in front of her was. Jamie narrowed her eyes at Nate; trying to give her best impression that if he tried anything with her that she would fight back with everything she had.

He looked up from his newspaper to see Jamie's death glare from across the cabin.

"Is there a problem?" Nate inquired in a polite tone, once again showing Jamie the proper way to treat strangers.

"No, no problem at all." Her sarcastic response startled him for the second time. Deciding to take the high road, Nate spoke first after their second suspicious exchange.

"So why are you headed to London?"

"Why do you want to know?"

"Just being kind, no need to get defensive."

"I'm not defensive!"

"Of course not, I'm sorry."

"If you really need to know, I am going to visit family."

"Oh, that's nice." He left it at that, not wanting to poke the bear any more than he already did.

The train came to a screeching halt, throwing Jamie to the other side of the small compartment and nearly onto Nate's lap. Nate helped the poor woman back onto her feet, who was shaking from the sudden fall. He looked out the doors that opened into the corridor, to see the hallway bursting with confused passengers, complaining about how late they were going to be because of this unscheduled stop. Nate returned to the cabin and closed the sliding door, causing the complaints of their fellow passengers to be somewhat muted.

"What on earth is going on out there? We weren't supposed to have a stop."

"No idea, the hallway didn't hold any sort of explanation."

The pair looked out the window, hoping to find some answers. The grassy hills stretched on for miles until they met with the overcast skies, not a single person in sight. The loudspeaker buzzed to life, and the conductor's voice echoed down the crowded halls and cabins.

"Ladies and gentlemen, we apologize for this inconvenient delay. However, we are having some technical difficulties but will be back on our way in about ten minutes. Thank you for your patience."

The passengers groaned simultaneously, each one of them not wanting to spend more time than they had to on the train. Alas, the passengers made it back to their cabins, leaving the corridor barren once again.

One of the train's attendants pushed a mid-sized cart to their door and knocked softly. Nate went to the door and opened it, smiling.

"Complementary snacks for our passengers; take what you'd like." The train attendant had a smile plastered on his face, but his eyes remained void of happiness. His cheesy red felt uniform was not suitable for a man of his enormous stature.

"Fantastic, Jamie would you like anything?" He beckoned his travel companion over to the treat-filled cart.

Jamie stood up and walked over to the cart, studying the contents intently, running her thin fingers over each of the options. She finally decided on a bag of chips, but when she went to pluck them out from amongst the others, the man's hand stopped her. She looked up at him, her short height and his enormity made quite a size difference.

"Is there a problem?"

"No, ma'am."

Two other men sprung out from the hall in identical uniforms to the first one. This took both Nate and Jamie by surprise. The two men that appeared from obscurity began to walk closer until Jamie and Nate were trapped in the back corner of the small room.

"Take the man too; he could be useful," the first man talked to the other two, giving commands.

The threatening men took cloths soaked in various chemicals and placed it over their noses and mouths until their vision faded to black.

When Jamie regained consciousness, she noticed the cold, damp, and dark room that she was in, with its only source of sunlight peeking from beneath an enormous iron door. She was overcome with fear, trying to free her hands and feet of the chains that bind them but without any luck. She was startled when she heard a similar sound of clinking chains from the other side of the room.

"Hello? Is anyone there?"

"Jamie, is that you?"

"Nate!" Her voice came out as a hoarse for help.

The two of them seemed to be trapped in this unfamiliar place, with no visible way out. Jamie's eyes began to adjust to the lack of light, making Nate's bruised face come into view about ten feet away from her.

"Where are we?"

"I have absolutely no idea."

At that moment, the men from before appeared behind the iron door, speaking in tongues. They took Jamie off of the chains that attached her to the wall and brought her toward the iron door. She fought with all of her might, landing a few solid kicks, but in the end lost the battle and was dragged into another room adjacent to the one she was just in.

Nate could hear Jamie's distant screams of pain and agony, which was a form of torture to him in and of itself. They went on for hours, but then suddenly they stopped. The footsteps approached the secluded, dungeon-like space, and the men appeared once again, but this time coated in the blood that was once pumping through Jamie's body.

They removed all of the chains that bound Nate and ignored the questions he peppered at them about Jamie and her well-being. They marched him down a dimly lit hallway and through another doorway, men almost twice the size of Nate on each side, holding his arms with a death grip. The faint whirr of a helicopter's blades grew closer as they marched through yet another hallway in the seemingly endless maze. The man who was giving the orders back in the train stayed behind and the other one accompanied Nate onto the helipad and into the chopper. Nate's mind was racing as to what they wanted with him. Before he knew what was happening, he felt a small poke in his right arm and was sleeping once again.

Nate woke from the familiar sleepy and foggy haze in yet another dark room. But this one wasn't like the last. No, it looked somewhat like a hotel room. He scratched his head as his eyes adjusted to the darkness.

Indeed, it was a hotel room, and when he drew back the curtains and looked out the window, he saw that he arrived at his final destination; London, England. The townsfolk were buzzing about on the sidewalk beneath him, looking more like ants than people from Nates' vantage point, completely unaware of the troubles that plagued his mind.

Was all of that just a dream?

His luggage was in the room, so he reached for his laptop. He scoured the Internet for any news articles about a missing woman fitting Jamie's description but found no such luck. There was no trace of her anywhere.

The relentless pounding in his head finally presented itself to Nate, as the adrenaline rush started to fade. The exhaustion of being thrown about and abused sunk in and Nate could not find himself handling the situation for another minute. He flopped down on the pristinely made bed face-down and passed out.

Waking from a dreamless sleep once again, Nate finally felt refreshed, and his relentless headache had finally eased to a dull throb that was barely noticeable. With another twelve hours of sleep under his belt, Nate still didn't know how to handle the information that swam in his head. So, he did what any other normal person in his position would do; he grabbed his jacket, and out the door, he flew, straight to the police station.

He pushed through the entrance to the station with such might that a random civilian would assume he, himself was about to be killed. Breathless and panting, Nate stood, leaning against the front desk, where the clerk gazed at him with narrow eyes filled with suspicion. Nate held up a finger to the woman, signaling that he would need a minute to catch his breath, for the frigid October air burned his lungs from the brisk run he had just taken. The desk clerk was totally unaware of the fact that Nate had sprinted ten blocks to get there, but virtually anyone could make assumptions based on his condition. When Nate's unintelligible panting slowed to a normal rate, he managed to choke out words to the unconcerned woman.

"Hi, I was recently abducted, along with a travel companion of mine, and I can't find her anywhere."

The words came easily, but the order they appeared in was unbelievable, even to Nate, who had experienced it first-hand. The clerk picked up the receiver of her phone and dialed, not even phased by Nate's tale. The formerly-suspicious clerk that before came off as a serious woman showed how taciturn she really was when she spoke into the phone. Her words were so quiet, Nate could barely make out anything she said. She slammed the receiver down to which Nate jumped at, and she smiled apologetically for startling him. She gestured for the uncomfortable-looking seating area across from her desk.

"Please take a seat and an officer will be right with you."

Another tight smile from the woman and Nate realized that he had to comply with her or leave. He shuffled to the blandly colored waiting section and plopped down with his arms crossed on the lumpy seat.

It felt like hours before an officer approached Nate. However, it was only a mere thirty minutes. The officer guided Nate through a maze of dimly lit hallways and opened one of the many identical doors that lined the corridor. The officer's hand gestured for Nate to enter the room first, and followed, closing the door behind them.

The room was very underwhelming, not decorated with anything extra, only one small table and a chair on each side, with a large mirror stretching across the left wall.

Nate took a seat at the table and retold his tale of his harrowing adventure to the officer, who nodded frequently at his words writing them down on a stack of papers in a beige folder. He didn't know why writing his thoughts down was necessary, for there was a recording device sitting on the table between them taking his words verbatim. Once Nate concluded his report on the action that had followed him the past few days, the officer put down his pen and sighed loudly.

"One moment please."

"Wait," Nate stood up with the officer and looked him in the eye. "I know I must sound clinically insane right now, but you have to believe me. This really happened, and this girl is really missing."

"We will do everything in our power to find her, sir. I'll be back."

The officer left the room, taking the file with Nate's words inside of it with him. Nate ran his hands through his hair anxiously, and his right leg refused to stop bouncing. He was so preoccupied with his thoughts that didn't even notice the absence of the silver band that was always present on his right-hand ring finger.

****

After she and Nate were taken from the train, Jamie remained in her chains for the same amount of time that Nate did. The ruthless thug that tortured her for hours and kidnapped her in the first place appeared in the doorway of the room she was kept in. He used the key that hung on a chain around his neck and released Jamie from her iron shackles. Jamie stood up from the grime-covered seat she was strapped in for hours. She took a minute to stretch her muscles, before connecting her right fist abruptly with the side of his face. This took him by surprise, not harming him in the slightest for his ginormous frame could take quite a beating.

"Damn it, Jamie. How about a little forewarning next time?"

She laughed slightly, shaking out her hand as it began to bruise, which soon will match the purple haze that covered other parts of her legs, arms, and face.

"Brody," she spoke to the man who she had assaulted, looking him right in the eyes as she did so. "You had that one coming, and you know it. Now get me the hell out of this nasty place."

The two of them walked side by side to the exit of the dark, cockroach-infested room, the size difference between the pair being almost comical. They walked down the endless hallways of the fortress, their steps echoing down the stone corridors.

"Did you get it?" Jamie's voice came out softer than before.

Brody just nodded in response, his face like stone.

"Good."

That was the last word that was spoken inside the tenable garrison. Jamie and her partner in crime exited the elaborate building to be greeted by a heavy downpour that watered the grassy hills of the outskirts of England. The dampness that hung in the air didn't phase Jamie or Brody in the slightest.

Under Jamie's wool coat, her dress that she had worn for days on end had been torn in numerous places, and all of the color faded out of each small flower that was printed on it. This was similar to her physical and emotional health with her face drained of color, in addition to numerous cuts and bruises scattered over her body. Brody had taken all of this out on her, for she had to make her screams of pain realistic for Nate's sake. She never was much of an actress, but for this role, she had to give it her all. Nate had something she wanted, and she got it.

A fleet of dark colored SUV's screeched to a halt in front of the two, nearly coating them in mud. Jamie and Brody entered the backseat of the same car, slammed the doors shut, and sped off without another word.

The rain patted softly on the roof of the hotel she and Brody were holed up in, creating a soothing sound that lulled Jamie to a dreamless sleep, which hasn't been gifted to her in the past few days. The skin around her wrists were red and irritated from the hours upon hours of being held captive in the metal shackles. However, those wrists were now free of the chains that had bound her. She was no longer in the dank dungeon, but in a plush room, with unlimited amenities surrounding her. Jaimie's head rested on a down pillow, and silky white sheets cloaked the rest of her body. Her side rose and fell with her breathing, the only sign of life that could have been seen from that entire room.

On her bedside table, barely noticeable compared to the elaborately decorated room, laid a single ring. It wasn't any sort of valuable engagement ring or anything with a large stone that was worth millions. No, it looked quite ordinary to the naked eye. If one were to look closer, one would see a small crest engraved in the silver. Jamie's family crest.

To be continued...

4.
American Uneducated System
Matt Mulattieri; Senior

America is known today as a place of sanctuary and the ability to exercise our own free will. From our symbolism of things like the bald eagle, Uncle Sam, and even the superhero Captain America, the amount of nationalism this country has is almost overwhelming. We live in a country where everybody believes there couldn't possibly be a better place out there to live in and take part in than in the United States. We show our muscles to the point where every other country describes us as cocky and only an illusion of personal freedom.

Underneath all of the patriotism and fireworks in our country that makes it so beautiful and mighty, there is still corruption that slithers underneath in the sewers of our amazing nation that makes it not exactly as solid as political leaders and nationalists say it is. Yes, we have diversity and opportunity, along with more freedom than most nations, but gradually our name is getting saturated into many other labels. America, our once great nation, is beginning to fall behind other nations and lose order. Racial inequality leads to unrest and innocent lives being taken. Elections have changed from picking who could lead the country that you would rally behind, into picking the lesser of two evils. But one thing stands tall in our nation as a symbol of stress and unrest, and only the student body of the country knows the pain it can cause in our minds.

The American Education System has stolen away the lives of kids in schools and universities. For myself personally, school is something very hard to juggle along with the rest of my life. Most kids are involved in some kind of sport, job, or club. I work three days a week for a company that has wonderful people in it but is understaffed to the point where I need to be there for it to run properly. Extracurriculars often take up the rest of the afternoon, making the student have to start studying or doing unnecessary amounts of homework later in the evening, without any sort of opportunity to be with their family or take a moment to meditate and calm themselves down. Students don't have the ability to have any free time without sacrificing either sleep or their grade point average.

But at the same time, there's the contradiction where colleges WANT to see you get involved in hundreds of different activities, sports, clubs, and charities on your college applications.

There is no right answer when it comes to being able to manage school in a perfect way, which completely destroys student's hopes and dreams philosophically. Nobody can handle multiple AP classes, a sport or job, a high GPA and a healthy amount of sleep per night in an endless cycle without developing mental illnesses or completely losing themselves and what makes them unique.

It is assumed that with the resource of technology and the internet that we are able to accomplish much more, much faster, which is true in most cases. This fact then leads to higher work amounts and higher expectations for students to get more work done, which takes even more time. Even with the advancement of technology, however, the work assigned often takes a large chunk of time to complete and keeps the student's on their computers for the majority of the night, and having bloodshot eyes the next morning from staring at Word documents all night.

I was able to conduct research and several interviews with classmates in order to gain multiple perspectives on the issue.

Michio Kaku is an American theoretical physicist professor at the City College of New York. His achievements include writing three New York Times best-sellers and making great strides in the field of quantum mechanics. In a conversation with Michael Schrage, the chief executive officer and president of Centier Bank, Michio claimed that the country's Achilles heel was, in fact, the education system. Michio Kaku even went far enough to say that the United States has "The worst education system known to science." America used to be the great gathering place for all of the genius minds to create, and build, and invent. It is to the point where the genius minds of people from places like India and China are returning to their home countries and "starting Silicon Valley's of their own." America used to be the melting pot of different cultures and ideas, which is what made the country so great. America used to be the brain magnet that sucked in all of the genius minds, and now all of the brains are going back, and different paradises of success and brains are being created from the United States

There are a variety of factors that can cause a dispersion of these genius minds. Part of it could be due to the realization that America is beginning to fall behind other nations, and that these genius individual's own countries have potential to hold their own Silicon Valleys and paradises of business and success and achievement.

Another reason could be with the racial tension that our country is currently facing. A study was done in our country on the race of Ph.D. candidates and found that 50% of them are foreign-born. In Michio Kaku's own system, 100% of the Ph.D. candidates are foreign-born. Michio Kaku claims that the number one thing holding the nation's economy and science field together is the H-1B Visa. With the H-1B Visa, U.S. employers have the ability to temporarily employ foreign workers in specialty occupations. Specialty occupations are theoretical and practical applications of a body of highly specialized knowledge in a field of human endeavor.

Some examples include biotechnology, agriculture, social sciences, education and health, law, theology, and engineering, along with many other different prestigious career opportunities. There have been many attacks on possibly getting rid of the H-1B Visa under the claim that "foreigners are taking our jobs." To dispute that, the Wall Street Journal responded that there are no Americans who can take these jobs since they are at the highest level of science and technology out of any other professions. Michio Kaku then finished by saying "They don't take away jobs from Americans, they instead create entire industries," and how problems like that are why the education system is such a weak spot in our country.

Neil deGrasse Tyson, a popular astrophysicist, cosmologist, and science communicator has also spoken out about our education system and his opinions on why it is flawed. Neil deGrasse Tyson has already spoken out several times on this issue, with his most famous quote regarding it being: "When students cheat on exams it's because our school system values grades more than students value learning." The main point Neil deGrasse Tyson stands behind is that there is too much emphasis on certain things in school that aren't as important as they are depicted to be. Schools are mainly focused on being able to score high on an exam that they wrote and teaching the kids how to pass the exam rather than the useful information. Neil deGrasse Tyson argues: "At some point you have to step away from the test and say 'I have a new thought that has never been thought before, and it is not a thought that you asked me to regurgitate on this exam, because it's a thought that no one has had before." The current testing system is flawed in that all of the exams are written by teachers who grew up and were taught information in an entirely different generation, and are teaching students the exact same way rather than adapting.

There are many people in the world right now who are successful that didn't get straight 'A's in high school. If you talk to successful novelists, inventors, attorneys, talk show hosts, comedians, or even politicians, a large majority of them didn't get straight 'A's in high school, yet still have made a success out of their life. People like Mark Zuckerberg, Ellen DeGeneres, Brad Pitt, Ted Turner, Bill Gates, Jim Carrey, John Lennon, and F. Scott Fitzgerald all did not complete their education for a variety of reasons but have made it big in America.

The American Education System puts too much emphasis on the importance of the test, making you think you're screwed for life if you bomb a test or final and go down a letter grade, when in actuality, grades don't even matter that much as they are depicted. Although Neil deGrasse Tyson agrees that tests are necessary because "it's a way to find out what you know," there are many qualities that are essential to becoming an adult that aren't taught or graded on a test. Tests only measure how well you can memorize information, not how hard of a worker you are or if you actually listen during class. Students differ greatly in that some are able to memorize and process information just by hearing it. Other students need to spend hours studying for the test, and still might not get a score as high as they expected. Not everybody is equally skilled in the ability to score high on tests, and even though testing skills won't matter after college, the education system forces the idea that poor test scores are equal to a failure at life. In Michigan alone, 12.8% of residents have Attention-deficit/hyperactivity disorder (ADHD), which hinders one's ability to focus in areas such as the classroom. Rather than filling in the bubble on a standardized test scantron, teachers should be asking our students to fill their thought bubble with new ideas to re-shape the future through questions and hypotheses.

I also conducted my own research on the topic of education by creating a survey online. The survey contained seven questions: What grade they were in, which grade was the most academically challenging, their own description of high school, the greatest flaw/privilege our current system has, what they would change, whether or not they felt safe at school, and their rating of our school. I then proceeded to send this out to my friends, my church, and the high school band to try and make it as widespread as possible.

The answers I received on the survey were a very large mix of different answers: some negative, some positive. A large majority of the students put down that they felt safe at their school, some putting down that their current school district is very well organized but pointed out that the average for the entire nation was much lower in rating than their school, specifically. The average rating out of ten, with ten being the best, was between a six and a seven, which is in the 'D' range for the American grading scale.

Most people would believe that a six or a seven out of ten is not the worst of scores, considering in other countries such as the UK, where scores such as a seven out of ten is around a 'B+'. In order to get an 'A' in Britain, you need only a 75% or higher, where America labels that as a 'C'. The fact that the American grading scale is much more rigorous even shows how much we expect of our students compared to other nations, who have easier grading scales and still are ranked higher than the United States in reading, math, and science. Has the United States not realized yet that strict standardized testing and high standards don't motivate the student body to learn or do so effectively?

The survey took a darker turn as I read some of the answers that some people put down describing their high school experiences. The following answers are completely anonymous and exact:

"It's honestly been the worst four years of my life. I wake up every morning and ask myself "why do I keep doing this when I could be exploring the world and finding myself." But I get up every day, see people I've spent the last seven to ten years with that I don't care for and don't care for me and I do my work. I come home every day, and I'm exhausted, and I sleep. I wake up and do it all again. I hate that this has been my life for the past four years."

"Very repetitive. Seemingly useless in what I want to do or need to do in my adult life."

"I think the school district I'm in is excellent, but I fear that in high school, we are fed too much information in a short amount of time and are sometimes guilted into taking AP courses. I also fear that we are over-scheduled and I think that is very unhealthy for people our age."

"I literally tried to commit suicide."

Is this not a wake-up call? The kids in today's society are being put through too much in their high school years to the point where a career would be much easier, work-wise, than managing their classes with subjects they won't ever use in the future.

I had an interview with one of my classmates, Jaya Davis, on the education system. One of her main points that she made was the biological discovery that during the mornings at the time school starts, the brain is still not fully functioning until closer to around ten in the morning, yet we still make school days start unnaturally early and last until the middle of the afternoon. Part of why students may be struggling in school could very well be the fact that everybody is completely exhausted and not fully awake or functioning that early in the morning, especially since the amounts of homework assigned prevent students with extracurriculars from going to bed at a decent time.

Another growing issue pointed out was the dress code in schools being too constricting towards women. Jaya stated: "Girls are being punished because it's being assumed guys can't control themselves when they see spaghetti strap shirts and a girl's shoulder. The problem shouldn't be what girls wear, but fixing urges, if any, that guys get from clothing worn in school. By taking us out of class and punishing women for wearing a shirt with spaghetti straps or that shows a tiny part of our boob, it's the education system telling women that our education is less important than our outfits for the day."

I also spoke with one of my old English teachers at Seaholm High School who I had the pleasure to meet through taking AP Language and Composition my junior year. After school, I decided to come into her room and conduct an interview with her to hear her thoughts on the education system.

My teacher believed that "where we are as a society is on par with where the rest of the world is right now for focus on education." However, she also mentioned how in this school year alone, she's had more sick kids and absences in her class than any other year. "More than ever, students are stressed out which is affecting their health, and part of it is due to the homework amounts which I feel aren't always related to what they do in class. Some homework guides the practice and skill, while other assignments are a complete waste and just serve as busywork." Mrs. Nayak also agreed with me on the lines of extracurriculars, stating "Kids are stressing out so much over extracurriculars since they have an elevated meaning to colleges. Colleges expect these poor students to do so much with such little time.

Kids in high school these days are suffering and going through hell, and nobody is listening to us. Everyone assumes that kids our age are just itching for something to protest or are whining because their grades aren't high enough. Either America is too ignorant to act on these issues or the student body hasn't conveyed the right words to the right person yet. I hope that by writing this piece that eyes will be opened and this document will be seen by an individual who can do something more than just compiling information, like myself.

To the Department of Education in the United States: It's time to start taking your heads out of your asses and reforming through research of other countries to see what works because clearly, our current system is a failure.

Works Cited:

"State-based Prevalence Data of Parent Reported ADHD Diagnosis by a Health Care Provider." *Centers for Disease Control and Prevention*. Centers for Disease Control and Prevention, 06 Oct. 2014. Web. 04 Oct. 2016.

Cosmology Today. "Michio Kaku: US Has the Worst Educational System Known to Science." *YouTube*. YouTube, 18 Jan. 2016. Web. 04 Oct. 2016.

Express55589. "Neil DeGrasse Tyson - Schools Are Failures." *YouTube*. YouTube, 26 Mar. 2014. Web. 04 Oct. 2016.

5.
Ares
Michael Arpasi; Junior

Luke has been training for this mission five years now. He started back in 2015 when NASA drafted him for this mission. He was put through strenuous situations involving stress control, g-force preparation, and combat readiness. He memorized all of the procedures and controls the spacecraft offers. Nothing could possibly take him by surprise during his 260-day long journey aboard the U.S.S. Ares to Mars.

The mission consists of three main points. First, a rocket launches ten American's into outer space. Once in orbit with the Earth, the rocket will dock with a larger spacecraft fit for the lengthy journey. The craft will reach Mars and orbit releasing pods to the planet with the crew and supplies to colonize the planet.

Luke is average height, has brown eyes, and clean blond hair. Luke graduated from the University of Florida with a degree in Astrophysics and Communications. Along with Luke are his two copilots: Charlie and Victor. The three of them were all drafted into this mission together. Charlie graduated from Massachusetts Institute of Technology with a degree in Astrophysics and Medicine. Victor came a year later and graduated from Stanford. He is renowned for his precision and ingenuity in engineering with a degree in Astrophysics and Aerospace Engineering.

Charlie was Luke's roommate during their training in NASA's HQ, they started together and finished training together. Victor was down the hall from them in the Engineering Wing's dorms. He wasn't supposed to be on the mission until NASA realized they were going to need someone with his level of skill in engineering to be aboard the craft during the expedition.

For this mission NASA recruited qualified American's to make the most effective colony possible on Mars. Two doctors, two botanists, and three engineers were recruited for the mission. Their objective is to set up a life-sustaining colony for the ten of them with sufficient energy, medicine, and food. Once the station is complete NASA will send thirty more Americans to assist in the construction of a city on Mars.

Luke never had much family on Earth. His parent's died while he was in college at the University of Florida. They had always supported him and his dream of becoming an astronaut and traveling to space. So when the day of September 27, 2020 had finally come he was ready to make his parent's proud and leave this planet.

The three astronauts have been packing their things for a month now taking into account the amount of weight NASA would allow them to bring. Each member on the rocket was allowed sixty pounds of cargo.

The members at NASA load their cargo onto the rocket and prepare the ten of them for take-off. Each member is equipped with a spacesuit and helmet to regulate airflow and pressure until they are out of the atmosphere and in outer space.

Luke, Victor, and Charlie suit up and prepare to board the ship. The three of them took the elevator to the scaffold to the circular entrance. Air blasts in towards the center of it for pressure release in the capsule. They walk the narrow hall into the open airlock. The smell of metal and jet fuel has filled the air surrounding them. Letting the three know this is it, there is no turning back now. The lock opens, and the astronauts are guided by flashing red lights to the cabin. Their boots clack and bang against the steel grates as they walk towards the ship. The hatch slid open from the sensor. Luke entered, followed by Charlie on his left, and Victor on his right. The three sat down in the individual leather seats supported by an aluminum frame for take-off.

In front of them was a vast accumulation of flashing buttons, levers, and screens on several different panels. Each with a different complex function for the ship's flight.

The rest of the crew boarded on the rocket after the pilots. They were led into the passenger section directly below the cockpit and above the cargo room.

"You ready for this?" Luke excitedly asks Charlie

"I can't wait," Charlie replied sarcastically.

"Shut up!" Victor says impatiently "I hate this part."

The countdown begins... "10, 9, 8, 7, 6..."

"Oh, I feel like I'm going to throw up," Victor says squeamishly

"No, you don't want to do that with your helmet on," Luke says jokingly.

"5, 4, 3, 2, 1..."

The engines ignite, and the crew is thrown backwards. With a screaming loud roar, the rocket blasts off of the platform and begins its ascension into space.

"I can't hold it in any longer," Victor says as his breakfast splatters all over the inside of his helmet. He then passes out cold.

"I knew he wouldn't last," said Charlie.

"It's alright we don't need him until we board the spacecraft in orbit."

****

The ship reaches outer space within ten minutes of their travel. Victor awakes in distress and panic as he realizes that he can't see through his helmet.

"That's what you get when you eat a large breakfast like that before takeoff," Luke says condescendingly.

"Screw you guys. Someone get me a rag," Victor says angrily.

No one gave Victor a rag. He felt his way out of the cockpit and towards the cargo room to grab one of his packed rags. He floats past the rest of the crew. However, none of them realized his misfortune because they were all passed out from the takeoff. Victor felt his way into the cargo hold, found a rag, and cleaned his suit out. This incident enraged Victor. He makes his way back to the cockpit and prepares for docking with the Ares.

The ship swings through orbit and slowly approaches the large spacecraft. Within minutes the two have locked together. A tube extends between the two creating an airlock chamber. A platform extends and the doors open. The first to enter the craft is Luke followed by Charlie, the crew and then Victor lagging behind. The crew floated through the main hallway towards the cabins.

One of the crew members, Caroline, the botanist, noticed Victor panting frantically and acting peculiar behind them. She fell back from the pack to talk to him.

"Hey, are you alright?" Caroline asked.

"Get away from me!" Victor shouted.

Caroline flinched back as Victors snap scared her. "Okay," she replied awkwardly and scared then floated back to the pack.

The ship was meant for a long distance travel. It is a cylindrical fuselage about thirty meters in diameter and two hundred seventy-five meters in length. Similar to the ship used for launch but about twice as large. Surrounding the ship is a hollow circular cylinder that rotates along the ship's axis. This circular cylinder simulates gravity in space. It rotates at approximately 1.185 rotations per minute, perfectly creating one 'G' of force. This area is called the SG-Zone.

Luke and Charlie lead the crew through the narrow main hall. The crew floats through a circular doorway and were lead down a tube with windows surrounding them. They entered the SG-Zone and everything floating fell to the ground. As the crew members experience normal gravity again, they began to stretch and yawn like they woke up from a long nap.

They were presented with a longer hall that stretched the length of the SG-Zone. Along that hall were doors and windows to dorm rooms, restrooms, and recreational rooms. There are five dorm rooms each containing access to one of the three restrooms, a double bunk bed, a small dresser, and with just enough area to stretch and get dressed. There are four Rec Rooms: a lounge, a gym, a kitchen, and a meeting hall. They are located every ninety degrees along the SG-Zone. In between the Rec rooms are the dorms and restrooms. On the main portion of the ship, there is a large engine room, a systems room, a cockpit, and a large cargo room.

Luke had everyone line up in the SG-Zone. He read the list for dorm assignments to everyone. Luke is paired with Charlie, Caroline with Grace, Victor with Michael, Leopold with his sister, Paula, and Emma with Stephanie. Each crew member went to their dorms and settled in. Victor takes his space suit off. His roommate Michael takes the top bunk while Victor takes the bottom. Michael begins to unload his carry on while Victor cleans out his space suit.

"How are you holding up?" Michael asks.

"Doesn't matter," Victor replies.

Luke and Charlie don't enter their room. Instead, they go to the cockpit to check on the ship's course. The two sit down in their futuristic white leather seats and lock in. Luke notices that the course is set and ready for travel to Mars. Luke gives Charlie the go to begin the main thrusters, and the Ares begins it's a long journey to Mars.

****

"Captain's log, it has been one hundred nine Earth days since we have left the atmosphere. We are traveling at about Thirty Thousand kilometers per hour, and I can't feel a thing. The crew has been great, everyone is getting along well. Well... everyone except Victor. Ever since his accident with his space helmet he's been acting more reserved and less outgoing. He has had numerous accidents following as well. Whether it be from motion sickness to failing to perform his job in the engineering room, or his attitude when we gather the crew together. He's always in a hateful mood and is very sick all the time. I worry about him."

The crew is eating breakfast after a short night sleep. Sleep in space is limited because there is no day or night. Everyone sleeps four hours then is awake for eight then sleeps another four and awake for eight. Breakfast isn't any better. Because they are limited on supplies, they have to ration everything they brought. The average crew member is given a protein bar and almond milk for breakfast and freeze-dried food for lunch and dinner all with water. While everyone was enjoying the morning, all of a sudden the ship shook, and a red light start flashing with a siren.

"What's that!" Luke shouts towards Charlie.

"I think we were just hit by something" Charlie concernedly replied.

Luke traveled through the ship up into the systems room to analyze the situation. When he arrived, he noticed that a piece of debris had struck the engine on the ship.

"Oh no," Luke stated

"Our engines are broken, and we're spinning out of control. Get Victor, we need him to go repair the engine outside of the ship."

Right as Luke said that Victor entered the room frantically. "What's happening?" Victor yelled.

"We need you to go outside and fix the engine, it doesn't look like that bad of a fix, but we can repair this from inside."

"What! Why me!" Victor yelled angrily.

"Because you're the mechanic."

"I'm an engineer, not a mechanic."

"Doesn't matter all that matters is that you're the only person who can fix this."

"Alright fine!" Victor yelled then ran out of the room to the airlock.

"Why is he always like that?" Charlie asked Luke.

"I don't know, space has changed him," Luke replied, frustrated by Victor.

Victor arrived at the airlock and suited up. The last time he was suited up he threw up all over it, so the experience of putting it back on is nauseating. The lock's aroma is that of filtered air, metal, and rubber. All things Victor knows well as an engineer. Victor might be disgusted from the suit, but he is ready to save the day. The lock is initiated, and Victor is set free into space.

Victor feels his way down the ladder following the guide lights on the side of the ship. He progressively inches closer to the main engine. Once he finally reaches the engine, he notices that the main fuel line had fallen out and was loose. Luckily the ship had a built-in backup system that prevented any jet fuel from exiting the Ares by closing the valve if it was ever compromised. He re-attaches the valve to the line. However, once he finished his job he notices that his oxygen levels are falling drastically. He finds a cut in his suit on his chest, and he patches it up with duct tape from his toolbox. His levels reach 2% oxygen, and he begins to slowly become light-headed. He tries to communicate with Luke back in the ship, but the cut in his suit also cut through his communications device. He's losing oxygen, passing out, and has no way of talking to Luke. He begins to feel his way back, but with each arm motion, he loses his feeling of touch and loses consciousness.

Somehow he makes it back to the lock, but he doesn't have a way of communicating with them to open it. For some reason, there was no one monitoring him through the window. He finds the auxiliary latch for an emergency open and opens the airlock. He floats back into the ship and closes the door. Steam and oxygen fill the room through the air ducts along the ground and in the ceiling. Victor tears off his helmet and takes a giant breath. He grabs onto a handle and begins to hyperventilate. The ship begins to realign itself and the course to Mars is set back in motion.

After a couple of minutes recuperating in the oxygen-filled container, Luke flies into the room in a hurry.

"What happened I tried talking to you, but you never answered once out there?"

"What happened, what happened! I almost died out there! You and Charlie never answered anything I said," Victor replied ferociously.

"What are you talking about I tried to guide you the entire time you were out there. Your communications device is broken"

Victor reaches down to his suit's tear and notices all the wiring for the device is frayed. He looks up to Luke confused.

"I don't understand why that happened, I never cut it on anything when I was out there" Victor replied. However Victor had a thought, what if instead of his suit tearing outside someone inside the ship tampered with his suit to kill him. Victor floated back a little in the chamber with an expression of fear and shock because of the idea.

"I don't know what happened Victor I'm glad you're back alive," Luke says.

"Okay," Victor replies.

"Come on, let's go relax a little. That was terrifying," Luke says as he leaves the room.

Victor stays back thinking of who could do this to him.

"Could it be Luke, why would Luke want me dead?" he thinks. *"No Luke is the only guy that ever liked me during training. It has to be Charlie. He's always been out to get me, whenever I was vulnerable or made a mistake he would be there to capitalize off of my misery. Yes, it's him… he's trying to kill me. He wants me dead. Only he could do that. He wants to kill me. That's why he made the tear in my suit. He's always the one who has to go outside to operate on the ship. He has access to it, and he did it. I have to stop him. I need to stop him. I have to kill him. It's the only way. I have to kill him and the rest of his friends before they kill me. Yes, everyone needs to die,"* Victor says to himself menacingly.

"Are you coming?" Luke calls back.

"Yes, don't wait up," Victor replies while leaving the airlock.

****

"Captain's log, it has been one hundred and thirteen days since we have left the atmosphere. Four days ago we had a piece of debris collide with our ship's engine. Luckily for us, the damage wasn't anything catastrophic. Our mechanic, Victor, was able to reach the breach in the engine's external fuel line and repair it. All with no communication device and with a tear on his suit's chest. I'm very proud and glad he was able to fix the ship and return safely. However, he didn't return the same person exactly. I knew he was acting differently before the spacewalk, but after I barely recognize his personality anymore. He doesn't bunk with his roommate Michael anymore, he doesn't eat meals with us anymore, he is very reserved now barely saying anything during our daily meetings. I think he is no longer psychologically able to handle the trip and I fear that he could compromise the mission. The only reason I don't act on this situation is because I don't have any legitimate proof that he is unstable. It's only a theory, but I hope to God that I never have to detain Victor. I hope he get's better and back to the way he was on Earth."

It was a normal day, Luke woke up and slid out of bed. He puts on his captain's jumpsuit and his shoes. He goes into the dining room for breakfast with everyone. As usual, everyone was already there eating, except Victor and his roommate Michael. Luke just assumes that they're running late and he grab's his breakfast then eats it.

Time passes, Victor and Michael still haven't left their room. Luke thinks that they must've just slept through their alarm. Luke leaves the dining room and walks towards Victor and Michael's room. He tries to open the door, but it's locked. He knocks on the door and waits a minute, but no one answers. Next, he pulls out his all access key and opens the door. Entering the room to find Michael dead on the floor in a pool of blood. He had been beaten to death by a metal wrench lying right next to him. Luke runs out of the room and pulls the alarm on the side of the hallway activating the ships siren.

The crew runs into the main part of the ship to the systems room. Luke enters in a panic looking to see who was there.

"What's going on?" Caroline asked.

Luke didn't reply, he was counting the heads of everyone there to see who showed up. He counted exactly seven different people excluding himself. Everyone was there except... Victor. Luke began to panic he flew out of the room and back into the SG area. He ran to his room, threw the door open and went to his dresser. Inside was a lock box that contained a gun for purposes of mutiny on the ship. He grabbed the lockbox, took the key to it off of his keychain, put it in the lock and opened it. Flipping the box open to find it empty. Victor had known about his gun and stolen it. The crew entered the room shortly after.

"What's going on Luke?" Charlie asks anxiously.

"We have a psychopath on this ship, and we don't know where he is," Luke replies in horror.

"What are you talking about?" Leopold asks.

"Michael is dead. He was beaten to death by Victor," Luke says.

"What!" Caroline shouts.

The crew begins to panic and shout different things. They ask how could he do this and why would he even want to. They become scared and worried about their safety.

"Okay everyone, we need to stay together and get back into the cockpit to take control of the ship," Luke states.

Everyone ran towards the cockpit as fast as they could. They all eventually reached the cockpit. However, as they entered, they found all the control boards smashed and destroyed. Electronics were freely floating all around the room. The only two things that were left intact were the operation seats.

"Okay, you all stay here I'm going to go check on the engine room. Charlie come with me I might need a backup mechanic," Luke says.

The two of them leave the cockpit and lock the door behind them so Victor can't reach the rest of them. They float down the small corridors of the main ship towards the engine room. They pass through the systems room and then the cargo room, both untouched by Victor's rampage. They arrive at the front door of the engine room to find nothing out of place. Luke enters to the lights turned off and an awful smell. The room smells like rotting flesh and engine oil. He feels his way on the wall to the left for the light switch and turns it on. Once the lights are on he is startled at the sight of Michael's dead body floating freely one meter in front of him.

Luke did not return to the body Victor left in the room, but he didn't see him in the room or on the way to the systems room. Luke realizes that Victor must have just left the body for him to find it and collect everyone together in the systems room. When he did this, he went into Luke's room and took his gun. He then waited for everyone to leave Luke's room and go to the cockpit to move the body into the engine room.

"Oh my God, that's horrible!" Charlie exclaims.

Luke moves around the body and examines the engine room. Oil is floating around everywhere. Victor compromised the main engine by destroying the main supply line to the fuel tank. If there was a spark in there, the entire place would explode. The two exit as fast as they can. They make it back to the systems room which is still intact.

"Okay, we need to find Victor fast," Luke exclaims.

"Check the live feed from the monitors around the ship," Charlie replies.

Luke ran up to the monitor and logged into his account. He opened the surveillance program and flipped through the cameras. Each one with a different angle on every room and hallway. There are a total of forty-eight cameras throughout the ship. When Luke logged on to the account, he was presented with an image of the systems room he was in. He could see himself and Charlie standing right beside him. He flipped to the next camera and was presented a view of the exterior of the ship in front of the airlock. Next, he flipped to the airlock, then the hallway next to the lock, then the engine room, and then the cockpit. The sight projected by this screen was both haunting and scary for the two. They were presented a horrific display of two dead bodies locked into the seats with bullet holes in their heads. The blood was rushing from their head and out into free floating space. The two zoomed in closer to the image and saw that the two strapped into the seats were Leopold and Paula. They surveilled the room even further trying to find a clue as to where and how Victor killed the two. They notice that there was no bullet hole or bullets floating around in the room. As well as a blood trail that led away from their heads and out of the cockpit.

"He's a psychopath!" Charlie shouts in terror

"We need to find the others," Luke says.

The two flip through the cameras everywhere until they finally find the crew. They are all being held captive in Victor's room. There are four of them tied up together on the floor with a sign near their feet. The words "Camera 34" were painted in blood on the floor.

"Change to that camera," Charlie says

Luke changes to that camera to find Caroline strapped to a chair in the lounge. She looks like she's been hit in the head and is badly bruised. Her hands are behind the chair and wrapped in duct tape. Her mouth is covered, and she can only mumble. She looks very worried and scared as a dark figure enters the camera. Victor looks up at the camera and waves. His face looks monotone and crazy. He is wearing his normal jumpsuit and shoes. In his hand is Luke's gun and in the other is a sign. It says "Bring me Charlie or they all die" painted in blood.

"How'd he do all of this so fast?" Charlie asks.

"I don't know, it's almost like what people do when they get lazy while writing," Luke replies looking towards the camera in the room.

"You know just rush the plot to the climax of the story."

"Almost exactly like that," Charlie says while turning to the camera in the room.

"I've got it, we can sneak around Victor and get to the hostages using the cameras and a feedback device to my tablet," Luke says.

"Good idea," Charlie replies.

The two set up their tablets and stream the live camera video to it. They devise a plan to have Luke go after Victor, and Charlie to rescue the hostages.

Luke and Charlie approach the SG-Zone, and they begin to feel gravity and fall to the floor. Luke is nervous but calm and steady he approaches the lounge while Charlie runs into Victor's room: all the while looking at the camera's to see where they are while making sure Victor hasn't moved. Luke finally arrives at

Victor's room and checks to see that he is still inside. He see's Victor and Caroline still in there. He knocks on the door.

"Hey Victor, open up, it's over," Luke says.

There is no response, Luke tries it again, but it doesn't work. He then takes out his all access key and unlocks the door but stays hidden in the hall. He then opens the door to find the four hostages and the blood sign at their feet. Victor renamed and rerouted the camera's to different rooms. Knowing that when he revealed himself, Luke would come for him and Charlie would rescue the hostages.

"Charlie!" Luke screams. He leaves the hostages there and runs down the circular SG-Zone to Charlie.

While he is running down, he see's Caroline running towards him screaming, "Charlie's dead! Charlie's dead!"

"What?" Luke asks. Caroline runs into his arms and hugs him crying and sobbing over the facts that Victor had just killed Charlie.

"Go over to the others I need to find Charlie," Luke says to Caroline.

Luke runs as fast as he can down the narrow hall, checking every camera ahead of him to make sure he won't be ambushed by Victor. He passes all of the dorms and all of the Rec rooms to arrive at the lounge. The lounge door is wide open, and Luke approaches slowly, fearing for his own life while still worrying about his friends. He peeks through the door. He finds Victor facing away from the door, standing over a dead body with a smoking gun in his hand.

"Why? Why would you do this?" Luke shouts to him.

"He deserved it," Victor replies intensely.

"No one deserves that," Luke shouts while charging at Victor.

Luke tackles him to the ground after hitting him from behind, Victor quickly begins to fight back as the two wrestle for the gun in his hand. Luke manages to point the gun at a wall while holding his arm down, but Victor won't let go. He punches Victor in the face, but he didn't budge. He tries again with two more. Still nothing. Victor head-butts Luke making him dizzy for three seconds. Luke still with all of his consciousness holds onto the gun and lies down on Victors' arm. Creating a sharp pain and a reflex reaction for his forearm to let go of the gun. Luke grabs the gun and stands up, holding it up to Victor.

"You killed my friend, and you killed my crew," Luke shouts.

"You never deserved to be on this trip we all knew that, you're clinically insane because of space travel. And I can't allow any psychopath to remain on my ship any longer," Luke says threateningly.

"No!" Victor shouts as he gets up to charge Luke. Luke pulls the trigger and releases a small caliber bullet right into Victor's corrupt and evil heart. Victor falls back in shock and fear. He slowly falls and hits the ground like a domino.

Luke falls to his hands and knees gasping for breath, he cannot believe he just killed a man. He looks over at Charlie's dead body and begins to tear up. He crawls over to it and holds his hand.

"I'm sorry buddy, I never meant for this to happen to you. I should've seen it coming. I did see it coming. I didn't think it would be this tragic, though," Luke says while tearing up and laying next to his best friends body. The rest of the crew has been released by Caroline, but they stay away from the room fearing Victor is still alive.

Eventually, the crew slowly steps out of the room and walk towards the where Luke is. After cautiously wandering through the hallways the crew finds the room. They don't enter it at first but right as they grabbed the door handle, the door opens, and Luke walks out.

"What happened?" Emma asks.

"Victor's dead," Luke replies in a monotone voice.

"What about Charlie?" Caroline asked concernedly.

"He... he didn't make it either" Luke replies sadly while looking down at the floor.

Luke and the crew walk away from the room. The now six of them have to find a way to survive and make it to Mars with all of the damage to the ship and low supplies. Luke with the help of some of the crew members hold a funeral for Charlie in the lounge room. Then put his coffin in the storage room to bury it if they reach Mars. Luke then takes Victor's body and launches it out of the airlock into cold dark space.

"Captain's log, it has been one hundred and fifteen days since the Ares has left the atmosphere. Our engineer Victor has killed four of the original ten of us. Including my friend and fellow astronaut Charlie. I saw the signs leading up to this tragedy, but I was too ignorant to act upon it. I guess I just hoped that Victor wouldn't do this out of the goodness of his heart, but this isolation takes the character out of a man. It turned his warm and hopeful heart into a cold and ruthless one. The Ares has been damaged severely in the engine room due to Victor, but we have managed to halt the problem for now. We have to reorganize the entire crew basis and priorities now. Moral is down with the crew, but I swear that these people on this ship will push through to the end of this mission and we will succeed. For if we don't all of this would've been for nothing."

6.
Backstab In Paris
Luke Knox; Junior

Malibu, CA, 2008

Raf and Nick were on their way back from a day of surfing when they each got a call. First Raf, then Nick letting them know that they had been accepted into Pepperdine University's International Program to study abroad. With this, they knew where they would be spending their second summer as students, in Florence, Italy. This was certainly what they had hoped for but expected nothing less than a "yes" as that is what they received all their lives. Michael, on the other hand, was astonished to get the call, having to run out of the library to properly celebrate the news. Unlike Raf and Nick, Michael came from a small town and had to work for everything he got, including paying for school, something many of his friends couldn't even imagine. There was a fourth friend, Charlie who was close with the other three in the group, including Michael, who the other two didn't know so well. Everyone in the group liked him, and he bridged the gap between the groups.

The four left on a Tuesday and arrived in Florence on a Wednesday to the apartment where they would be spending their next few months. The first day there, they slept and tried to get rid of any jet lag they were experiencing. The next day they planned to go to the new art gallery across the street, Brooke Galleria. It was very spacious with thousands of pieces, new and old. The one thing they had in common were they were all expensive. They left mid-day, and when they arrived, there was extreme traffic. Raf had high anxiety about the situation as he knew nothing but the spacious beaches of Malibu. Because of this, the four agreed on a central meeting spot and decided to split up with Raf and Nick looking at the West Wing and Michael and Charlie the East Wing. About thirty minutes after they began browsing, Charlie urgently needed to use the bathroom and found one about ten minutes later. The two got separated as Michael was left confused and shocked that this many people were allowed in at one time. There was so much noise that Michael couldn't even believe it was an art gallery. Eventually giving up, Michael headed back to the central meeting place the group had established. Charlie showed up a few minutes later, and the two decided it was no longer a good idea to be separated from the other students. They called and texted both Raf and Nick non-stop and heard nothing, so they headed to the West Wing to investigate. On their way there, one of Raf's shoes, a Rick Owens geobasket was laying on the floor. Charlie was shocked as he recognized Raf's shoe and knew he would be distraught if any of his high-end clothing was getting trampled in an environment he couldn't control. The shoe was large and was pointed to a storage closet that they opened. Within the closet was a nightmare, a sight that no one would want to see. Their two best friends dead.

Room 1 (Michael)

"Why would I do such a thing, I barely know these guys. This was my chance to get to know them. I've been looking forward to this trip for a year".

Room 2 (Charlie)

"The fact I am even here is absurd. Those two were my best friends, and I know who did this. I can prove it".

The two students were heavily interrogated for forty-eight hours straight with just water and bathroom breaks. They gave up all information on where everyone met, their childhoods, why they would or wouldn't do certain things, met with psychologists among other doctors, and were exhausted. They contained the two in separate rooms for a number of days. By this time, everyone was convinced Michael had committed the crime. Michael had run off when he finally escaped Charlie's sight and gotten rid of the two "friends" he had really hated the whole time. Or so they thought.

When they finally let Charlie leave, he was distraught, almost not physically or emotionally able to keep up a conversation. The more he thought about the loss of his friends, it appeared, the more it continued to haunt him that he could have done something to stop it. Michael, on the other hand, was defensive the whole way through and was extremely frustrated with the situation as his life would soon be over for something he could not control.

The result was set in stone when a letter came to the police station from Charlie. The first line read "I'm sorry" and the rest was a shocking depiction of how and why he killed Raf and Nick. He revealed that he had been jealous of the two ever since he began having to third wheel their friendship. "That was supposed to be me out surfing every morning" he revealed, "they have ruined my college experience, and for that I need revenge."

To be continued...

7.
Captain Pace:
Space Adventure
Karen Gallaway; Senior

Hop on board!
And join Captain Pace,
On this exciting journey
Through outer space

You'll see Venus
You'll see Mars
Maybe even
Some shooting stars.

So fasten your seatbelt
Get ready to fly.
Up off the Earth
And into the sky.

Let's go see the sun
But don't look too close!
Its rays are so hot
A weenie could roast!

The sun shines on Earth
And gives us light.
But when it's gone,
That means it is night.

On to Mercury
The hottest of them all
So much heat,
For a planet so small

Now we're at Venus,
Sister planet to Earth.
Earth is bigger, though,
For what it's worth.

We are passing by Earth,
Where the living things roam.
You might see your school,
You might see your home.

You'll also see clouds,
And water and land.
All the things,
That make Earth so grand!

There is our moon!
That grey, circular rock.
Let's all stop by,
And do the moon walk.

On to the Red Planet,
The color of flame.
We are looking at Mars.
That's its real name.
Oh no! The Asteroid Belt!

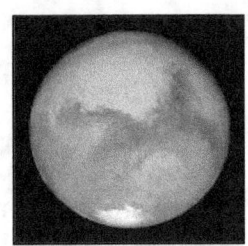

Hold on tight!
The asteroids are tough
They put up a good fight.

Coming up next
Are the planets of gas.
You better get ready,
For these next ones, we'll pass.

We've arrived at Jupiter
The biggest we'll see.
Its dark spot is huge!
Wouldn't you agree?

Saturn is next.
Those rings are great.
There are so many!
Way more than eight.

There is Uranus
So pale and blue.
It has twenty-seven moons,
Yes, really! It's true!

Last is Neptune,
Very far and cold.
It also has rings,
There are five, I'm told.

We are passing old Pluto
No longer one of them,
Just a small dwarf planet,
In our big solar system.

But Pluto stays strong
Orbiting around
Though sometimes his path
Cannot be found!

Our adventure is ending,
It is almost done,
Thank you for coming,
We had so much fun!

Now we are back,
To Earth, our home base.
Hope to see you next time,
When we visit a new place!

8.
Dear Dad
Haley Dolan; Junior

Dear Dad,

I'm not the best at telling stories, but I'll set the scene for this one as picture-perfect that my head can remember. It was 2000, September 26th, around eight o'clock at night, I happened to be in the backyard at the time, playing with my lunatic of a dog, Petey. Before you ask, no, this isn't one of those lame stories of a girl that gets a dog, and they become the best of friends and braid each other's hair. In fact, I absolutely hated Petey when my drunk, alcoholic Aunt Cathy brought him home as a birthday present. Don't worry, though, I'm not some horrible person that didn't say thank you for this scruffy, lopsided dog, but in all honesty, I'm much more of a cat person.

Anyways, on this particularly cool September evening, Petey was lying next to me as I read the newest Harry Potter book; *Harry Potter and the Goblet of Fire*. I distinctly remember hundreds of disgusting flies swarming up in my face and irritating the hell out of me, but that's beside the point. I was at the part in the book where Harry runs into Voldemort while he's finding his way through the maze, he's seconds away from his long anticipated death, and my aunt comes screaming out of the house as if someone had stabbed her. She bursts through the door and screams, "I've got it! I've got it this time, Spence! I really think I have it!" Here I am, staring blankly at this insane woman who I'm supposed to believe I'm related to, while she screeches about a senseless crossword puzzle. "Wow, great job Cath! How long's it taken you to get that word? Three days now?" I joke. She purses her lips, desperately trying not to murder me with her sarcasm.

My Aunt Cathy is basically that obnoxious lady on your street that you dread talking to every time you see her power-walking her way past your house. I'm not too sure how annoying she was when you knew her, but I'd like to think she wasn't always this crazy. She's constantly roaming through the neighborhood with a crumpled paper bag in her hand, over-done makeup, and an atrociously tight pair of yoga pants on. As much as she drives me absolutely mad, I do admire the way she paints. I know—a power-walking, booze drinking, yoga pants wearing fifty-two-year-old that paints? Trust me, I'm totally aware of how ridiculous it all sounds. However, she's quite the ridiculous woman.

As she stumbled on inside, I noticed a tiny, rustic looking piece of paper crammed in the pocket of her shirt. Of course, me being the curious teenager that I am, I was desperate to know what that suspicious slip of paper said. I slid inside and peeked at my aunt from behind the staircase. She was sitting in her makeshift studio, painting away, a beer in one hand and a paintbrush in the other. I'm standing there, my head running wild with all of the possible secrets hidden on that yellowish piece of paper, and she softly speaks "I see you," without even turning her head. She has a way about her; you might think you're totally alone and there she'll be; waiting for you as if you were expected. I think it's because she's a lonely old woman that always wants company, but she claims that it's a "gift." See, I told you she was crazy. I quickly muttered something that not even I could make out.

We stood there in the dimmed light and musty air without saying a word for at least half a minute. She glanced up at me, amid uncomfortable silence, and said, "Now I know you aren't one for words, but speak child!"

This relieved my nerves, so I stared down her scrawny eyebrows and thin circular glasses and shyly spoke, "I'm, um, hungry."

While this was true, I was still dying to ask her for the piece of paper. However, I've learned that you may never simply ask for what you want. You need to manipulate your way in until you've obtained what you desire. At least, that's what my old hunchback teacher Ms. Fisk told me she did with her husband.

A short backstory on Ms. Fisk—imagine a woman that is likely to be around five foot four if she stood straight, that stands at about five foot one due to her fishhook of a back. She has mousy brown hair that she once tried to dye blonde, but it turned a lake fish green color instead. She has absolutely no boundaries, which usually gets her sent to the principal's office. I even heard this rumor that she once told a boy passing notes with a girl that if he didn't read them out loud, she'd fail him. After he refused to read the notes, she read them herself. I don't know what the notes said, and man I wish I did, but apparently he nearly got expelled, and she was nearly fired. Apparently, she "invaded his privacy," but I find the whole thing perfectly civil. Imagine that; a teacher that gets sent to the principal's office. Hilarious right? Anyways, as crazy as she might sound, she truly is a remarkable teacher. She has no sense of style but could deliver a speech on Shakespeare's life story. Let's just say that Ms. Fisk and Aunt Cathy are not the best of friends. My aunt has resented her ever since I received one 'D' on a research paper that I spent a solid eight hours on. I got over it pretty quickly, but my aunt isn't the best at letting things go.

Moving on, Aunt Cathy slowly made her way into the kitchen to cook me dinner, but realistically, I knew that I would be getting a bowl of cereal with an overpowering amount of skim milk. While she shuffled over to the cupboard, I quietly walked into her studio. As I stepped onto the crooked and faded wooden floor, I glanced over at the painting she had been working on. It was a picture of a blackish grey sky with at least ten doves flying through. There was a young girl that appeared to be between the ages of seven and ten sitting at the end of a dock that overlooked a lake. To her left side sat a bottle of vodka, and to her right sat a children's book. As I'm standing there, mesmerized by this thought provoking painting, my aunt barges through the already broken door yelling "dinner's ready!" I walked out into our pea-sized kitchen and was surprised to see a sandwich sitting on a plastic, almost white plate. I looked over to Aunt Cathy to thank her, but she had already made her way back into the studio.

Once I finished my sandwich, I realized that my mysterious snooping had carried me into the latest hours of the night. Cathy hardly ever sleeps, which is totally creepy, but I make sure to be asleep by ten-thirty at the latest. I glanced over at the clock and nearly had a panic attack when my tired eyes read 12:52, especially since it was a school night. I ran up our staircase covered in the most hideous, ghastly carpet you can possibly imagine and was asleep in my bed by 12:56. Impressive, right?

I awoke the next morning with bags under my eyes and curly, dirty blonde hair shooting out in directions I didn't even know were possible. School takes me eleven minutes to get to on a good traffic day, and thirteen minutes on a bad traffic day. I wake up every single day at six twelve, and yes, I'm one of those people that refuses to sleep in on weekends. Why waste the day, right? I plan my outfits the night before and lay them out nice and neat to save as much time as possible. Sorry, I'm probably boring you with my strenuous morning routine. I'll move on. I got in Cathy's car to drive to school because she likes to walk almost everywhere she needs to go. I personally think it's to show off her backside, but she claims it's simply good exercise.

We can skip the hours of seven in the morning to two-thirty in the afternoon because the point of this story is not to tell you about what I learned in school. Let's be honest, what kid really wants to tell their parents what they learned in school? Do they really think I'm going to give them a history lesson on the Civil War or teach them Trigonometry? That's what I hear kids complain about at school; the kids that have parents. Don't get me wrong, I absolutely love Aunt Cathy, but she's not really into the whole school thing considering she dropped out her junior year.

Once I got home and ran around the back to see if my Aunt had left Petey out again, I noticed something that I had never noticed before. Cathy was wearing the exact same shirt she had worn the day before. Maybe it doesn't sound that weird, but I had never seen someone lack the decency to change their shirt. Did she always do this? Was my aunt wearing the same shirt every day for the span of my life and I had never noticed? Did she just really like the shirt? The whole situation left me flabbergasted. I figured it was time to stop being so mischievous and go ahead and ask her what the deal was. I walked inside and immediately received a huge, "Hey, kid! Have fun at school?"

"I guess so," I muttered.

She walked over to the kitchen to grab another beer and microwave some tacos. I sat down and analyzed the shirt as if it were my job. I stared at the wrinkled pocket with the still suspicious slip of paper, and the yellowish tint that the collar had obtained.

"Hey Cathy, weren't you wearing that shirt yesterday?"

She looked at me as if I were the crazy one, glanced down at her shirt and laughed.

"How funny! I must have forgotten that I wore it yesterday. It is my favorite shirt you know." I didn't know, but for the sake of her sanity I pretended I did.

"Oh yeah, that makes sense! But, um, what's that little slip of paper in the pocket?" Suddenly, my aunt got very quiet. She looked as if she would faint, get sick, or even both. It almost seemed as if she was losing balance, but quickly recollected herself when she saw the worry in my dark eyes. "You okay?" I asked.

But still, without saying a word, a troubled look was shooting through her eyes. She tried to make something out but sounded more ridiculous than I did the night before. Before I could say anything else, she slowly moved to the stairs and increased her pace with each step. While I still had absolutely no idea what my aunt was hiding on the filthy piece of paper, I knew for a fact that it was something my eyes were never supposed to wander upon.

I felt as if my head were about to spin off. My Aunt had never looked at me with such disappointment. Between the moment I had asked her what the slip of paper was, and the millisecond of silence before her eyes nearly spun back into her head, I knew I should have shut my mouth. I dropped down and sat on the hideous steps, replaying the look of her peachy face transition to a glowing blue. I sat for a few minutes but quickly started to walk up the stairs, praying that she didn't resent me for the question I should never have asked.

As I anticipated another awkward encounter, slowing my pace with each step up the rickety staircase, my aunt sprinted down with a small suitcase trailing behind and a fresh face of makeup. I stared in awe at the nerve of this woman, literally running away from her problems, and to where?

"Cathy, what the hell are you doing?"

"Oh dear, I told you last week! I'm meeting a friend for dinner, and then I figured I would just sleep over for a girl's night, you understand right?"

I most definitely did not understand. First of all, my aunt did not have any friends, and if she did, my snooping certainly would've uncovered them by now. But what could I say? In her mind I had done some terrible thing by asking her what the slip of paper said, so maybe this was her way of telling me to drop it. However, if that's her motive, she doesn't know a thing about manipulating people because not saying anything about the situation only provokes my curiosity more.

"What's your friend's name? I don't remember you telling me."

"Her name is Pam," she said softly.

"So what am I supposed to do while you're gone? Are you coming back soon?"

"Like I said, I'm only spending the night. You should spend the night doing teenage things," she grimaced as she threw me a five dollar bill.

I suppose there was no stopping her now, within about three minutes she had exited the front door, suitcase in hand and a six-pack of beer gripped under her arm. I wished to believe that she was coming back tomorrow morning, but her history hasn't led me to believe so.

I went to collapse in my bed that night at exactly 9:45, but I had probably woken up about seven times, checking to see if my aunt had returned.

10:52, no one; 11:36, Petey turned his head, but still no Aunt Cathy.

12:40, I sipped some warm milk to calm my nerves, yet it didn't fill the emptiness of being without the company of my Aunt. I hadn't realized how comforting she truly was. I always thought that she was more of the child, and I was the guardian, but I guess I'd never had to spend a night alone. I suppose I'd never thought of it before, but she's really all I have.

The following morning, I awoke at five forty-seven, though I didn't need to be up until six-twelve. I sat in the kitchen, engulfed in an oversized sweatshirt tightly gripping a large cup of coffee. I hadn't ever liked coffee before, but Aunt Cathy loves coffee. I eyed the clock as it clicked to 5:57, and then to 5:58, and so on until 6:04. I skipped breakfast that day, which I've also never done before. I usually drive to school at 6:50, but I was slightly surprised to see that my Aunt had taken the car, and therefore I had to walk.

The day went by obnoxiously slowly, with each class dragging on to the next. I didn't ask any questions in any of my classes, and usually, I always ask questions. I only ate a few almonds and drank some lemonade for lunch. Finally, as the clock rang 2:30 PM, I sprinted out of the school. I ran all the way down my street until I reached my small, green house. My stomach dropped.

I ran around the back to see if our car had returned to its rightful place, but it hadn't. Petey was still inside, a gloomy look plastered on his face. I opened the door and didn't see any trace of my alcoholic Aunt. Oddly enough, there was a glass of water sitting on the counter.

Did I drink water this morning? I was sure that I hadn't. For the second time in a matter of minutes, my stomach sank. What if someone was in my house? Cathy doesn't drink water, at least not until she needs to.

I slowly reached into the kitchen drawer and grasped the most menacing knife I could find. Hesitantly, I walked up the stairs to find whoever was in my house, praying they were not bigger than five feet and four inches. As I turned the corner to look in each room, I saw her. Aunt Cathy was sitting in her room, clothed in the most beautiful dress I had ever seen, holding a crumpled picture with the suspicious note that caused her to leave. "Cathy?"

She quietly turned her head, wiping a tear. "Oh, um, Hi Spence."

"Is everything okay?" I closed the door and sat in the finest chair of our whole house. It was purple, with velvet fabric and lion's legs.

"There's something I need to tell you, or rather, show you."

I moved closer as she motioned me to get a peek at what she was holding. I sat on the bed next to her and looked at the picture in her hand. It was of a much younger Cathy, likely around the age of twenty. Next to her sat a man, who looked a bit older, but not much.

"Cathy, who is he?"

She didn't say anything, just handed me the note. Her hand shook as it's crumply edges brushed my fingers. Once I grasped the note, she scooted away a bit, glancing down at the note and then back up at my eyes. Finally, the note I had been dying to read, was sitting right in my hands. The note read:

Dear Cathy,

I know it has been some time, but I miss you. I really miss Spence too. I don't know exactly how to go about this, considering I haven't been present for the last twelve years, but I want to come back. Since Jennifer died, I haven't been the man I promised to be, as I'm sure you've noticed. I need to see my daughter, and if you'll let me, build a relationship with her. I can't even begin to apologize for my inexcusable absence, but I guess sorry is a start. Twelve years is a long time, and a day hasn't gone by that I haven't missed the two of you, so if you'll let me, I must come back and be the father and brother-in-law I promised Jennifer I would be. I've disappointed both her and you two enough. So I'm begging you, let me come back. Call me at 555-568-9942. Please.

Sincerely,
Stephen

I looked at my aunt after I had finished reading. More tears fell down her face, so I wiped them with the sheets. I didn't really know what to say, but after a terribly long minute I muttered,

"So, is Stephen like, my father?" To be honest, I already knew the answer. He had to have been, because who else would he be?

She nodded yes. I had a million questions, but for the following few minutes, words seemed to be as difficult as calculus. I gave her a hug, unsure of what else I could do. After a long-lasting and comfortable embrace, she began to explain why she hadn't told me about the note when she got it; March of 2000.

She was terrified. Terrified of losing me to a man that hadn't been there since the day my mom died, and of letting his, or I guess your, negativity back into her life. You must be wondering what I thought happened to you, and to be clear, I didn't really know. I had asked if you were dead, but Cathy always just said, "He isn't here, and he won't be here. I'm here." She didn't like to talk about you. So now that I know, Hi.

When I discovered that you left me in the hands of my Aunt alone, I was absolutely enraged. How could you have left me when one horrible thing happened? So what mom died, I had to deal with that without you. You weren't strong enough to handle that? I suppose that's what scares me the most. You say that you want back into my life, but if you weren't strong enough the first time, why would you be this time around?

I'm not too sure why I'm even writing you, but I am. I guess there's a part of me that's always wondered about you, like what color your hair is, what you like to do for fun, if you're smart, and everything in between. Cathy didn't want to write you back; she was too scared. See, that's where your advantage is, I hardly know anything about you. As of this point forward, you have an almost clean slate. With her, apparently, you're a pretty bad guy. I'm going to give you the benefit of the doubt, so come find me, and we can talk. My phone number is 555-534-8872. If you're really lucky, maybe, just maybe, you'll get to know me. And by some miracle, you may even become my Dad again.

Sincerely,
Spence

9.
Double Trouble
Sarah Coburn; Senior

It was a brisk winter day in the town of Downsville. The winter season was picking up its pace. The snowflakes descended from the sky and joined a pile full of its friends.

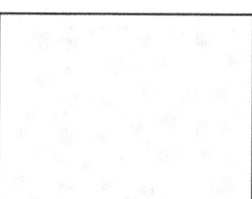

Parker Dunfrey, otherwise known as Eisenhower Elementary's toughest and roughest bully, was ready to take on Monday's adventure. Parker was never alone for his attacks. His sidekick, Maverick Mulley, stood by his side: loyal and ready to dominate.

"Ptuit! Take that you dweeb!" Parker and Maverick shouted after they finished their daily white-washings to a particular fourth grader. This fourth grader, Little Jimmy, was a year younger than these two. He was scrawny, quiet, and often forgotten. All he ever wondered was what *he* ever did to deserve Parker and Maverk's cruelty treatment. He wished it didn't have to be him.

While Little Jimmy was wishing one thing, Parker was wishing another. It was nearly Christmas time, and Parker's desire was to be on the nice list for once. Every year when he was eager to find presents under the tree, there was nothing. But Parker couldn't seem to figure it out. Why was he on the naughty list?

Parker realized that he had forgotten his lunch outside after he and Maverick shoved Little Jimmy's face into the snow. But when Parker found his belongings by the playground, he heard a whimper coming from around the corner.

"Ah-boo-hoo-hoo."

A feeling of guilt rose up in Parker's heart. He felt cold and lonely inside as if he felt bad for Little Jimmy. Parker decided to walk over to him.

"Uh um uh... hey Jimmy."

Jimmy sniffled, rubbed his eyes, and looked up. "What're you doing over here talking to a guy like me for?"

"I um uh just wanted to see if you're okay," Jimmy replied.

Little Jimmy didn't say a word. He just twirled his fingers and sniffed a couple times more.

"No?" Parker whispered.

During this moment, Parker knew that he had gone too far. He did not enjoy the feeling of pity building up inside of him; it had to stop for good. So, Parker made his way over to Jimmy.

"I didn't know that I damaged you this much," he admits while looking at Jimmy's tear rolling down his face.

"Yeah well it's not a big deal really. Oh, here—Do you want my lunch?"

"No, I've got mine right here." He holds up his lunch sack. "I really am sorry Jimmy. I hope you can forgive me. I understand if you can't."

There was a brief moment of silence, but soon Little Jimmy nodded his head, and Parker strolled away.

The next morning, Parker seemed quite different. When it was time for him and Maverick to give their weekly swirly in the bathroom, he held back. He didn't desire to be the  school bully anymore. Did he really mean what he said to Little Jimmy?

Of course, Little Jimmy was joyful and relieved about Parker's reassignment. But, one particular person did have a problem with this. Patrick's buddy, pal, and friend who had his back the whole time—Maverick.

Maverick's attempts to persuade Parker to come back failed each and every time. When he shoved students in the locker, he celebrated by leaping up and down the halls, attempting to drag Parker along with him.

"Sorry, I can't." Parker walked away.

When Maverick was throwing snowballs at the fourth-grade class after school, he made a pile for Parker to join him.

"I can't do that Maverick! That is mean!" Parker stormed off.

When Maverick took the lunches away from the students in his homeroom, he saved some for Parker. But when he tried giving them to him, Parker said, "I told you Maverick, I am done with bullying others. It is wrong. I want to treat others the way I want to be treated."

Maverick finally took the hint. Parker would not and will not budge. He scratched that plan and created a new one: he would be the replacement of the toughest and roughest bully. He disowned his fellow friend. For good.

The new bully in town was one not to mess with. He was bigger, stronger, and angrier. He desired to be better than his former sidekick.

To prove that Maverick was the worst, he went overboard. To change it up he not only wanted to target more students, but teachers too. Maverick was a sneaky one. One day after recess, he returned to class a bit early to take action on his plan. He grabbed pens, pencils, a stapler, and tape from the teacher's desk and threw them in the trash. He shredded some paper and poured coffee on top of the files on her desk.

"Excuse me!" Before Maverick could finish is duty, he was interrupted. He slowly looked up, set the coffee down, and stood in silence. His teacher came back and boy, was Maverick in some deep trouble.

After a trip to the principal's office, Maverick was granted the punishment of being suspended. He sat outside of the office in disappointment and regret.

Parker saw him as he walked by, and was very startled by what he had seen. He walked over and sat beside him. Once Maverick described what happened, Parker expressed that bullying won't do any good.

"It makes us feel better at first, but then I feel guilty and wish that I have never hurt anyone on purpose."

Maverick realized that his former partner was right. His actions not only hurt others but he hurt himself too.

The two boys made amends with one another. They would still be partners in crime, but this time, they would perform actions of kindness.

A few bitter, cold days passed, and Christmas Eve came along. It was the middle of the night, and Parker was tossing and turning in bed. All he could think about was if this Christmas would be different from the others. The repeating crackling of the fireplace put Parker to sleep.

When morning came, the bright reflection of the snow from the blazing sun woke him. He rushed down the stairs and searched everywhere for a present, but nothing was found. He was disappointed and sat down on the couch. But all of a sudden, he sees a box jiggle out from behind the Christmas tree from the corner of his eye. The box seemed as if it were shaking or vibrating. Parker walked over and lifted the lid to peek through.

A creature popped out and licked Parker right on the cheek!

"A puppy!"

Parker was so thankful. He scurried to put on his coat and shoes, scooped up the puppy, and ran outside to play with his new pal.

10.
Dreaming Of You
Mackenzie F.; Senior

The wind blew the screen door, slamming it into the house waking the sleeping women. She struggled to open her eyes; it was as if they had been sewn shut. Her vision was blurry, through the corner of her eye she managed to read the clock; it was half-past three. She peered out the window to see the rain pouring down on the sidewalk, but then she heard something coming from the hall. Her heart was beating so fast it was ready to jump out of her chest. She listened carefully to the floorboards squeak; someone was coming toward the bedroom door. The hinges on the door squealed as the person behind the door slowly pushed the door open. At last, she heard a familiar voice.

"Sorry sweetie, I didn't mean to wake you." He sounded tired as he crept toward the bathroom.

"When are these late nights going to be over?" she mumbled back to him. He ignored her and proceeded to shut the bathroom door. She turned to her other side, the silk sheets rubbed against her soft skin, they felt so smooth. He finally came out of the bathroom and crawled into bed next to his wife of twenty years. He even kissed her on her rosy cheek and then turned away from her, closing his eyes, and went to sleep. She laid there awake lost in her thoughts. She knew she could not fall asleep with her heart still beating so fast.

In her hours of restlessness, she got up and headed to the bathroom. She grabbed a towel and put it under ice-cold water. She pressed the towel against her face, it made the hairs on the back of her neck stand up. When she went to put the washcloth in the woven laundry basket, what she saw in the bin put her in a trance, it would permanently scar her forever. It was her husband's work shirt with a cherry red lipstick smear on the collar. She picked it up and held it in her hands. It smelled of cheap perfume and cigarettes. Suddenly, every memory she ever had with him flashed through her head and just like that, they were all gone. She could never forgive him, he finally broke her. She knew what she had to do. Since he killed everything she believed in, now she would kill him.

Without hesitation, within the next second, she kicked down the door shaking the bedroom walls. She ran out of the bathroom, her face red hot, she was out for blood. Her husband, terrified, jumped out of bed.

"What's going on?" He was shaking barely able to stand. He glanced down and saw a red stained shirt in her clammy hands. He instantly became pale, as if he had seen a ghost, but little did he know soon he would be one. He could not bear to look up at the woman he betrayed. Her eyes were filled with callousness. He had never seen her look like that before; he knew something detrimental was going to happen. Then, the next thing he heard from her was...

"Run!" She said it in such a deep voice it sounded as if she was possessed. She darted toward him ripping their wedding picture off her nightstand. She hurled the picture towards his head it gashed him right in his forehead. He collapsed to the ground pressing his hand hard against his open wound.

"You're crazy!" he yelled out, crawling towards the bedroom door leaving a path of blood on the floor. She ran over to the broken picture frame on the floor picking up the sharpest piece of glass she could find. She ran the staggered blade down her finger. The glass pierced her skin drawing blood. She licked the warm blood off her finger; except this was not the blood she was out for. She crept out of the bedroom, stepping into the hallway onto the cold hardwood floor.

Honey, where did you go?" she said calmly joking. The only thing that responded was from outside the house. Nothing but the howls from the wind was her answer. She followed the puddles of warm-blood down the stairs. He was standing in the living room with the gun in one hand and his cell phone in the other.

"You don't want to do this!" he cried out to her. Now, she was to treat him the way he treated her, she didn't even acknowledge anything he said, it went in one ear and out the other.

"How could you do this to me!" she shrieked. "You're going to pay for this," she said as she put her foot out in the front of the other, stepping towards him, grasping the piece of broken glass in her hand firmly.

"I'm going to call the police, and if you try to attack me again, I will shoot you."

"Oh ha ha, nonsense," She laughed like a crazy women. "You wouldn't dare shoot me, sweetheart." She sounded sincere.

"I promise, oh, I will, don't you make me do it."

"That's funny honey because you don't keep your promises."

"What are you talking about?"

"When I said 'til death do us part, I meant that. Unlike you, I keep my promises." She darted towards him with the piece of broken glass held straight out in front of her. He raised the gun.

"Please stop!" he begged, but it was too late, she threw the blade towards him. He fired his only shot straight into her heart. At that same moment, the blade slit his throat. The two bodies instantly collapsed to the floor, filling the living room with a dark red pool of blood. The warm blood began to seep into the tiniest crevices of the dark wood floorboards and completely submerged the white fur rug, like a wine stain that would never come out. The house fell completely silent as the husband and wife lay in puddles of their own blood.

Suddenly, someone spoke. "Honey, wake up are you okay?" The woman, in a daze, couldn't comprehend what was going on, *how could this be possible*? she thought. The women opened her eyes quickly to see her husband lying next to her.

"You were shaking." The women jumped out of bed to find her and her husband's wedding picture still sitting on their nightstand. She scurried to the bathroom to find her husband's white work shirt unstained. She came back out wiping the cold sweat off her forehead.

"Yeah, I'm fine, just a frightening dream."

11.
For I Rest On The Moon And They Live On The Stars
E.D.; Junior

Children are not children anymore when they are worried they're carrying a child themselves. Now there may be identifiers of 'adulthood' or 'adult-like symptoms' but I believe one of the most pivotal and most terrifying points in any juvenile's life is pacing a room waiting for one stripe to appear on a pregnancy test. Here's a story, with no particular meaning or significant ending or hidden metaphysical messaging. Maybe just more of a prettier side to despair.

During the day, I'm ignoring what might be, but at night, with no one to distract me from my thoughts, all I can do is go deeper and deeper into WebMD and feed my paranoia. There really isn't any real proof of me being potentially pregnant, but that doesn't stop me from believing the fake proof I've manufactured. I pushed myself through two weeks of either being at a point where I've talked myself out of the possibility and can sleep for the night, only to wake up in the middle of the night to tightly grip my knees and gently rock on my bathroom floor bawling. It's getting hard to function without slightly/majorly emotionally breaking down so, come the end of class, on a brisk Friday afternoon, I'd have my friend drive me to the nearest convenience store so I can spend my mom's money on a pregnancy test.

Three-thirty in the afternoon and class just got out, and the people fill the halls like water. There's even more selfish pushes and shoves than usual because it's Friday and people can't wait to steal a shot or five of Fireball from their parent's liquor cabinet. I pass all the familiar faces from elementary to middle, and now high school on my walk to my friend's car, wondering if they've ever had a heartbreak, or watch as many Minecraft videos as I do, or have ever been as worried as I am right now.

I wonder about people often.

We're laughing and giggling as if nothing mattered and I was happily going through another five-minute phase of, "I can't be pregnant." But after we park and make that pitiful walk to the planned parenthood section and I sit right on the dust-covered tile and look up at the wall of lube and PlanB and remind myself, "I would be that bitch to get pregnant."

Along with the pregnancy test, we childishly skip around the store looking at the aisles of months' early Halloween candy but eventually making it to the counter. The cashier makes almost too much effort to not point out the obvious, actually never said a word.

I wish he would have talked to me.

We leave, and the pink of the pregnancy test packaging is peaking through the almost transparent 'Have A Great Day" printed plastic bag, so my friend kindly stuffs it down her pants.

We make it back to her house, and I head right to her pantry for a marshmallow; a daily routine for me.

"I'm not sure if I'd be angry at you or not if it comes up positive," she says. I don't reply and continue chewing my mouthful of fluff. We make our way upstairs. I drop my backpack and realize I haven't taken it off yet today.

My back hurts.

I open the colorful blue and pink packaging to have a hairball of anxiety plant itself in my throat. I giggle it off because I can't be pregnant. I nervously and sloppily pee on the test and rest up against her cold radiator, pants still off and rest my tired worrisome eyes in my fingertips. I whisper to myself, "But then again, I would be that bitch to get pregnant."

My friend tiptoes over and puts a cheesy plastic gold crown on my head, "Look what I found," she nervously says through a smile.

She keeps me sane.

The next one-hundred-twenty seconds seemed longer than every math class I've spent staring at the clock, longer than all those hours spent staring at the ceiling just trying to fall asleep, longer than the time after someone texts you, "We need to talk." With my head down, pants off and crown slipping off I tell her to look at it first. I flash the still piss covered stick at her, and she gives a little gasp, then reveal it to myself like some twisted game show.

Not pregnant.

I knew it. I knew I knew it. I let out a good relief cry and then pull my pants up off my ankles. She embraces me, and I cry a little more and then almost instantly the hairball was gone, and I could breathe, and see a little better. I lie on her shaggy carpet and just breathe. She brings out a big piece of paper and a pencil and says, "Draw your baby."

Draw my baby? I can't even begin to comprehend me being a mother. Even the word is sour off my tongue. Someone, another someone, has to fully rely on for character development? Yeah, no thank you, I'll kindly pass for now, but nonetheless, I start with a rough sketch of the eye.

I love drawing eyes.

But realize this is looking more like a vegetable than anything, so I pitch it and start new from a different perspective. Babies are babies, they all resemble a naked mole rat but what about where they came from. Not chapters two through three in the heath textbook but what if the purity of a newborn isn't tangible to us. I'm not spiritual. Never was, and most likely never will be, but I admire the concept; but with something as so imaginary now as motherhood, now I can be more formative with my baby. I draw a crescent moon with a content face and little glowing orbs almost hugging the stars.

Per say, I rest on the moon, and they live on the stars.

I sit here day in and day out in my what was once a white law chair that is now ivory.

Maybe 'I' am God. It's nice believing in something.
Per say, the moon is our mother and the stars home her children.
Before they are our children, they are her children.

They illuminate a soft aura of all different shapes and sizes and color similar to a string of out of date rainbow Christmas lights.

They're laughing and giggling as if nothing matters, satisfied not knowing their purpose, just gently floating.

They dance to their own harmony that they sing with the stars. They're very good singers.

Some sleep in the clouds or bundle with the thick cosmos and leave behind them a small train of comfort dusted in sparkles.

They play in peace, ignorant to the world below, probably for the best.

Forever in a playful orbit, she and I watch from afar the purest thing known before any knowns."

She didn't respond but simply took the little photo, ripped it out of the sketchbook and propped it up on the desk.

"I like that." she reiterates.

"It's fun pretending that maybe that purity is existent somewhere."

12.
Homesick
Siena C.; Junior

**"You can't make homes out of human beings
someone should have already told you that."**
— *Warsan Shire*

The July before freshman year, I ventured down the tree-lined streets to my best friend's house for a going-away party for their family. At the time, I don't remember feeling anything incredibly distinct - perhaps a little fear sitting back on its haunches, for the time being, a little nostalgia in nooks that are hard to reach, bubblegum-sticky. I felt like my middle school friendships were waning, like I was waning, like home was waning. Like time was running out. Like I could see the sidewalk speeding out from under me, *I'm sorry, girl, I have to go now, don't you know?*

A burst of swing music punctuated by group laughter erupted from a window as I neared, honeyed light spilling from the eyes of Mallory's house. I pushed open the door with both hands rather than knocking, as the years had taught me to, dished out polite smiles to mothers who I had watched and wondered if this was their dream life for years upon years, padded down the carpeted stairs to where the others waited.

My other friend, Avery, was crowded against the wall beside Mallory, the glow of an iPhone screen flickering across their faces and washing them out to facelessness. There was an uneasiness climbing up the knobs of my spine, but it hadn't quite reached my brain yet. Avery's younger brother got up to bump my fist and grab a plate of pasta from the kitchen upstairs, but Mallory and Avery just looked up, eyes like rivers, murky, rumbling with something knowing. I felt like I was running along the bank to keep up, these days.

The next thirty minutes were relatively uneventful, consisting of dancing to a trashy pop punk song and lazily attempting to organize a skit with the distractedly giggly younger kids, Avery and Mallory authoritative in their girlhood and seniority. I sipped on flat Coke and laughed absentmindedly and tried not to mind the ghosts of eighth grade and this summer moving furniture around up in my head.

The other girls there sat beside me for most of the time, but the other two were magnetic, sparking and inseparable. The clock had hit past nine, the party only having been in swing for just under an hour, but the stacks of paper plates in the corners of the room leaned right with fatigue.

Avery leaned in to Mallory's ear, hand cupped to protect whatever she said in the way that girls often do as if they could preserve a little sacredness in their palm in whatever knowledge they share. And as every young girl feels once in their life, I felt the pupils on me like tracer bullets that froze in front of your face and followed you around for the rest of your life, tasted their whispers on the roof of my mouth, bittersweet like youth and bared teeth.

I can't say for sure what they said to this day, and I don't know if I'll ever truly see again whatever happened within me that night, I just know I heard my name—"Look at her..." and a light switch flicked on within me—burning from the inside out, blinding heat through my eyes and ears, until I was hard to look at. A lighthouse, finally stuttering on and illuminating the rocks on the shore.

I saw every year go to ribbons behind my eyes, the photographs of my relationships with these strangers finally developed and hanging on a string before my eyes, and without really registering what I was doing, I felt myself get up. Pad up the carpeted stairs. Pass the parents who called for me in their half-remembered dream. Departed from the house in a false halo of honeyed light.

Walked under the purpled sky, homeward bound, or at least to where I lived. The crickets were muted in my ears, the leering silhouettes of the thick-trunked trees lining the sidewalks bending down to peer at whatever must have been in my eyes.

I could hear the clamor of a pool party happening down in my backyard when I finally walked up my own front steps into the next chapter, but I headed for my room, laid on my back, and didn't cry.

We don't make eye contact in the hallway, three years later.

****

"You see, I usually find myself among strangers because I drift here and there trying to forget the sad things that happened to me."
— F. Scott Fitzgerald, *The Great Gatsby*

I have loved many strangers, but not many as quickly as I did the kids I met at camp a summer between high school years. I clung to them, and they clung back with the special kind of ferociousness that belongs to a group of teenagers who know they have only a week.

I remember the glint of my friend Eliza's braces in the yellowed hallway light, the night we snuck down to the basement laundry room, the last night there - my friends and I a pack of quick silhouettes and bright pajama pants, blurry laughter and urgent hushes. Every floor the elevator hit, I could feel another version of myself left on the floor above.

And how it felt when not only was a particular boy there but the others, all of the kids scattered around the laundry room in stolen swivel chairs and in laundry baskets. How it felt to hop up on the washing machine beside him and look the end in the face as we touched hands, safe for a last night, listening to the *chug-uh-chug-uh-chug* of the washing machines underneath us, and the heavy rhythm all of our hearts inside of them.

We talked for two weeks afterwards, blinking away sleep as the phone glared unflinchingly at the dusky circles beneath my eyes, his little siblings babbling in the background of every call.

When we stopped, I picked up every self from the floors and went on.

****

"In the world I am
Always a stranger
I do not understand its language
It does not understand my silence."
— Bei Dao

Tasha is a girl who lived down the hall from me when I spent two weeks at a camp in the South. She had come from Asia when she was a little girl and was a fervent Christian; she liked acapella groups and Vietnamese food and jogging, she wrote everything down in gel pen and often cried when she was happy and felt inadequate compared to her older sister. We spent countless lunch hours sitting across from each other as she giggled so hard she wept at my school's mascot, and I remember so distinctly her words on a four in the morning hike as we reached the top of a local mountain at dawn. There was a brief silence as we watched the world stretching awake all around us in dripping shades of oily rose and gold before she spoke, her eyes unfocused on a trio of teenagers further down the mountain who had taken off their shirts as they mirrored the rebirth they saw. "I think it's amazing how this happens every single morning, even when nobody is around to see it."

I thought, at the time, *I think I have a problem with loving strangers more than I love a lot of the people that I go to school with every day. I think I love inevitable things. Is that bad?*

I said, "Yeah."

I left her behind a little over a month ago, sitting in the passenger seat of a rental car with my Dad, the songs playing from his phone that I listened to when I was twelve because he hasn't downloaded new music in so long.

I unzipped my backpack to get a bottle of water and drew out a letter marked with my name, and a Bible verse written in the corner, in green gel pen.

****

"For you I have so many words / but I forget where we were."
— Ben Howard, *"I Forget Where We Were"*

Maybe we fear strangers because they represent the unknown, what we haven't felt yet, but I know that this is often where we are truly safe: surrounded by those who haven't yet hurt or seen or heard or healed you, standing with your head bowed in a blind world.

And so I'll write for a thousand strangers in the way that those in love with everything do until I can learn to understand the stranger that I am.

I ran into Avery at the town smoothie place four months after the July before freshman year, making small talk over the chaotic whir of blenders. Her head was tilted to the side slightly when she spoke to me, maybe not recognizing me. Or at least I hoped masochistically.

"Why did you leave Mallory's party that night without saying goodbye?"

I smiled.

****

"Two people who were once very close can
without blame
or grand betrayal
become strangers.
perhaps this is the saddest thing in the world."
— *Warsan Shire*

The night in July we drove home from Chicago, I had my knees pulled to my chest in the passenger seat of my mother's Chrysler, watching the road speed out from under me. *Terribly sorry to rush you, girl, don't you know? I can't quite help this turning.*

I am going to write every stranger I collect as I move on and in and out of these places where we are scared to go, of homes and heads and heartbeats and washing machines. The only way to keep short things is to find the place where they'll live for a thousand years.

The city lights don't speak to us too, but I often watch them as I go, finding the strangers in them that blink at us in confusion, for perhaps we look a little different than we did when we came.

13.
In-Between
Holly Booth; Senior

Shutting my laptop, I glance over at the clock that reads 2:38 am. I reach quietly flipping the switch on the lamp, and my blackberry starts to buzz. I rummage to find it tangled in-between the sheets.

"It's in the middle of the night, Jeff. We have a long trip tomorrow," Alice shouts while softly gripping my wrist.

"It could be an emergency. I have to take it" I say halfway out the bedroom door. I sit on the top step of the staircase, take a deep breath, and answer the phone.

"Hello, Bill. Just finished and emailed the presentation for Sunday."

"No need to send it to me, you'll just present it yourself when you're in Boulder," Bill snaps.

"I have my family vacation to our house in the Hamptons that starts tomorrow," I say kindly but still firm.

"I'll see you Sunday, or Lance will be taking over the project," he hangs up without giving me a chance to respond. I make my way back to the bedroom and finally shut my eyes.

"What did Bill want?" Alice rolled over looking me dead in the eye.

"Nothing Alice. He just wanted to make sure the presentation was emailed."

Alice slowly rolls back to the far end of her side of the bed.

My Alarm loudly beeps, and I'm up by 5:04 am. After getting out of the shower I put on my freshly ironed dress pants, no pleats, a button-down collared shirt, blue tie, and finish off with my new apple watch that Lucy and James bought me. I have absolutely no clue how to use it. My blackberry makes a single buzz in the back pocket of my dress pants.

Start packing your plane leaves at 10:00 am. Sincerely, Bill.

In the closet, I pull out my giant brown luggage and pack my nicest suits. A shadow emerges from the bright hallway.

"Honey, why are you packing so early?" Alice whispers, coffee in hand. She looks at the briefcase stacked on top of my suitcase.

With her eyes glued on the luggage, she says "Don't do this again Jeff."

"I will lose my job if I don't." I clinch my fist tightly.

"You've had new offers for jobs every week!" She slams her half empty mug on the shelf.

"I can't do this right now I have my flight soon. You guys leave without me."

"If you leave, don't bother coming back!" Alice yells back.

I rush towards the archway with my luggage, forcing Alice to jump out of my way. Lucy, and James with his blanket in hand, stops me right before the door.

"Are you leaving again?" Lucy says. I don't respond and jump into the car waiting in the driveway. Staring from the front window is Lucy and James. An intense, sharp pain hits my chest. I reach into the deep pocket of my briefcase and take three pills from an orange prescription bottle to ease the pain.

Miles away from the airport a crowd of cars comes to a halt. The driver slams on the break forcing my body to slam forward into the back of the passenger seat. My shoulders, neck, and jaw begin to ache.

"Don't you know how to drive?" I yelled at him. He tries to speak, but the only words that he can get out of his mouth are, "Sorry, sir.

Finally, we make it to the airport, and I can barely pull my luggage from the intense aching in my chest. I arrive at my gate and pull out my blackberry. I see an incoming call from the home phone. It's time for first class to board and I quickly press decline on my phone. I get in front of the line to board and hand a tall, large, man with a long beard, my ticket.

"Excuse me, but you have to wait and board with the rest of business class," the flight attendant says.

I look down at my ticket. "I will not sit with the low class. I paid for first class, and that is what I will get."

"You're holding up the line. I need you to step to the side and sort out your ticket issue, sir."

I clench my fists, feeling another wave of aches and pains. I don't move, and the attendant eventually hands me the correct ticket. As I enter the plane, I overcome the stench of stale peanuts and sweat. When I get to my seat, I am finding it harder and harder to breathe. I quickly sit down and order two gin and tonics while taking some pain pills along with it. It's taking forever for the other passengers to find their seats and get settled, so I order another drink.

By the time I finish my third gin and tonic, the pilot announces it's time for takeoff. I fasten my seatbelt and watch as we get further and further into the air. I now feel a severe amount of pressure on my chest. I reach, trying to grip my upper body but my arms feel numb, so I can't move. My breaths are getting shorter, I keep gasping for more air. My vision gets blurry, and all I can see is black. I can still feel my body in the seat and the plane heading in an upward direction. My breathing is starting to get better, but the pain is still there.

"Help!" I yell over and over, but still, I can't hear or see anything.

In the distance appears a bright white light rapidly coming towards me. It's coming dangerously close so I shield my face. A gust of wind hits me hard and lifts my body floating, almost like I was in a deep body of water. The space is now completely illuminated by the bright light. My vision is starting to clear, and I can see a figure standing yards away from me. It's a man dressed in all white. I squint my eyes to get a better look. His beard, eyes, and nose all look familiar. I get my feet back on the ground. He turns in the opposite direction and starts to walk away. I run after him.

"Pops?" he stops and turns around.

"Welcome to the In-between," he smiles.

"What is happening to me?" I say in a panicked and shaky tone.

"You suffered a fatal heart attack, and you are now here."

"So I'm dead, and I'm in heaven?"

"Yes, you have died, son but you are not in Heaven and not in Hell either. You are in the In-between, a place between Heaven and Earth until you can earn your way to heaven," he starts walking again, and I join him.

"How do I do that?" I ask him.

"That is for you to figure out," Pops smiles at me again.

We arrive at a giant mirrored door with nothing behind it. I can see in the reflection that I'm not in my work clothes. Now, I'm in a soft white button-up shirt and flowy white pants. Pops opens the door, and I can't believe what I see. Pops directs me through the door. Above us are big puffy clouds that are so close you can almost reach your hand up to touch them. The ground is a thin layer of water that reflects the beautiful blue sky above. I look up toward the clouds, and I'm blinded by the light.

"Is that Heaven?" I turn to Pops, he nods.

I keep walking further in the water, but suddenly Pops stops me. He looks down, and as soon as the water settles I can see Earth below me. Even though it seems to be thousands of miles away, I can see the world so clearly.

"Look, Jeff," Pops nudges my shoulder.

I can see Lucy and James sitting on the patio steps in the backyard of our house, dressed all in black. Alice comes out from inside. She sits down next to them and holds both of them in her arms.

"When will he be back?" James asks Alice.

"He's dead. He's never coming back, James" Lucy whispers back.

Alice holds them tighter and begins to cry.

"Oh, James, Oh Lucy, and Dear Alice!" I yell.

The ground begins to shake, and the water makes waves. I can't see them anymore. A tear runs down my cheek. I fall to the ground trying to look through the water for Alice and the kids.

"Why did this happen to me?" I shout.

"Jeff, we need to keep going, we don't have much time." He reaches his hand to help me up.

The water stops moving, and I can now see the world again. But now it's dark as night. I can see down into our living room. Lucy is wearing her tutu and is getting her ballet shoes on.

"Lucy, let me get a couple pictures of you all dressed up," Alice says holding her phone out ready to take a picture. Lucy has the biggest smile across her whole face. James joins, hugging his big sister for the picture.

"Where is your father? We will be late for your first recital," Alice says reaching for the home phone next to her. I can hear the phone ringing and then hear myself telling Alice that I'm still working.

"Your father isn't going to make it tonight he is very sorry," Alice says laying a hand on Lucy's shoulder.

"He never comes to anything!" Lucy shouts taking her ballet shoes off then throwing them down on the ground.

The ground shakes again, and the waves come back.

"Lucy, I'm sorry!" I yell.

The water lays flat. I see another flashback coming, and it's from this morning. In our main bedroom, Alice walks into the walk-in closet. She finds me packing for the business trip instead of our family trip Alice had all nicely planned out.

"I've had enough," I say to Pops.

Tears rush down my face. The ground shakes once again. As the water gets more still, I can see multiple flashbacks at a time. I see the first time where Alice and I met in a coffee shop, the day I asked her to marry me, the day Lucy was born, the day James was born, James' first soccer goal, and many more memories washing over me like a tidal wave.

I'm now being lifted into the air, floating slowly towards the bright clouds, leaving my body behind. I've never felt so light, so weightless or so calm. I keep rising until I'm deep into the clouds. The warm sunshine welcomes me into this strange new world. I know I am in Heaven now and can finally be at peace. Pops is there smiling at me.

I say, "This is Heaven right, Pops?"

"Yes, Jeff, you learned the error of your ways on Earth, and you have been forgiven, and your family knows how much you love them." He rests a hand on my shoulder.

I can still see the Earth so clearly, but now I am not seeing the past but seeing the present. I am with my family as they go on. I vow not to miss a thing. I am so happy and at peace.

14.
Jessica's Unfortunate Night
Corinne Sickman; Senior

The woods were silent, having been vacant for years. The locals stayed away, out of fear of an incident similar to the last. It had been nearly fifty years since then, and no one had been brave enough to enter the woods since. Until October 22, 1989; a day this group of friends would never forget no matter how hard they try.

Chris had been driving for hours and needed a place for him and his friends to stop for the night on their way to Colorado. As Michael, in the passenger's seat, looked at the map, he noticed a large wooded area a few miles up the road. He told Chris to get ready to pull over and told Josh and Jessica to get ready to grab their stuff and set up camp, before sunset.

They turned onto a small, overgrown, dirt road and drove for a few more minutes until they reached a gate with an old rusted sign hanging off of it which faintly read "no vehicles beyond this point." They parked, grabbed their tent and sleeping bags and began to walk along the path. It was overgrown with tall grass, the smell of rainfall surrounded them as they walked alongside an ominously dark river, with a steady flow of water running through it. After ten minutes, they came upon a small, flat area with an old picnic table and what appeared to have once been a small fire pit.

"Yo Michael, come help me find some firewood," said Chris as he turned away from the camp and toward the woods. His luscious blond hair flowing in the light breeze. Michael jogged to catch up with Chris, and Josh stayed behind with Jessica to set up the tent.

"Hey Jess, I'm going to head down to the river to wash up, I'll be back in a few.," said Josh, playfully.

"No, don't leave me alone, that's not funny," she responded.

"Haha you'll be fine, don't worry," he said as he headed toward the river.

Jess began to read the instructions for the tent and attempted to put it together. She got as far as assembling the poles before hearing a sound in the distance, followed by what sounded like the cracking of a stick. Thinking it was Josh lurking in the bushes trying to scare her, she turned quickly, but no one was there. Averting her attention back to the tent she fumbled to stick the pole through the tent openings. Once again she heard a noise, seemingly closer than the last. "Josh is that you? Josh... this isn't funny!" she said with an anxious tone.

Jessica heard the sound once more. It reminded her of something she'd heard in a horror movie. She quickly turned back to the tent to find one of the poles missing. "Alright boys that's enough, I know it's you. This really isn't funny." She glanced around the woods in a circular motion. Suddenly, she felt a presence hovering over her. She turned abruptly. As she opened her mouth to scream for help, the dark figure jammed the missing tent pole directly down her throat, impairing her ability to speak. She fell to the ground in anguish. Before being able to understand what had happened she was stabbed with another pole, this time directly through the heart. Her final sight as she took her last breath, was the ghostly pale and seemingly familiar face of her cold-hearted attacker.

A few moments later, Chris and Michael returned to the campsite to find Josh hunched over Jess's body. Josh, unable to speak, remained on his knees and began to cry at the sight of his dead girlfriend. He began to repeatedly shake her body hoping and praying she would wake up. Chris grabbed Josh and pulled him off of Jess, holding him tight in an attempt to console his friend. Michael, in such shock, was unable to move and just stood there staring at his friends.

A few minutes later, Chris said in a weary voice "We need to get out of here. Pick her up, and let's get her back to the car." So that's exactly what they did. No one said a word on the walk back.

When they reached the car, Josh said, "I'll drive."

"I don't think that's such a good idea, I'll drive." Michael murmured, still in shock.

Josh raised his voice "No I'm fine. I am going to drive."

So they got into the car. Michael in the passenger's seat and Chris in the back seat with Jess. Josh started the car and began to drive further up the base of the mountain. As they passed a sign which said "lookout point .5 miles" Chris realized they were going the wrong direction. He told Josh to turn around.

Josh ignored him and began to accelerate. Then he lost it and began to yell things like "This is all our fault. If it weren't for us, she would still be alive. We don't deserve to live."

Chris realized what was happening, they were headed straight for the lookout. He yelled to Michael "We have to get out. You have to jump... Now!" Michael hesitated, giving Josh the opportunity to grab hold of his arm. Josh, being much stronger than Michael overpowered him and Michael realized there was no escaping Josh's grip.

With the cliff rapidly approaching, all Michael could see were the lights of the small town below. He looked at Chris and said, "Jump, you can get out alive. You have to make it back and explain all of this to our families."

Chris hesitated but knew what he needed to do. He flung open the door and dove out just as the car reached the drop-off. He got up and stood at the edge of the lookout as his three friends and his car soared through the air. Having no light, no means of transportation or communication he lay down on the lone bench which overlooked the small town below. He lay there, in shock, until dawn. Then, he made his way down the mountain and to the small town below, where he asked to use a phone and contacted the police.

They conducted a thorough investigation but found nothing.

To this day, no one is certain of what happened in those woods. And no one is willing to return to try and find out.

15.
Lessons Of Many Lives
Brigitte Gagnier; Senior

The fresh, crisp air blew through Bimal's hair as he reflected on the life that he has come to hate. There are so many journeys he has yet to experience, so many people to meet, and so many lives to live and he could not be more eager to get to them. Bimal has just begun his journey as a soul, and it's off to a start that is less than what he would like it to be. Bimal has been born into a rich family that lives atop a rolling grass hill along the English countryside. Bimal was born to a very wealthy family that values only their things and their image within their early twentieth-century society. Bimal was born "Harry," and was given a nanny named Caroline who has taken care of him since infancy and he had grown very close to her, finding comfort in her emerald green eyes. The memories of Harry's family are far less substantial than he would like them to be.

Every morning he is dressed in freshly pressed clothes, and at age seven he wants nothing more than a childhood filled with fun and adventures, which is far from what he experiences. Harry has blonde curly hair and ice blue eyes that encompass Bimal right inside of them. Bimal is as pure as a soul gets. As Harry, he cares so deeply for the people around him, and all he wants is some level of care back from the people whom he needs most- his parents. Bimal knows that within every life there is something that he must learn and throughout his first life he can't seem to quite decipher what it is. Caroline becomes his ultimate guide and the person whom Harry looks to for everything, compassion, love, guidance through the life that he's living. As he grows up Harry is home-schooled, and he is taught by the best teachers and become very well educated. Harry seems to sometimes forget that this is one life of many as he grows up. Harry must remind himself that inside Bimal is who he truly is, Harry is just the shell that carries him through this life.

The one thing that Harry feels a connection to more than anything else in his life is animals. Growing up, one of the few things that brought him joy the horses that his family owned. Harry would get up and run out to the stables. The joy the smell of hay and the sound of hoofs colliding with the concrete brought Harry were something that no one could take away from him- not even his parents. Harry had his own pony, Prince. Prince was a small white pony that Harry had learned everything from. Harry had more love for Prince than he ever imagined that he could have for anything in this life. Harry and Prince were inseparable, and Caroline was overjoyed that Harry found something that brought that level of comfort and joy. Harry felt as though he could do anything when he was with Prince and Prince became his best friend. Caroline would take Harry to the stables, and Harry would run in the pasture with Prince, he would brush him with the stiff bristles of the brush caring for Prince the way that he longed for his parents to care for him.

As Harry grew older, he found that his purpose in this life was to show others love, care, and compassion. Harry knew what it felt like to just exist and he knew that he wouldn't let any other person that had a part in his life feel that same way.

One day Harry came into the stables, and he looked at Prince, he looked at his older tired legs and the way Prince's brown eyes were glossed over. Harry knew that Prince didn't have much longer and he knew that Prince was no longer enjoying the life that he had. Prince was given all the love in the world by Harry, but he had gotten to a certain point where he knew that Prince was just existing. Harry learned to be selfless, he learned to love that horse more than he loved his own feelings. He knew it was time to let Prince go. Letting something that he loved go evoked emotions so deep that it changed him. It didn't just change Harry, it changed Bimal who lay deep inside of Harry.

As Harry mourned the loss of Prince another animal that came into his life. Caroline had always warned Harry about the dangers of snakes. Harry had not yet had an encounter with a snake, and as he walked through the pasture that Prince used to spend his days grazing on the tall lush grass, he came across a green snake. Shaken and flooded with fear Harry could not move as his ice blue eyes met the piercing red eyes of the green scaley snake. This wasn't an ordinary snake, this snake was large and could move faster than the blink of an eye. As time slowed, the snake talked to Harry, whispering things he refused to believe. He knew better than to believe that nothing in this world was worth loving, that no one was worthy and that this life was for no one but himself. Bimal focused on the task at hand and brushed off the snake. As the rest of Harry's life passed him by, Bimal didn't feel as though much more was to come of it and let it go. Bimal was ready for his next life and his next adventure.

As Bimal reflected back on his life as Harry, he thought about what was to come and what he could and would do differently to make a difference in the world, instead of just learning things for himself, after all, that was a traveler's job.

Bimal is shot directly into his next life, and this time Bimal is not a man, nor a woman- Bimal is a dog. As Bimal rummages around the bin of toys with his brothers and sisters, a pair of small gentle hands lift him from the ground. The little girl pulls him to her chest, and the scent of warm vanilla fills Bimal's wet nose. "I want this one," the little girl said to her dad as Bimal wagged his tail in excitement. Bimal is quickly wrapped tighter in the girl's arms as he heads for his new home and his new life. "Let's call him Oliver!" the little girl exclaimed to her dad as her eyes glistened with happiness. Oliver it was, and Bimal could not be more excited about what was to come.

As the little girl grew up, Oliver stood by her side rain or shine. Oliver was there as she learned to ride her bike and fell countless times. Emily became the center of Oliver's world and

Oliver the center of Emily's. As they grew up, they grew closer until Emily was old enough for college. Oliver didn't know what to do with himself or where to go or who to trust.

Bimal had felt lonely before, but he had never experienced this kind of loneliness.

Oliver sat and waited at the door waiting for the day that Emily would walk back through the door, and one day she did. Oliver was overwhelmed with joy and his heartache quickly disappeared as the two reunited.

Emily and Oliver moved to a new house that Emily bought, and their journey together continued. They went on walks in the smooth autumn air, went boating in the summer and had ice cream for dessert almost every night. Oliver felt a connection with Emily that he had never had before. He devoted his whole life to her happiness.

One day as they walked in the forest on a brisk Sunday morning, a snake came slithering out of the thick green brush. Immediately Oliver recognized the red eyes. He barked profusely, but Emily didn't notice the snake until it was too late. It dug its fangs into her flesh as poison seeped into her blood. She fell to the ground as Oliver chased after the snake, and it disappeared just as quickly as it appeared. Oliver was flooded with fear as he ran to find help. He came upon a small cabin and barked until someone came to him. He ran as fast as his legs would carry him back to Emily, and by the time they got her to the hospital, it was too late. Emily was gone, and Oliver alone.

Oliver didn't know what to do. The immense pain that overtook his body was almost unbearable. He had didn't have the desire to eat, to play, or to live.

Bimal had never stooped this low in his lives, and he didn't know that his pain was something that he could or wanted to endure. Bimal changed with the past life in a way that taught him to care so deeply and purely for others, and now he was wondering if that was worth it if, in the end, this is what life had become. Bimal was also filled with rage as he came to the realization that the snake was what had caused all of this pain and anguish. He now decided to set his eternal life to finding the snake not for revenge, but for closure. *Why? Why would he cause this? Why would he do this to hurt someone so badly that it was nearly irreparable?* As those thoughts flooded Bimal, the life of Oliver was over, and the next was about to begin.

Bimal's earliest memory of this third life is at age seventeen, as Charlotte. Charlotte was born into lower class family in twenty-first century America. Charlotte worked so hard to get to where she was. Despite the financial challenges she faced, her family stood by her side, always pushing her forward to be the best that she could be. Charlotte had all of Bimal's knowledge and character. Charlotte was kind, generous, and knew what real hurt felt like. Charlotte was one of the kindest people anyone would meet in their lives. She was also reserved and was cautious to let people in because she knew what could and would come of it when it ended. She not only didn't want to let herself get hurt, but she also didn't want to be the cause of others feeling that same way.

As Bimal looked through Charlotte's eyes at the world, he saw the world differently than Bimal had ever seen it before.

As Charlotte grew older, she began to let people in and experience the world. She traveled the world to see how people lived, cultures she had never experienced, and things she had never known.

Rather than living the life of every person in world Bimal realized that living one life that truly meant something and going to observe others lives was so much more fulfilling. Bimal knew that he was going to make something out of this life if it was the last thing he would do.

Charlotte went on to graduate college and become a pediatric emergency room doctor. Charlotte was happy with where she was in her life and Bimal finally felt like all of these lives that he lived were worth something.

After five years as an emergency room doctor, Charlotte had seen so much that had changed her. Lives she couldn't save, people she couldn't help, and parents that she had to tell their child didn't make it. This shook Bimal to the core, but he knew that he was there for a reason and if he did everything that he could, then Bimal's purpose would be served.

One day a young girl is rushed in, she had been bitten by a snake. After the girl is rushed in Charlotte saw her mom and dad rush in as the girl's dad tied her golden retriever outside to the bench. Charlotte's stomach dropped. Bimal knew that girl meant more than the world to those three. Charlotte would not let this girl lose her battle like the girl Bimal loved did. She saved her. Charlotte saved the girl. Bimal felt like he had beaten this grey shadow of a snake that followed him around from life to life, and the battle was over. Charlotte finally had good news to deliver to a family and Bimal couldn't be happier with the person, the being, that he had become.

Every life was meaningful, and every life had a different purpose. Bimal became more and more of a person throughout each life he lived and wouldn't change a thing that he experienced. He had defeated the evil that followed him, and now he had the decision to be done. To either spend eternity whatever way he wanted or help more people. Bimal decided what any pure soul would, to help others.

16.
Locked Away
Erika MacArthur; Junior

My eyes snap open. The throbbing inside my head is nearly unbearable. As I slowly sit up, I expect to be met with the familiar image of my TV facing opposite my bed. Instead, I am lying on the wooden floor of a stuffy wooden attic. My heart starts racing as my body scrambles backwards on hands and knees until my back hits the slightly slanted wall. *Okay, okay, okay...I must be dreaming.*

I close my eyes tight, take a series of deep breaths, and reopen them. All I see is the same barren, dusty storage space, dimly lit with a single flickering light bulb several feet above me.

"Hello...?" My voice comes out raspy and broken. "Is anyone there?" I try to sound firm and confident in order to hide my confusion and fear.

After the sound of my voice settles around the room, the eerie silence takes its place once again. The heavy nothingness sits on top of me like a confining blanket. I never knew something could be so silent where I could feel it in my head. Suddenly, a voice with a sharp command cuts through it like a knife.

"Listen up" she bluntly states. It startles me as my instincts take over and I fly to the opposite side of the room. My brain, in its mad frenzy of processing information, decides it's a voice I don't recognize.

"Who are you? Why am I here? What do you want with me?"

"I'm here to help you get out of here. Let me be your eyes and your ears. I need you to trust me."

My heart stops for a whole other reason. It's not the mysterious room I woke up in. It's not the unknown voice coming from an unknown location. It's the phrase "trust me." So many times those two small words have been directed at me, and so many times I believed them, only to be burned and devastated by them later. Friends, girlfriends, even my parents have used those words to deceive me.

"How can I trust you, I don't even know who you are. What if you're trying to hurt me?"

"There's a key hidden somewhere, that's your ticket out of here. Once you find that the rest is easy. If you want to get out you need to listen to me, you have no other choice." She's right, my two options are either go against every instinct I've built up over my life or sit in this room until I die. It's almost an impossible decision, but in the end, I have no choice. I need to trust her and hope she doesn't let me down. *Easier said than done.*

"Okay, let's do this."

"First you need to get out of here. Use that ladder in the corner and go downstairs."

I reluctantly do as she tells me to. I slowly make my way over to the ladder and cautiously go down it.

Once I'm down, I survey my surroundings and realize I am in a house that reminds me entirely too much of my childhood home and all the trauma that occurred in it. *Why does this house seem so familiar?* As I continue to slowly creep along the wall, I hear what sounds like flowing water filling up a bathtub. As I round the corner, I see the bathroom door slightly ajar with steam billowing out of it.

Suddenly, memories flood my vision like I'm in the front row of a movie theater. The foreign house transforms into my former home, and my mind is filled with images of a three-year-old me and my father. I'm standing in front of the bathtub with his hand bunching up the collar of my t-shirt. Water comes raging out of the faucet, steam fills the entire room and fogs the mirror. The heavy heat makes my labored breaths even harder to come by. His voice fills my head clear as day, "Maybe next time you'll think twice before you draw on the wall. If you get in now, it'll be over quick, *trust me*" Just before he throws me in the stranger's voice snaps me back into reality.

"He can't hurt you anymore, you need to go in there and search for the key, it might be in there." *How did she know I was thinking about him?* Questions of who this woman is pop into my head again, and I still have no answers for myself.

"I... I can't." Just the thought of what lies on the other side of the door causes flashbacks to flood into my head, how was I supposed to dive into one just because some voice told me to? "You're supposed to be here to *help* me. Not traumatize me." She takes me through the trust speech all over again until I'm cautiously pushing the door open and entering the room. The steam makes my breathing difficult, just like it did when I was three. *Or maybe that's just the impending panic attack.* My only thought is to get in and out as quick as possible. I search every possible area of the bathroom, the medicine cabinet, under the sink, around the toilet. Everywhere until just one part remains, The Tub. I try to calm myself with a series of breaths before reaching into the scalding water. It pricks at my skin, I internally hear my younger self-pleading to be let out, I force myself to keep looking. This continues until I yank my hand out of the water. A hand red from the heat, sleeve soaked with water, and a dizziness in my head from the memories is all for nothing.

Frustration switches places with fear and I shake my arm like a wet dog in a futile attempt to dry it. "No key! You said there'd be a key!"

"I said there *might* be, if it's not there that must mean we need to keep going, it's here somewhere," she promises.

I continue through the halls, each room results in nothing. Every closet, every bedroom I anxiously sort through, all for no reward. Eventually, I finish with the upstairs, and I need to make my way down the stairs to the main level. I gingerly walk down and peer my head around both corners as a safety measure before I enter the kitchen. Inside is a seemingly normal kitchen, complete with a toaster, microwave, granite counters, stuff everyone has in their kitchen. What catches my eye is the piece of paper stuck to the fridge. It's not the ominous *"Be back soon"* carelessly scrawled across the page that sends me into my second anxiety attack in an hour. What sends me spiraling into a panic is what the note resembles. It triggers another traumatic episode for me. My mind is filled with the memory of a ten-year-old me bouncing down the stairs and into the kitchen, only to be met with a note. It simply reads *"Went to dinner, food is in the fridge. Be back soon! Love, Mom"* I didn't think anything of it at the time, except maybe that she wasn't there to cook for me. I didn't think anything of it until there was a knock on my door. Their car was struck by a drunk driver on the way back, and she never survived, never made it home. I was stuck with my dad, the same man that instilled my irrational fear of water. *Life isn't fair, life isn't fair.* The mantra that became my life's motto slipped back into my mind. *How did my number one tormentor make it out nearly unscathed but my sole protector in life didn't?* I feel tears begin to form in my eyes as I slowly spiral farther and farther from reality. Each episode from my past brings a new, stronger wave of panic. Each harder to banish than the last.

I slide down the wall and take a series of rapid breaths. My chest is in the middle of collapsing as the walls close in on me when I hear the sound of a slamming door and footsteps approaching. The sound, in reality, is muffled by the world I'm trapped in, but the footsteps pound loud and clear. *Are those footsteps or my own heartbeat?* I can't tell. I hear the voice, "RUN!" she commands. Somehow, amongst the chaos, my subconscious is able to lift me from the ground and carry me away from the approaching danger. I run out of the kitchen, my entire world still spinning. I make my way down a hallway, and hide until the footsteps fade away from me.

My new place of solace isn't much better than my last. As I look around and take in my surroundings, I notice various pictures hung throughout the halls. Almost every household has pictures hung up, nothing special here. Because I am so on edge, the pictures shape into portraits of all the people in my life that I've trusted only to be betrayed or abandoned. My dad, my mom, childhood friends, and an ex-girlfriend. It is her face that puts another vivid memory into my head. I see a broken adolescent, his buzzed hair just beginning to grow back. I had just returned home from deployment, I was traumatized and was suffering from PTSD. Before I left, she told me she would be here waiting when I arrived back home. Except when I opened the door, all her stuff was cleared out—no clothes in the closet, no shoes in the front hall, not even a letter with an explanation of where she went. The final piece of faith and hope I had in others was instantly tarnished. To this day, I still don't know where she went, all I know is she left me to deal with my disorder all on my own. Leaving me with more walls built up than I ever imagined possible. Even thinking back to those times makes me extremely anxious and angry, which is why I try to repress any recollection of it.

The increasingly familiar voice reminds me that I still haven't been successful in finding the key out of here and that there is one final level I haven't ventured down to yet, the basement. I quietly maneuver my way to the steps and quickly go down, careful to avoid the source of the footsteps. It is there that I'm met with a shelf littered in cheap trophies that triggers a memory that just about sets me over the edge. On the trophy shelf, I see a medal that reminds me too much of the Purple Heart they gave me when I returned home. Suddenly, I'm back in combat, under heavy fire. The air is so heavy with gunpowder and sand that it hurts to breathe. The sharp smell of sulfur fills my nose as my ringing ears try to differentiate the difference between explosions and the deafening shouting surrounding me. I'm stuck hiding behind a truck, unable to move because of constant firing from both sides. I watch helplessly from behind cover as the only men I knew I could ever really trust, die, one by one in an effort to save me and to save each other. I was the only one to survive, and they gave me a damn medal for it. They gave me a reward and a ceremony for hiding behind a truck. The medal is a constant reminder of the immense guilt that eats away at me constantly. I am no longer able to snap back into reality and see a house, I'm stuck looking at the faces of fallen soldiers. This has to be the moment I give up any hope of ever finding the key out of here. The line between reality and illusion has become blurred too much.

However, with the last bit of reason I have left I catch a glimpse of a key on the mantle. I make my way over to it as my chest closes up with anxiety. I hear every past experience in my head all at once like some twisted medley. I'm not one hundred percent convinced I have the strength or willpower to make it all the way across the room. Just then, she gives me one last message that pushes me forward, "You did it." With that, I fly to the mantle and lean against it for support, as soon as I grasp the key my entire vision goes white and there is an intense ringing in my ears.

My eyes snap open. This time, instead of a dimly lit attic, I am in a sterile, completely white room. My nose is filled with the smell of intense cleaning product instead of heavily accumulated dust. The steady sound of machinery beeps and whirs as I steady my breathing. The monitor next to the bed translates my pounding heartbeat into a fury of rapid beeps. I blink the blinding light out of my eye, and it dawns on me that I'm in a hospital. *I've been in the hospital this whole time?* The sudden spike of the heart monitor causes a group of nurses and doctors to come storming in. I watch their expressions go from worried to taken aback. After a long pause the doctor that appears to be in charge comments, "You're awake..."

He correctly interprets my raised eyebrow as a sign of confusion and continues, "You've been in a coma after you were struck by a drunk driver." My fate was determined almost the exact same way my mother's was so many years ago. My mind is whirring, trying to wrap itself around the hyper-realistic experience I had just found myself in the middle of. It is at that moment I realize the house was never a house at all, it was my own consciousness that I was trapped inside of. The familiarity of it stemmed from the creation of my own mind. My mind had created a house of horrors filled with every single one of my repressed memories I had failed to properly deal with and had locked away instead. Another thing I notice is my girlfriend standing behind the doctors, a worried expression etched across her face. Then suddenly, all the loose ends become tied together. I now recognize the voice inside my head as her voice, whatever she was saying, in reality, guided me through my illusion until I woke up. She saved my life. Almost instantaneously, I feel the walls blocking me from trusting collapsing like a line of dominos as I shakily smile up at her.

17.
Looking For Jermaine
Victor Donati; Senior

It rained all night. No rest for the weary, as Jerome couldn't get any sleep. All he could think about was getting jumped by a pack of feral dogs while he was resting. The thought alone sent chills down his back. Everything was wet, and the air was cold. Not cold enough to need a heavy jacket, but cold enough that your breath makes a little cloud when you exhaled. Jerome slept in a rusted yellow car. In fact, the car wasn't even yellow, but he could tell from the few places that the orange rust had not washed over. The windows were smashed out, and the car was slowly being eaten by vines and plants that surrounded the area. A mouse scurried on the floor in front of him as he came to his senses. Jerome was alone. He carried a backpack full of the following supplies: a half-filled canteen of water, three slices of meat, a pair of sunglasses, a lighter, a four-inch knife, one chocolate bar, a small radio, deck of cards, five yards of rope, and forthy-three silver coins.

Jerome climbed out of the car and surveyed his location. He was on the edge of a forest looking out into an expansive field of waste deep grass. On the horizon, he could see lights half way up a mountain. The ground was soaked and he sunk a bit in his boots. His surroundings smelled of fresh dew on the morning leaves, and pollen. It was the beginning of spring. Jerome had narrowly survived the winter only by living off sunflower seeds. He had fallen sick during the last Month of winter. His brother, Jermaine had saved him by finding food and water for him. Jermaine had disappeared a week ago. Leaving nothing but a Knife.

Jerome wore high black boots with barbed wire laces, and baggy grey cargo pants held up by a raccoon tail used as a belt. His olive green parka jacket and holed shirt kept his chest warm. He was now ready to start the day. Step after step, he started towards the lights in the distance. His mission: to find his brother.

Two months ago he had woke up alone, without his brother by his side. Jerome theories that he left in the middle of the night, but he wonders why. *Why didn't he leave a note? Was he taken by someone or something? Is he still alive?* The thoughts lingered in Jerome's mind as he walked. Now his only lead was his brother's knife, that he had found a hundred yards away from the cave that they slept in. As far as Jerome's location. *Who knew?* Maps were rare, and if you found one good luck reading it. The only map Jerome had seen in his life was written in some sort of language with short groups of markings clumped together. However, Jerome did know one thing. His brother once told him that they were in a place called the Alps. Wherever he was, he knew that he was in the mountains. The sun, barely up, hung hot and heavy. It warmed his face as if someone had lit a fire in front of him. He looked back, the car he had slept in was in the distance. He had only walked a couple hundred yards. The grass surrounding him was as expected, about waste high. It brushed his hands as he walked. Then he heard something.

Jerome stopped walking, it sounded like the faint hum of a motor from behind. Jerome crouched low in the grass, fearing he would be seen. The tall grass scratched his face, but he didn't notice. Peering through, he looked back in the direction of the old car, and the forest beyond. The hum grew louder and louder. He now knew that it was some sort of vehicle. Then, like a fish emerging from water, five bikes flew out of the forest. They carried people and Bots alike. Bots are advanced artificial intelligent robots. In some ways, they were better than humans, and in some ways, they were worse. Jerome was told that after the food shortage of 2029, the Bots survived and essentially became their own race on the planet Inhabiting cities and towns. They were not treated the same however because there were some religious skeptics saying the only life should come from God, not man. Jerome's thoughts on bots were indifferent. He had met some helpful bots in his past and, he had met some that tried to kill him. Bots come in all shapes and sizes, the ones speeding toward him on small blue and green bikes were tall and lean. They didn't have a face that resembled a human at all, as one sensor or eye was in the middle of their tall bottle shaped metallic head. They had varied numbers of long robotic arms. Some had four, and some had only two. It looked like some of their arms had been ripped off.

The humans in the pack were rough looking. From a distance, they seemed angry. They carried large guns and explosives strapped around their backs. Their faces were scarred and twisted as if there had seen many victories and defeats over their lifetime. They wore gold and silver bracelets that gleamed against the morning sun. Their shirts and pants were littered with bullet holes and waved against the wind. Jerome knew they were pirates, looking for something to make some coin off of. He ducked lower in the grass hoping they would fly by and not notice him. However, they were headed straight for him. He pulled out his knife and feared for the worst. "*Hummmmmmm, zip, zip, woosh*! The grass around him blew like he was in a tornado. The Pirates passed him. They were traveling the same way as Jerome. A few seconds later the Pirates were out of sight, and Jerome continued on. This time, he was more alert.

Jerome never knew his parents, it was always him and his brother. He often asked his brother, Jermaine, where they were and got the same reply every time, "Mom and dad are looking for us just like we are looking for them." That would always relieve him of his anxiety for the time being. Jerome had been with his brother for as long as he could remember. They had never been separated before until now, and Jerome feared the worst. "*Kaboom!*" an explosion rocked Jerome to his knees.

He looked up to see a cloud of smoke and fires at the town he was headed for. "Damnit!" Jerome exclaimed. He started to run towards the flames. He was still about a couple miles away. Frustrated now, as the town might have the key to his brother's whereabouts. The knife that he found was made by the blacksmith in this town. They called it "Westwend Pass" because there was a trail that extended from the town through the mountain. Jerome had visited it before with his brother. It was his only idea of where to start looking.

He had waited four days for Jermaine to return before he left to search on his own. Now at the base of the mountain, Jerome's lungs had exhausted themselves. He would have to walk from here. The road was littered with garbage and waste. Empty plastic bags, shattered glass, metal scraps, and ash forced Jerome to watch his feet. As he climbed, he remembered that he hadn't eaten anything today. He quickly grabbed that chocolate bar and wolfed it down. It tasted sweet, and the sugar upped his glycogen stores. The higher he climbed the harder it became to breathe. The rarified air forced him to walk even slower.

As he was nearing Westwend Pass, the smoke looked blacker. He could smell the soot and ash, it smelled similar to a bonfire he once made. The town was not completely destroyed. Three shelters were burning and produced a great deal of smoke. The remaining several shelters had survived only to collapse in the later hours. The bar in the middle of the town seemed untouched. People were everywhere. Jerome could only describe the scene as chaotic. A group of bots had taken it upon themselves to attempt to put out the fires. Children were cowering behind their mothers while men scrambled to prevent any more losses and aided the wounded. It was the most people Jerome had seen in his life at one time. Feeling overwhelmed he merged into the crowd unnoticed by anyone.

He made his way straight to the forge. Not caring to look anyone in the eye. Head down, Jerome minded his own business. He wasn't here to be a hero or anything. Luckily, he remembered that the shop was located on the outskirts of Westwend Pass. This meant that it was probably avoided by the pirates, and left alone. Jerome looked up from the ground and entered the small shop through a curtain.

The shop was empty, except for the flies and the mice. A strong stench of gasoline pierced Jerome's nose as he entered. Hot metal was bubbling out of a cauldron. It seemed like someone had left abruptly as there were swords and knives glowing red with magma as if they were just about to be hammered to completion. Pictures hung on the walls, as well a sole map. Framed and in good condition from what Jerome could see. It seemed to be a map of the surrounding land because he recognized some of the physical features. It was unbearably hot inside the shop, few windows meant the hot air was trapped inside for the most part. Jerome took a long drink of water and wandered around the shop. He looked at all of the different objects such as gates, grilles, railings, light fixtures, furniture, sculpture, tools, agricultural implements, and weapons.

"Hey!" said a rough voice near the entrance. "The shop is closed now. Go home!"

"Wait. I need to talk to you" piped up Jerome. "Have you seen my brother? He bought a knife from you about four months ago."

The man stepped into the light. He was small, only about five feet tall. His beard made his face look like it was bigger than it was. His hair was brown and curly. When he talked his eyes moved like a rodent looking for predators. The man was plump, and you could tell that he didn't get out much. He wore a white apron that had turned black from all of the time spent forging iron and steel. The thing that struck Jerome was the blacksmith's hands. Covered in dirt and soot. It looked like the dirt crept into every wrinkle, crevice, and fingernail in his old hands. You could tell he loved what he did and became consumed by it because he didn't care to clean his hands very often. His craft came at the sacrifice of his body.

"What did he look like, kid?" the man said. "I see a lot of people 'round here."

"Long black hair, tall but skinny, he had a small beard as well."

"I do recall seein' a fellow like that, but it couldn't be."

"Couldn't be what?" said Jerome.

"Well, the t'ing is I saw a man by the complexion you described. However, it was not here. I saw this man you speak of, outside the Blybixson wasteland while I was scavenging for scraps." said the man. "He seemed disoriented and confused. I thought he must have contracted a disease and I made sure to stay away."

"Which way to the wasteland?" said Jerome

"Listen, son, I would not advise you to wander that way. There are things in the wasteland that young lads like you won't be able to defend themselves against."

"Like what?"

"Don't bother, son. It is not likely your brother survived."

"Which way is the wasteland?" repeated Jerome.

"I have said too much, get out of here. For your own good."

"Just tell me—"

"No! Be gone!"

And with that, the Blacksmith proceeded to pick up one of his swords which was cooling off. Steam was pulsing off the sword as he palmed the handle. Jerome was taken aback. He hadn't found the information he needed, yet he was so close. The Blacksmith walked towards Jerome. His steps thundering against the concrete floor. Jerome had only one option. He leapt onto the nearby table kicking candles and scrap metal rattling to the floor. He smashed the picture frame out with his fist. Blood oozed onto the floor. Gripping the map by his index finger and thumb he removed it. Jerome could feel his heart pounding in his ears as he knew the Blacksmith would be upon him by now. He turned just in time to see the hot blade cut his left ring and pinky finger, clean off. With adrenaline running through his veins like a river Jerome didn't feel the total extent of what had just happened. He jumped over the blacksmith and bolted for the curtain covering the exit with the map in hand. Sprinting out into the fresh air, Jerome didn't look back and made straight for the pass. People stared and pointed as an eight-fingered, bleeding kid ran through town.

Jerome didn't stop running until the pain started to kick in, and that wasn't very long. No one followed him through the pass, the old blacksmith must have realized he couldn't keep up with Jerome. Jerome could feel the pain now. He could only describe it as if someone had set fire to his hand. Bandaging it up with the rope helped to slow down the bleeding, but it would from now on, be a liability for him. He had glanced at the map before, but now he could really study it. From what he saw in the forge, the map had a wasteland on it. If the blacksmith couldn't tell him where it was, Jerome would find it.

The map was not as difficult as Jerome theorized. It was small about the size of a little flag. It was black and white, and written in ink. The labels were not legible but from the small pictures he could tell where he was. Westwend Pass was more or less in the southern part of the map. And to his surprise, the wasteland was only beyond the next mountain. If Jerome stayed on this road, he would hit it.

Outside of Westwend Pass the air was colder. Around Jerome the tops of mountains had white caps, luckily he was not up that high. The dirt road he walked was littered with boulders on the edges, and there were multiple times Jerome had to go out of his way to avoid them. He walked through a large valley. Small bushes and other greenery were found on the side of the road. No one was out here, once again Jerome was all alone. He spotted something stuck on a nearby tree branch. It looked like a piece of blue cloth. Intrigued, Jerome walked closer. He could tell it was old by the rips and pieces that were missing. On the cloth, there was a symbol that Jerome had seen before. It was a large yellow star, with ten other smaller stars surrounding it. He recognized it as the flag of the European Federation.

Jerome had heard stories about the E.F. He knew was a coalition of European countries that was created in the year 2032. After widespread famine and drought rocked first world countries, an estimated one billion people died. The E.F. was created to strengthen the world in a time of desperation. However, It may have only divided it, considering the three-way war commenced only seven years after its formation.

Jerome picked up the tattered flag and placed it in his backpack. He was thirsty and hungry from the effort he put out to get the map, so he took a swig of his water and had a slice of meat. The meat was not from an animal. This meat was grown in a laboratory, the next evolution of factory farming. Invented in 2030 by American scientist, Christopher Lakewell, to combat the food shortage of 2029. The method involved growing cells in a laboratory setting which was more efficient on time and price. However, there are claims that the meat does not contain a sufficient amount of nutrients and some people were poisoned.

Shaking out the last few water drops into his mouth, the canteen was empty now. He started walking down the dirt road again. His hand bothered him. It still was unbearably painful. The only thing that kept his feet moving was the thought of seeing his brother again. Doubt had started to grow in his mind. He recalled what the blacksmith had said about his brother. It didn't settle well with Jerome, but he had to figure out the truth. *Was Jermaine still alive? If his brother was still alive would he be the same?* Jerome became lost in his thoughts.

The sun had started to settle down in the sky. Night would be upon him soon. Jerome now had to find some type shelter. Last night, finding the abandoned car was a blessing. He doubted that he would have the same luck tonight. All he could see was this winding road, surrounded by tall mountains with white peaks. It was beautiful. Sometimes Jerome forgot that. There was no cover around him. If something decided to make a meal out of him, there was nowhere he could run. Creatures come out at night that Jerome would not like to confront. Things such as feral dogs, bears, and mutated insects.

He continued walking as it became dark. His legs were tired, and he dragged his heels against the ground. He thought about stopping and taking a rest, but the fire inside of his soul continued to move his tired body along the road. Insects started chirping, and his vision became faded. The fact that he was still walking was remarkable. Finally, he could not continue anymore. He collapsed on the road face down in the mud. The last thing he heard were dogs howling in the night.

Jerome awoke in a hut. With a roof, a door, and windows. A teapot was screaming on the stove. The morning sun shown through the window onto his face. Jerome rubbed his eyes. Clearing his vision. Music was playing in the background, and Jerome recognized it as old rap songs. A man was in the kitchen tending to the stovetop. He was average height, black skin, middle-aged and wore a dark khaki jacket. He moved with precision and didn't miss a beat to the music. A thin goatee outlined his expressionless face. He seemed to be absorbed in the music. Jerome could smell fresh eggs on the stove. He had only had eggs once in his lifetime. He hated them.

"Aye you up?" said the man

"Yes" replied Jerome. "Who are you? Where am I?"

"Welcome to the Sanctuary. My name is not important. How are you feeling?"

"Great but my hand is in pain" Jerome motioned toward his two knuckles that were missing fingers.

"Ah, of course," said the man. "AT-eighty-eight!" a small bot waddled into the room. It was about the size of a toddler and had the shape of one, too. Two robotic arms emerged from the basketball-sized metallic body. Its hands were like claws but had the precision of a surgeon. It carried a tray of small metallic pieces and instruments. It came right up to Jerome. And spoke in a muffled, radio-like speech.

"What seems to be the matter," said AT-eighty-eight. Jerome unwrapped the bandages from his finger and showed the bot.

"I can fix, hold still." With that, a long needle went into Jerome's hand, he yelped in pain. "Still. Remain still," said the bot.

It began working furiously on his hand. Cutting, and attaching tiny metal fingers to the injured spots. To Jerome's surprise, he didn't feel a thing. The bot was finished in minutes and administered another shot into his hand.

"Ouch" squealed Jerome.

Jerome's hand became tingly like it was returning from a long slumber. It looked strange. The metal fingers had merged seamlessly with his flesh. He wiggled his fingers in a wave-like formation. The mechanical fingers responded as if they were real. Jerome was amazed.

"Done," said AT-eighty-eight, and it sped off into the other room.

"Breakfast is ready.," said the man. "Eat up, you have a long way to go."

Jerome ate all the food on his plate. As he was eating, he thought of a billion questions to ask the man. *Where am I? How did you find me? Who are you? Why are you helping me?*

"I need to get to the Blybixion Wasteland," said Jerome.

"Are you kidding me, kid?" said the man with a look of bewilderment. "There ain't nothing out there for you."

"Oh yes, there is, this!" Jerome pulled out Jermaine's knife to show the man. "I need to find my brother, he was last seen just outside the Wasteland."

"Listen, kid, The Wasteland is no place for a person with a bright future like you. However, I understand your concern. Before you go, let me tell you something. The Wasteland used to be a thriving city. It went by the name of Turin. It was destroyed during the three-way war, turned to dust and ashes to be exact. Now it is a place for bandits, pirates, and like to conduct their nefarious business. Be wary, my friend. Best of luck, I wish you Godspeed in finding your brother."

Jerome stood up from the table and thanked the man for saving his life. With that, Jerome walked out the door. His spirits were through the roof. He had never felt better. Talking to the man gave him an inspired confidence that he could actually find Jermaine. For the first time in a long time, Jerome didn't feel alone. Outside, the wind was blowing. Jerome had to put up his hood to protect his face from the harsh conditions. He looked behind him, at the old hut, except it wasn't there. Jerome squinted his eyes, but to his disbelief, the hut had disappeared. He had only taken a couple of steps outside, yet it was gone as if it had just been a dream that materialized and vanished. Jerome wondered if it was even real. Nevermind that, he had a mission, and he had to stay focused.

He found the path with ease from the map and started in the direction of the Wasteland. It seemed to be high noon, as the sun was high in the south sky. Jerome would probably reach the outskirts of the Blybixion Wasteland in a couple hours. Jerome became lost in his thoughts as he walked.

Everything around Jerome was grey. A couple of meters in front of him a tattered and rusted metal fence stuck out of the ground, partially covered by ash. To his right, was a sign that read "Stay Away" in red paint that was faded and crooked. On his left was a group of rotting metal poles that were probably from a long time ago. The Mountains were on his six and a dessert on his twelve. Grey dust blew like sand and limited his visibility to about thirty meters. His boots were sinking a couple of inches in the ash and slowed his walking pace. He stared into the grey abyss that was the Blybixion Wasteland. Jerome had arrived.

His brother was obviously not here. But Jerome had faith. He most likely went forth into the Wasteland. Therefore, Jerome would do the same. He checked that his boots were tied up nice and tight, zipped his jacket all the way up, put on his sunglasses and stepped foot-over-foot.

Jerome trekked through the Wasteland for hours. Overall, there seemed to be nothing there. Sometimes he would see metal scraps and other debris scattered around. But for the most part, there was just dust. It got everywhere. Jerome had already stopped twice to empty his boots from it. He breathed it and tasted it with every step. Jerome could only compare the taste to a dry sand. His sunglasses protected his eyes as it never seemed to stop blowing.

Then his surroundings changed. He was well into the third hour when he started seeing tracks in the dust. Bike tracks. Jerome knew what that meant. He also knew that they were recent considering how fast the dust covered everything. More metal appeared out of the dust in the shape of dismantled buildings. Jerome seemed to be walking on a sea of ash above the destroyed city. He had seen small critters darting in and out of cover. Not to mention the snake he almost stepped on. He didn't see it as it blended in with the grey surroundings.

In the fifth hour, the storm stopped. Jerome could see the sky again, It was nighttime, and a full moon was out, it lit up his surroundings with a soft glow. Jerome had never seen the moon so big and white. Around the moon were the most beautiful arrangement of stars he had ever seen. Different sizes and colors reflected off his eyes in the moonlight. Jerome came to the conclusion that one day he must leave this Earth. He had heard stories of a large number of people leaving in search of a better home. He wondered it they were still out there, still looking after generation upon generation had passed.

He could see for a good distance now that the storm had ceased. He could tell that he was in the heart of the city, half-destroyed buildings surrounded him. In the distance, he saw a light. It was small and faint, but it definitely was flickering. Jerome moved closer to investigate. The closer he got the more footprints he saw around his feet that weren't his. It was a campfire, five beings sat around it in heated conversation. Two bots, three humans. Jerome recognized them as the ones that he saw on his way to the Westwend Pass. They seemed to be arguing about something. Jerome moved in, hid behind a hunk of metal, and listened.

"It's your fault we got robbed," one of the humans said to the bot. "If it wasn't for your bot brain we would be halfway to Baystonville with three sacks of silver coin."

"Nonsense," said the bot in a choppy voice. "You were on watch when the bandits attacked. It was your fault."

"Just be glad they didn't steal the bikes along with the coin," said another human. "We can still make it to Baystonville and join the others."

Jerome sat in silence and watched as the conversation escalated to the point of a fight. The human and bot were about to brawl, but the other three pirates held them back. They were obviously in a difficult predicament. After a short time, four of pirates retired to sleep. The last one, a human with long brown hair, was set to watch the camp. Jerome formulated a quick plan in his mind. If he could steal one of their bikes, he could ride around the Wasteland, and find his brother faster. He would need a distraction as the campfire, and a guard were between him and the bikes. Jerome crawled to the left and picked up the biggest piece of scrap metal he could find. Being as quiet as possible, he crept up behind the pirate at the campfire.

Jerome lifted the metal bar over his head. He didn't have time to react, the pirate whipped around and punched Jerome straight in the nose. Jerome fell on his back dropping the metal bar on top of himself.

"Well, well, well, look what the cat dragged in." said the pirate. "I know someone who will pay a pretty coin for this."

Jerome's hands and feet were tied together, The Pirates all woke up and took turns talking to Jerome. Jerome said nothing. His nose was definitely broken, and it throbbed with pain. At some points in the interrogation, he was hit again. Luckily, not in his face. The Pirates took his backpack and searched through it. They made sure to eat all the food. Now satisfied, they went back to bed. It seemed that they were making their way to a town called Baystonville that was just south of here. Jerome had never heard of it.

Jerome, tied up and immobilized, slept in the dust. This was the end, his story was finished. There was no daring escape, no one to rescue him, no one on his side. He stared up at the stars and thought about his brother. He had let him down. Jerome closed his eyes and slept.

He was woken up by a kick to the stomach that knocked the wind out of him.

"Wake up," one of the pirates said while towering over him.

Jerome was blindfolded and tied to the back of a bike. He thought he heard them talking about other captives, but he wasn't sure. He heard the start of an engine and lurched forward.

Jerome didn't remember much of the ride. The blindfold protected his eyes from the dust, but it didn't stop him from eating it. The pirate that drove the bike he was on was large. Jerome could tell because he didn't feel the wind as he was in the pirate's slip steam. The ride lasted an hour before Jerome started hearing other noises, besides the *humm* of the motor. It sounded like voices and other people not identifiable. Jerome suspected he had entered the outskirts of a city. He tried to take off his blindfold, but it was no use. His hands were tied behind his back, and he couldn't rub it off with his shoulder. He would have to rely on his other senses for now. The bike slowed down as the entered the city. It now took left and right turns at random. Swerving in and out of people and other obstacles in the streets. Then they stopped.

Jerome was pulled off the bike and into a room. The blindfold was removed. Everything was dark. Jerome couldn't see anything. Then he heard voices and people talking. He could see the outline of a couple people. They seemed to be discussing a transaction. Four hundred coin was transferred from hand to hand, and someone told them to "Put him with the others." Hands grabbed Jerome and hauled to his feet, he was dragged to another room. This room was brighter, yet still dimly lit. There were other captives in here. People and bots of every shape and size tied with their hands behind their backs. Sitting, waiting, for something. Whispers were heard momentarily throughout the room. Jerome tried initiating a conversation with the person behind him.

"Hey, where are we?" Jerome asked.

"This is Baystonville, we are slaves of the city.," answered a voice.

"Why?" asked Jerome confused.

"The mayor, he wants to build a giant city, like the ones of old. A place that was similar to the time before the Armageddon, before the famine. He wants to revive the human race."

"How can he do that? This is ridiculous" said Jerome

"The quickest way for advancement is slavery, every major civilization was built by slaves.," replied the voice. "We are all here, captured by snatchers, or bandits, or pirates. Against our will."

Then an idea popped into his mind. He started on the ropes around his wrists. Jerome took his two metal fingers and rubbed them against the rope. Back and forth, back and forth. He felt tiny pieces of the rope begin to fall apart. Soon he was halfway through the rope. The good thing was his nervous system wasn't repaired in the two fingers so he couldn't feel a thing. Jerome continued for about an hour. Then his wrists were freed. He used his hands to untie his feet and stood up. He then turned and untied his compatriot, who in turn, untied another captive. Jerome moved on to another captive on the far side of the room. Jerome couldn't see him clearly, but he was tall and had long black hair. Jerome untied the man's hands and looked up at his face.

"J...Jermaine." Jerome stammered in disbelief.

The man looked down upon Jerome and smiled. It was, in fact, his brother. They embraced each other for a moment.

"How did you get here?" Jerome asked.

"I was out picking berries when I got jumped by a group of raiders. They took me to the city, and I was put here to work."

Jerome was delighted. All his hard work had paid off. However, they were not free yet. They needed to get out of this room. They went to the door, but it was locked. They were stuck. They waited for some time for someone to open the door. Finally, they heard footsteps outside. Someone was coming to take them out to work. Little did they know the people inside were free from their bonds. As soon as the door was opened they escaped, trampling the doorman. They entered a long hallway with a door at the end. Jerome and Jermaine sprinted toward the exit. They could hear footsteps behind them, and they knew they were being chased. They reached the door and opened it, into the fresh air. The brothers ran up and down the streets until they were sure they had evaded the guards. Jerome and Jermaine now had some catching up to do.

18.
Learning Love
Max Joelson; Senior

do you like me?

☐yes

☐no

☐maybe

i just wanna say that i know

your sad right but i wnt

want to make you feel good

i am sorry your sister left
you and

those boys said those mean
thins i woodn't do that

love Max

Roses are red,
Violets are blue,
i really, really
like-like you.

meet me by the swings at
reccess

love ur secret admirer

p.s. happy valentines
thanks for being such a good
friend in elementary school.
please don't leave me in middle
school even though i am not a
cool kid sorry i am not cool.

i love you

I feel like I know people well and then magically the next day they are gone. Relationships materialize and disintegrate so quickly I cannot believe it. I would do anything for that not to happen to us. I know I have been shy lately, that is my fault. I just don't really know how you feel or where we are and that is scary for me. Not being in love in like being on a hamster wheel and i do not wanna get off. But maybe you are the one to get me off. I love you, i trust you. Keep me safe.

Love,
Max

Emily,

I am different from everyone. Please, take this chance on me. I look at you, and all I see is you. The background you live in, the world, just melts away instantly. I know I am younger, but I'll look after you. You can break my heart, but just not yet. Please.
Please please please please please please.
Just a chance.

Sincerely,
Max

listen, i am not gonna lie. when i first was with you, i was going through a really difficult time in my life. i was diagnosed with some mental illnesses, and i had a really hard time coming to terms with who i was. i was really self-conscious, and i was an asshole. but, i've changed a lot with who i am, and i accept and love the person i am today. i just really hope i can get another chance because to be honest there's not many girls i imagine being with, but when i am around you, i feel awesome and just want more. the other day, i experienced what should have been a really shitty day, but i got to spend a little time with you and that made me consider it really good. you're gorgeous and i respect you, and i love the person who you are. however if i had one chance, and it's gone, i understand, cause i really messed up last time. i just hope you can look past it, and that i can have a chance to redeem myself as something more than a friend.

  Subject

iMessage

This is really unexpected especially because we haven't talked in awhile until recently

Max you didn't mess up it's not like that at all

I look past everything regardless because I value our friendship

Sun, May 8, 00:50

hey i am really sorry but for some reason i like never got these messages until now. i know it's really late so I'll just talk to you tomorrow.

Max I just want to be straightforward with you I really value our friendship and I wouldn't want to ruin that and that's how I've always felt I hope you can respect that

And don't think you messed anything up because you didn't, I've always just wanted to be your friend I hope you feel the same way too

Subject

iMessage

yeah hahaha

see you got it

Haha okay working on it right now

didn't mean to rush you lol

Okay so we had a brief chat

She said that she thinks of you as one of her best friends and doesn't want that to change
She hadn't really thought about you like that before and she feels that what you guys have right now is really great and shouldn't be messed with

I'm sorry I know that's not really what you wanted to hear :/

no i am completely fine with that

okay good

yeah we are all good thanks for helping

   Subject

iMessage

19.
Mountain Runner
Caroline Radecky; Senior

It was a cold winter day, the roads were all closed. No snow plows and no salt available in the little town of Windsor. The town, however, was filled with warmth and love, but there was no way to get there. The townspeople used their skis and snowmobiles to get from one place to another, but outside the town, nothing was moving.

A new girl named Jacqueline, and her Bernese Mountain dog were moving into the small ski chalet at the end of the long winding road. She was going to take a couple of classes at the local college and possibly try out for the ski team. Jacqueline was a very shy girl coming to pursue her dream of skiing but not only skiing but starting a new life. She would go to classes for a couple of hours then head up to the mountain with a cup of hot chocolate and her skis. Hiking up to the mountain could be quite treacherous for an unskilled person.

After finishing up a few touch-ups in her new ski chalet she called, "Skier's Peak," Jacqueline fell onto a fluffy stuffed chair and fell fast asleep. She dreamt of the crazy drama back home and the rude and snobby kids. She even dreamt about the rich kids who got whatever they wanted and cried when they didn't get their way. "BANG!" the newly mounted skies fell and crashed onto the ground waking her from her disturbing dream.

"Argh!" she said out loud as she thought about the crazy people but felt relief that she no longer had to deal with any of that nonsense.

After a cup of java, Jacqueline decided to take a hike up the mountain and explore her new surroundings despite the massive storm. Jacqueline packed ski boots, pasta, skis and headed out. She hiked for about four hours and realized she's far from her ski chalet; not only far, but she could see her ski chalet from the top of the mountain. "I made it to the top! Whoo Hoo!"

Jacqueline looked up and felt the cold snow falling on her face. She smiled and slowly turned around. "Wow, check it out!" the Olympic team's training resort for the winter season.

"I'm going to be on the Olympic team one day."

She put on her boots and skis and flew down the hill feeling more free and happy than she ever remembered feeling.

Jacqueline makes it back home to her little ski chalet after the day of hiking and skiing. She sits down at her computer and looks up ski racing, but nothing showed up. She then types in ski racing "Windsor Olympic team" and tons of articles blew up on the screen saying click here to join and train with the Olympic team today! *click!*

Jacqueline gets an email from the coach of the ski team saying, meet here tomorrow at "three o'clock" for our meeting, all are welcome, just bring paper and something to write with. The next day, she shows up to the meeting with her friend, Skylar, the tall blonde, brown eyed friend. Skylar is one of Jacqueline's good friends who supports her but also has always looked up to her as a god. They sit down, and the coach introduces himself as coach Jake.

"Today you're here because you signed up to join or U.S. Olympic team for 2014 Winter Olympics, am I correct?"

"Yes," Jacqueline responds in a quiet voice.

Jake begins to talk, "dry land workout in the morning and afternoon, and we will start training as early as "Five o'clock," before the ski lifts open." "You have to commit to us no matter what condition you're in, the training can be rigorous and extremely painful, but it's the only way of life in order to achieve something so big." Jake hands them contact information and explains a little more. "Thank you for meeting with me; give me a call anytime today and let met know your decision."

Jacqueline looked at Skylar and was a little confused. She thought they would ask more questions about her experiences skiing or where she has been in her life in the mountains, and what she wants to strive for during this season. She goes home with Skylar and sits down in the kitchen next to the fireplace. Rethinking about signing up or committing.

But Skylar chips in the silence and says isn't this what you wanted in your life.

"I think you should sign up and begin tomorrow."

Jacqueline looks at Skylar and says, "You know what you're right, I'm going to start tomorrow with a positive attitude. I'll call you later and let you know what happens. Thanks, Skylar."

****

The phone rings at five forty- five in the morning. Jacqueline answers and guess what, it's Jake; "Get up we have training in fifteen minutes!" See you there. Jacqueline jumps out of bed scrambling to find her ski boots, helmet, gloves, speed suit and skis and realizes all her stuff is packed far away, so she decides to just put workout clothing on and run over to the training facility. She gets there at exactly at six o'clock tired and very cold. They start the morning out with easy stretches and a mile run, all in an hour or so. Jake pulls Jacqueline aside and checks on her making sure she is okay and feeling confident.

****

The next morning, Jacqueline wakes up. Starts to pack all her stuff into her ski bag shoving so many things in because she doesn't know what may happen. She is preparing for everything that could go wrong. She grabs her flask of coffee and starts to drive her 2009 Jeep Grand Cherokee down the road which takes an hour because of snow conditions. Bumpy as the road is, the sun is out, and the birds are chirping. It's a beautiful day with no clouds to be seen, only the sun. Jacqueline finally makes it into the ski town where all the roads have been blocked off due to the snow conditions. She tries to find other ways to the mountain, but there are no other ways showing in her GPS. So she decides to park her car and start walking. She drops her pair of skis down into the snow then sits down and looks at the mountain and starts to have a little panic attack because she's not up there. She walks about one mile and runs into a tall blonde hair, blue eyes and super-tan man.

He stands there and looks at her for a while then finally decides to ask, "Are you okay?"

Jacqueline says back, "Yes, my name is Jacqueline, I'm new here and am training for the Olympics with my team up there on the mountain the only problem is the roads are blocked with snow."

He replies "Hi, Jacqueline, my name is Mountain Man I'm the guy you need for the job because I have the snow plowers at home," says Mountain Man, he starts to walk to his MM Snowplow company cabin and gets in the big truck. He looks back at Jacqueline and motions her to get her car and drive behind him.

Jacqueline starts going up the mountain thinking of the tall, handsome, blonde man that is helping her get to her destination. It's like she can't get him out of her head. They get to the top of the mountain with no interferences. Jacqueline looks at her watch, and it says 6:45 am, she screams, "Thank you" to the mountain man and makes her way up the chair lift.

After a long day of skiing, Jacqueline decides to call the mountain man's number from the card she received after he plowed the roads. They meet up at a little coffee shop around the corner and order two hot chocolates to go. Jacqueline invites the mountain man to her house, and they talked and talked until they finally glimpsed at the clock seeing one o'clock roll around. Finally, the mountain man looked into her eyes and asked her to be his girlfriend, even though they just met and she says yes.

****

It was the day of the 2014 Winter Olympics. Jacqueline was on the chairlift going up to the mountain, ready in her ski suit. Looking around the crowd, Jacqueline notices that the love of her life isn't there. She starts to freak out because she thinks, *Oh no did he leave me, or whatever happened to him?* She decides just to focus on the race and figure out what's going on. She gets into the starting gate "3 2 1 racer go," she pushes out of the gate overwhelmed and a little un-concentrated half way down everything's going well then... All of a sudden, Jacqueline's down with the best time and a gold medal. As Jacqueline is getting interviewed she notices a tall man .. and realize its mountain man cheering her on. She runs out past the fence and hugs him with a big smile. "I thought you were gone," Jacqueline said. "No sweetheart, I need to show you where I have been," Dane replies.

They pack up all of Jacqueline's ski stuff and start to drive for one hour back down the mountain into the woods, over a bridge, and past a creek. Dane had Jacqueline close her eyes and open them as soon as they passed through the trees she opens her eyes and sees a huge log cabin house. The smell of fresh wood, a large fireplace built with stone around it, spacious and cozy, that was brand new. Jacqueline's mouth was wide open, and she was so surprised and happy that her dream came true her own log cabin house in the middle of nowhere with the love of her life.

20.
Not Crazy
Danielle Amboyan; Senior

Journal made by Isabel Jenkins

FIRST DAY OF SUMMER
I'm not sure why, but I have a really good feeling about this year. My best friend, Erica, and I are going to take on new adventures. That's why I decided to keep a journal. So I wouldn't forget anything important in my life that's going on right now. I want to read this as an adult so I can see what I was thinking and how I felt. Erica and I are a perfect fit for each other. We both love to go rock climbing and high ropes' climbing... that's mostly why I got a job at Highropetopia. I wanted to meet new people that I would have things in common with, maybe even a new addition to my friend group! We need someone else to side with one of us... to tell us when were wrong and when we're right. Ugh, wish me luck!

Later, Ryan threw a party to welcome summer. Everyone who is anyone is going to be there.

Erica got ready with me at my house. We got dressed in our new summer tanks and planned to arrive fashionably late. When we got there I've never seen a more beautiful human being, he was standing in the corner talking to Ryan; he must be his cousin or something because I've never seen him before. Everyone was talking about this new Maverick kid like he was some type of celebrity. Erica said it at the same time as me, "DIBS." I automatically pretended like I didn't hear her because I knew he was my ticket to a great summer. I ran up to Maverick and started to talk about our summer and where he came from. Well, I tried at least. The music was so loud I could barely hear him. Turns out, he just moved here from Birmingham, Michigan. Ryan is his new neighbor and wanted him to come and meet everyone. After that, I didn't understand anything else he was saying. I couldn't stop looking at his face and how flawless it appeared. His skin was so clear and his eyes were the darkest brown I have ever seen, kind of like he was hiding something dark inside of him. A mysterious boy... I like that.

MY FIRST REAL JOB AT HIGHROPETOPIA

I am in charge of handling the customers and writing down any of the complaints the costumers have. Erica went for the common lifeguard role at a swim club, but I wanted something different. HighRopestopia seemed like the perfect fit for me. And the staff is so nice! And guess what. MAVERICK WORKS HERE TOO. I can't believe it. We have so much in common too. I can't believe this is actually happening to me. But I don't really see him. He works on the actual course and is always on the ropes helping people out. I first saw him at lunch. We sat together and ate our homemade lunches together. Enjoying the smell of the woodchips and the fresh woodsy air. We talked the whole entire time... I really hope this leads to something new.

END OF THE WEEK- FRIDAY

I'm starting to get the feeling that Maverick only wants to be friends. He keeps talking to me about all of his personal feelings, and I'm just not into it. At lunch, he follows me around everywhere like a sad puppy. Maybe I can change his mind. But then again, he is one of my best guy friends right now, and I would take him over any of the other losers at my school. I just hope he doesn't talk to my ex, Brandon. He always calls me psycho and I don't know why. I have the feeling it has to do with me keying his car... Hm. Weird ;) ugh whatever, though. He deserved it. Let's just say never ignore a girl for ten hours.

4th OF JULY

I took Maverick to our country club fireworks they have every year. It was only us, and I did that on purpose. He came to pick me up around seven-thirty, so we could get something to eat before and head over to the club. He opened the car door for the restaurant and me when I walked out! What a gentleman! Then we went to the fireworks. I packed a blanket for us to sit on. We saw Erica and Ryan walking so we invited them to come sit with us to watch the show. I figured they were on a date because I didn't see anyone else I knew around them. The show started, and the colors were surrounded with great *booms*. I looked at Erica and Ryan and let's just say I couldn't see their faces... if you know what I mean. I looked to Maverick next, and he FINALLY made a move. I think it's clear to say we're more than friends now.

THE LOVE OF MY LIFE

This is officially the best summer ever. I love that I see Maverick almost every day at work and if I don't, I see him later that night. He treats me better than anyone else. He gives me gifts out of the blue all the time! I think I have about three stuffed dogs and one ginormous teddy bear; it's like five feet tall. I'm seriously so happy, maybe the happiest I have ever been. And guess what! The other day while we were at work (after hours) we were climbing the course. He took me on the black diamond, and I needed help to get down because my clamp got stuck and wouldn't unhook. He repelled me down with him at the same time. While we were going down, I had word vomit. The three words people are terrified, the three words people count on came out. "I love you." AND HE SAID IT BACK. Honestly, I can see us getting married and having a life together.

MEETING THE FAM

Maverick finally took me to go meet his family. Not to sound weird or anything but now I know why he always smells like cinnamon apples! He has candles all around his house lit with that same scent. His mom is seriously the cutest thing ever. She made a huge feast just for me. We ate steak and potatoes with gravy and grilled veggies. It was sooooooo yummy. I met his grandma, grandpa, and his younger brother. He is a legit exact replica of Maverick. It's scary. We talked about how we met and how we work together. I asked them a whole bunch of questions in return about when they moved and if they liked Westport so far. I really liked them, and I'm almost positive they liked me back. I mean how could they not? I'm the best package for their son.

WEIRD VIBES.

Maverick is starting to become kind of distant. He's taking twice as long to respond to my texts, and at work, it seems like he's avoiding me. I asked Erica what to do, but she got really weird and told me to ignore it and said I was overreacting for no reason. The only thing I can do it cry and cry because I love him so much and I can't imagine a world without him. I am really starting to worry and think there might be another girl. Maybe it's Polly from work, who never stops talking. I always see her eyeing my guy. Looks like it's time for my detective side to come out.

OUT WITH ANOTHER GIRL

I spotted him... With Erica... I am so depressed, and I am not so sure what to do. My life feels over. All I want to do it sleep and watch old movies from the 90s. Right now, my best friend is *Clueless* and *Sixteen Candles*. The person I loved and my best friend are going behind my back. I can't believe it. I am devastated. I am speechless.

I saw them walking out from his back door and around the house. He thought he could hide this from me? Ha. Little does he know that I was already suspicious of him and was watching him for the past three days? That doesn't sound crazy, I'm just looking out for myself. I guess looking back on it now, I should've asked him first before I went into my stalker mode.

He betrayed me... and I now know what I must do.

ERICA MY BFF

I went over to Erica's house today and pretended like nothing even happened. I told her how I saw him with another girl while I was driving by his house to drop something off but I didn't get to catch a glance at her face. Aw man, you should've seen her face. It was priceless. On the inside, I was so happy to trick her, but I had to keep in character. I had to show her how upset I really was. The tears kept pouring out, and my breath became heavy and choppy. She kept on saying things like, "Aw sweetie you don't deserve him," and "He just doesn't know what he has." I hate her. What a two faced 'B'. I must get down to business and start my plot now that she doesn't suspect me.

PART 1

Every month or so Erica gets her hair done at the salon for some highlights or a new color to touch up her roots. I had to get in there and switch the hair dye. So I did. I called the salon and made an appointment under my aunt's name so they couldn't trace me. When I walked in, she was getting her hair washed and was facing the ceiling. I knew this was my chance to move. I got up from the waiting room and asked where the bathroom was. I knew what hair color she was getting because it's the same for every visit, and what best friend for ten years wouldn't know that? I grabbed a random color and went for it, squirting two or maybe three colors in the bowl. I placed the containers back, and walked back to the waiting room, and then left. Her hair is her biggest insecurity, so I knew this was the way to go. I hope it looks great! Sike.

PART 2

HAHAHAHAHA it's red, oh no, not just any red but with a blue tint. It looks awful, and the best part is, is that her mom is making her keep it because she doesn't want Erica's hair to get fried. However, I wish it were ruined. But I guess I will have to deal with the red. Oh wow, that was the best idea ever. And the best part is, she called me to tell me how her hairdresser messed up, but on the line, I was so surprised and everything. It was great.

Now it's time for Maverick…

MY LOVE, MAVERICK
While all of this drama was going on with Erica, I was ignoring Maverick. I couldn't look at him or talk to him at work. I knew if I did, I would slip into that gross lovey phase I was in earlier this summer, aka, only a few weeks ago. He has no idea about what I did to Erica, and it's going to stay that way. I thought about it for a while, and the only place I could think of is HighRopeitopia. I didn't want to hurt him from the high ropes course, but I could come close to it. While everyone was eating lunch, I slipped into the equipment room and tampered with his clips. Not both, only one. It was the most important one, but at least the backup was there! It was time. He's so good at balancing on the wires and going from obstacle to obstacle with no problem at all, he makes it look effortless. Wait I need to stop. Okay back to the clip. All of a sudden his foot slipped and the safety clip didn't do its job (Hm weird) He fell for about a foot. I wanted him to fall because I wanted him to see what it felt like to lose to something you love. I've never heard a girl scream before. His face was priceless. He was terrified. I didn't show any sympathy at all. All of our coworkers ran over there to see if he was okay. No one could tell if he was hurt or not because he was crying too hard. Good. And of course, he wasn't hurt, he's just a baby.

A FEW WEEKS
I haven't seen Maverick since that day at work. He quit shortly after the "accident" due to his new fear of heights. School is about to start, but no one has seen or heard from him. I haven't been picking up his phone calls or responding to his texts. He's not worth my time.

Erica has been locked up in her room and refuses to leave the house because of her hair. She doesn't want anyone to see. Honestly, I don't blame her. It's hilarious.

Well, to say the least, I would say this is the best summer ever. I had my first love, my first breakup, and my first revenge plot.

Just remember.
I'm not crazy...

21.
Outside In
Siena C.; Junior

APRIL 1ST, 2016 - 11:32 PM.
I feel the sun on my arms, hear the murmur of trees for miles. Everything I used to fear is caught between my teeth, and I am standing at the intersection of shadow and light with my own decision of where to go.

My bedroom longs for me to return rather than my longing for it. The entire world pinwheels, breathless around me until the possibilities splatter me in shades of everything, eager to catch me up on what I missed while I was gone. The soft wind greets me, the flags lining the street flapping on their poles, the blackberry bushes dotting the dirt rustling. Maps unfold on command under my fingers like the trails run the same course as my veins. My heart beats in tandem with the sun, and together we learn not to long, not to scrape our chests empty in the shape of a hole that nothing will fill, not to sit perched among the stars only to spend all of our time waiting for the moon. My heartbeat exists alongside all of the others.

And I breathe the same air, in this world, too - everyone's, the kids at the high school I would go to and the foreigners and the President and the tigers stalking around in their Gardens of Eden.

But before any of these things I am alive. I am alive. I am alive.

APRIL 3RD, 2016 - 6:12 PM.
Google rattles off the definition of agoraphobia as irrational or extreme fear of public spaces or gatherings. The books my

mother thinks I don't know are wedged behind her tacky 80's sweaters in the closet generally, have the same consensus.

I disagree, I think. I haven't refused to leave the house for four years because of filled space. The people don't scare me, nor the things: I don't tremble at the thought of the smiling peaches in the fruit bins at the grocery store, it's the spaces. The possibilities. The boxes left unchecked gaping at me emptily. What *could* happen? *Fear or phobia of the empty spots in a fill-in-the-blank question*, I scratch into a 2008 copy of WebMD.

APRIL 10TH, 2016 - 1:45 PM.
There is a girl beyond the fence. My neighbor, I think. Now that spring has woken up from its long sleep it's mild enough for her and her friends to bike home together. They explode down the road like a shaken can of soda every afternoon around two, barreling past the kitchen window. The sight lasts behind my eyelids for a few hours.

I'm not sure if it's them that's so enchanting or the fact that this girl knows everything I don't know about this planet. I wonder if our lungs would look any different if they were laid out next to each other.

She has this crazy grin like she knows exactly when the world ends.

APRIL 13TH, 2016 - 4:02 PM
She is not afraid.

APRIL 13TH, 2016 - 7:27 PM
Questions for apocalypse girl:
1. Is it zombies or meteors?
2. Will we all hopelessly collide in the end?
3. Will we be looking at the sky?
4. Would you hold on if you knew the inevitable anyway?

APRIL 14TH, 2016 - 3:31 PM

I think she may be friends with the mourning dove because her own harmony drifts through the window like a paper airplane delivered to the wrong house, too. She plays basketball with her friends - I tap my foot to the *thunk, thunk, thunk* until it drives my father crazy - and snaps at her younger brothers in Hindi. The words escalate and escalate like a glimpse of an unfamiliar orchestral scale.

Her family looks a little like the photo insert in a picture frame when you buy it, minus the tacky outfits.

She caught my eye today and the window in between us was a silent third party. She waved. The sun swayed in the sky.

APRIL 15TH, 2016 - 12 AM
I want to go outside.

APRIL 16TH - 11:21 PM
I want to

APRIL 18TH, 2016 - 2:42 AM
I want

APRIL 23RD, 2016 - 4:23 PM
"Nia, this is Dr. March. He's here to help you."

I blink at the mirror on the wall behind him and wonder if I would look any different if I went outside. Everything on me is dark, now: brown skin, short dark hair, my mother's serious and dark dark dark eyes, dark heavy eyebrows. Like shadow curled in on itself, I think, looking at my knees tucked up under my chin on the old kitchen stool. Like something you'd find in a haunted house, except I haven't been to enough places to have one to haunt besides my own home.

"Nia. That's a pretty name. It means purpose."

My stomach churns at this.

I realize Dr. March's hand is floating in front of me. It looks like a bear trap, and I shake it cautiously as if I'm afraid that it'll snap shut on me. *Chomp.* I decide I don't like this.

"You never like them," my Mom will say later, shaking her head in a way that twists my stomach left and right with it, "but it's the only way you can get better." I grit my teeth and pretend I'm my own bear trap, crushing everyone's words and turning it into something I can digest where I won't have to see it.

My Dad will say some meaner things I am not writing down because I pretend he didn't say them.

Spanish is a pretty language: I see Puerto Rico in my dreams, my smart and solemn mother and my mirthful and young father. How they would look when they stood in the salty sea wind with feet under cool sand: like a pair of twin trees, strong and sure of each other. And the taste of alcapurria from the Luquillo kiosks, the contrast between the mild evening weather and the rush on my tongue, biting heat like if I were to touch the stars above. The sound of bikes reeling past vast stretches of crowded, colorful spaces and the crackle of my own native tongue on the radio. This is probably why it is so much more fearsome to be yelled at in Spanish rather than English. It feels more like a heat-seeking missile that struck with precision, in the fiercest and most loving parts of myself. *Home.*

Maybe if we went back I wouldn't be so afraid all of the time, I sometimes think. And then I feel sorry for blaming Puerto Rico for my own issues. We all know the problem is me.

My parents know.

The grim parade of doctors in and out of my life, they know.

I know.

Puerto Rico and the alcapurria kiosks know, lonely under the yellowed rush of stars since I abandoned them.

APRIL 25TH, 2016 - UNKNOWN
What if I die here?

APRIL 25TH, 2016 - UNKNOWN
Nia means purpose.

APRIL 25TH, 2016 - 10:02 AM
I had a dream that I sat on a bench in Puerto Rico with apocalypse girl, sunny and vast and magnificent.

I ate alcapurria while she chattered on in Hindi and I nodded between mouthfuls, somehow still understanding her.

She pointed up, and I looked to see the sky crash down on top of me, except it looked like a big window of my bedroom.

APRIL 25TH, 2016 - 7:30 PM
Things I would like to experience here in New Hampshire:

- The awful winters: the clean blue-gray light, the season stretching out like an ex-lover borrowing your couch, bringing nothing but memories and slushy gray residue of the month you thought you loved when it was clean and white.
- The spring: Seeing my own reflection in a puddle, for once. Wearing my favorite soft black t-shirt one day and then my Puerto Rico FC sweatshirt the next. Seeing the first flower blink its eyes at the world, knowing we have almost made it again, though we always forget that we

usually do in the end.
- Autumn: The world collapsing in warm shades, burning my tongue on a good drink, making a crown of leaves that go *crunch* under your own excitement.
- The summer: Everything.

APRIL 27TH, 2016 - 5:37 PM
I have the best news, and I am shooting off so many sparks I fear that the paper will catch on fire when I write it.

Apocalypse girl cracked our kitchen window with her basketball! Isn't it great?

She has a name now, too. It's Stella! This means "star" in Latin. I feel that it is appropriate because her eyes are shiny in person but still dark like mine. The difference: I am still and unmoving and stuck in one place. Everything about her is frenetic, moving like the *tick-tick-tick* of spinning bike wheels.

Anyways, Mama and I were in the kitchen "studying" trigonometry, though it was more her on a wrought monologue about triangles while I traced the zig-zag patterns the sun threw onto the table with my finger. She was halfway through a rant about thirty-sixty-ninety triangles she thought I wasn't listening to when there was a sound like a bird mistook our window for the door to a new beginning and smacked into it headfirst.

Mama's chair scraped on the floor as she murmured a Spanish expletive and hauled herself up to investigate, and I peeked out from behind her, expecting to see a wilted red cardinal like a fallen rose and instead, finding something better: a spiderweb of cracks in glass, flourishing across the entire window sheepishly. There was something magic and personal about it: broken, fractured, yet suspended in place by laws of nature.

The most magic thing of all was the distorted sight of round eyes like new moons peering at us from outside of the window, Stella's image splintered by the upset glass. I swallow hard as my Mama's words do the opposite, shooting up her throat. She storms to the front of the house in the rod-straight way of hers that means business, and I trail behind her, attempting to look less small and frightened than the mirror always tells me when it whispers in my ear.

"I am so, so, so sorry—"

My mother's eyes soften, ever so slightly, when she sees Stella's hands fumble with the pockets of her red varsity jacket, fishing out a few crumpled bills. Her knuckles are scratched a little, to my own fascination. What universes has she touched?

"Keep it."

Stella blinks owlishly, like a night thing.

"I guess this was God's sign we should be polite and introduce ourselves to our neighbors anyway. Would you like to come in?"

As if the expression she wore just moments ago was a mist shrouding her, it dissipated, giving way to a lopsided grin. I had to look away.

"I kinda gotta babysit my brother."

And then, she leaned right a little bit, and as if I dreamed it, stuck her hand over the threshold to our house, past my Mom, towards me. I reckon to an outsider, it must have looked as strange and inevitable as the sun and the moon: I, unlit in a black sweater with wide eyes, her washed out in breathless light in a pair of cherry red Converse.

"Antonia, right?"

I managed a tragically uncertain-looking nod. *If you can't handle speaking to another human being your age, you certainly can't handle adults or crowds or for that matter, the peaches in the grocery store bins,* I thought, flushing. Who cares that it is an untouchably cool, tall, everything-I-am-not, did I add cool human being my age. I feel a little like I'm staring at a test I decided not to study for.

"Nia is fine."

Nia was very good. Great. *Superb*. Peachy, if you will.

"Cool. I'm Stella. Nice to meet you. And, um, Mrs. Tavares. We were trying to play HORSE, but I guess it kind of ran away on us. And into your window."

It is such a peculiar way to put it. I was beside myself with joy.

"Go run and tell your mother not to worry about it."

Stella's face says she's not going to tell anyone at all, but her head bobs convincingly, long black hair near dark brown in the brilliant sunshine. I bow my head and scratch at my eyebrow, so nobody sees me smile.

When she waves and backs down the cobblestone without tripping or looking back once, I race upstairs so quickly to write that I think I left the scared me standing at the bottom of the stairs.

APRIL 30TH, 2016 - 6:07 PM
After a few relatively still days, Stella came back in the form of a note jammed halfway in our mailbox.

When are you free this week?

Her letters lean right as if they were caught in a wind. I trace my finger them a few times while sprawled out on my bed in the midday light.

I can't quite decipher whether she is incredibly oblivious to think that I would have anything to do or if she is trying to be polite. As friendly as she is, she doesn't strike me as the careful kind, and the idea leaves me soft at the edges all day.

Uncapping a purple marker, I draw a sun and a moon. On an invisible bridge between the two, I write in block letters, *whenever you are.*

It stays taped up on my window where I hope that she will see it before the light dies.

APRIL 30TH, 2016 - 9:45 PM
The shades roll down over the window on her pale yellow house like an eye winking at me. On it, a lined sheet of paper taped to the material reads: *See you tomorrow.*

APRIL 30TH, 2016 - 2:43 AM
I am not going to die here.

APRIL 30TH, 2016 - 11:26 PM
"You can't be seeing anyone else until you're willing to see a doctor first, *hija*. You are sick."

My mother was slouched against the worn wood headboard we lugged all the way home from Puerto Rico, sitting at the center of a garden like a rose herself, faded dark green vines and patchy red flowers spiraling from all of her edges. She peered over wireframes at me, legs crossed in a pair of old sweatpants from her university in Puerto Rico. I try imagining that she is only doing this because she is a Mama who time traveled from the past to warn me of a great danger. It doesn't work.

"I don't understand why you aren't happy for me."

Her eyebrow distorted as she smeared a hand across her eye as if I had deprived her of a long sleep. My gut twisted when I considered that I likely had, for years.

"I'll be happy for you when you're better, so you can properly enjoy your own social interactions."

I take her words into my bear trap, *snap*, and crush them between my teeth.

Glancing out of the kitchen window this morning, it was as if the world was setting the scene for me: rain pattering on the roofs of the neat English-style homes lining the slicked suburban street, limiting the world to my own dry house. Stella could've come over, without the freedom to suggest going anywhere outside, and I would be free of explaining a single thing.

The world will have to assume that I am thankful for its efforts anyway and move on.

When I turned eleven, I had my birthday party planned out for my backyard, decked out in papery red streamers tacked up along the clothesline, fresh-picked poppies woven into my hair and around Mama's wrist, paper cups dotting the plastic table we unfolded among the unmown grass waving in the breeze. The air smelled like the meeting point of soil and sky, the distinct thickness of rain that distressed me. My Dad reminded my younger self that the world has a funny way of always finding a way to open the door for you, even when human beings keep theirs locked tight.

There was not rain that day. There was a hurricane.

And I sat inside, eleven years old, watching the paper streamers melt in the unrelenting dark rain and the plastic table limp across our backyard in the breakneck wind, knees pulled to my chest. In a last-ditch effort to cheer me up, Mama remarked that perhaps the hurricane was mad because I didn't invite it, and my Dad quipped that clearly, I had my reasons, it was not a very amiable guest. I didn't talk to my parents for three days. Later on in my life, I didn't talk to the Earth for four years.

Today, I saw Dr. March at the time I was to see Stella, and before I curled up to sleep, I stared at the parallel window and watched the red streamers melt down to nothing.

MAY 1ST, 2016 - 7 PM
A new month starts, without me.

MAY 2ND, 2016 - 6:21 AM
Sometimes I believe that the greatest pain of going outside would be realizing how breathtakingly beautiful it is to exist in open spaces and spend the rest of my life mourning the four years I refused to live under the sky.

MAY 10TH, 2016 - 9:34 PM
There have been three times in these four years that I have tried to go outside:

     1.   When my neighbor's dog ran into the street, and I kicked open the door like my hands would be burnt by whatever was on the other side. I had flown out like I was a prey animal being chased by a predator on the inside, certainly not a rescuer. All of a sudden, I remembered who I was, and I couldn't feel my legs and arms and face and brain and heart and soul. I flattened myself against the front of our house, screaming like a siren until I didn't need to tune out the sound of all of the windows along the street opening like wide eyes. I was carried back inside. The dog was fine.

2.   When a boy who went to the middle school nearby, Davey Ettick, stopped by my house every day in March to dare me to come outside with this big grin on his face. The boredly antagonistic jeers coming from his mouth were borne from a dull knife that is just beginning to be sharpened for adulthood. I lurched forward and shoved him down the front steps. When my parents grabbed me, I laugh-cried so hysterically that our neighbors pried open their windows only to hear me say: *What are you gonna do, ground me?*

3.   I wanted the flower that lived beside the porch so badly that I dreamt of it. I skinned my knee when I tripped on my way back inside, with the petals crushed in my sweaty palm. My heart rattled the bars of its jail cell so loudly that I cried, because I had killed it, and all of a sudden I knew why my brain told me I wasn't allowed to go outside.

MAY 14TH, 2016 - 2:01 PM
Sometimes I think I am the dumbest human being to not walk the planet.

There was a knock on our door today, three sharp raps. For once, I thundered down the stairs to open it before either of my parents could even think of standing up. Stella was standing in the gray post-rain light in a soft t-shirt. She held a bright yellow box of Popsicles in her right hand.

"I waited for you yesterday."

I couldn't decide whether my heart shattered or simply swelled three sizes bigger at that. I swallowed hard before I answered.

"I'm sorry. Family problems."

"Figured as much."

I pressed my lips together, moved to the side so she could come inside. She stood still, and I shifted on my feet a little bit to resist the urge to move myself back into place, like a human barricade between her and this place that trapped me.

"Let me make it up to you."

"Don't have to. I've got grape Popsicles, because all educated people like them, and I thought maybe we could sit out here and eat them or something?"

And then I was a sinking ship, my gaping holes filling with cold saltwater. I think I visibly flinched at her words because her eyebrows drew together.

"I can't. Sorry. Come back another day."

It came out all in one breath. When the door closed, I felt it close inside me too.

MAY 15TH, 2016 - 3PM

There were three sharp raps on the door today at precisely one o'clock.

I open the door to see Stella shouldering a yellow box of red Popsicles. Her face splits into a grin as soon as she sees my expression.

"Stella, I closed the door on you because I don't—"

"You don't like grape popsicles? I knew it. I brought cherry today."

It looks like a laugh threatens to spill out from some sunny place inside of her, and my expression begins to mirror hers.

We both laugh so hard that I nearly fall from my perch within the house to outside, and tears blink in the sun at the corners of Stella's eyes like distant stars. I think we woke up anyone trying to take a nap in the neighborhood, wheezing for breath.

"Your mom told me, you don't have to talk about it."

I blink rapidly at her, a soft guiltiness chafing against the warmth within my chest as I think of this small favor my Mom did for me in comparison to how I have treated her lately.

"Would it be okay if we sat in the doorway? I like to see the neighborhood, and this is a good spot."

"Me too."

And then, I sink down onto the threshold between home and the world unsteadily, as if I had a limb problem rather than a brain problem. My heart has sped miles away from my body, tires squealing.

Stella plops down beside me and peels the wrapper off of a Popsicle to hand it to me. She began to tell a story of how her Dad accidentally sent a text to his coworker that he had meant to send to her Mom, and the planet hummed quietly around me as if to say, *Welcome home.*

MAY 17TH, 2016 - 5:31 PM
"I hear you've been outside, young lady," Dr. March remarks while peering at me over his glasses. My heart doesn't move until a slow smile spreads across his face.

"That's remarkable. You do realize that puts you so much closer than the day you were before, right?"

All I can do is stare at him until the feelings within me are so intense that I have to move my gaze to the floor or his salt and pepper hair or bear trap hands.

"Never, ever, ever ignore your own progress. You did that, Antonia. That was you."

MAY 18TH, 2016 - 10:48 PM
Things I am learning:
- Stella likes 80s hip-hop more than anything. She hoards her father's cassette tapes like a time machine shoved in a cardboard box below her bed.
- How to curse in Hindi. I teach her in Spanish.
- She laughed the loudest at the story of the first time I rode a bike and cursed the devil when I fell off, leading my parents to call me "Hell on Wheels."
- She is often angry with the fact that the high school boys' basketball team makes the school PA system every day for losing, while the girls' team meets silence at their wins.
- The mourning dove that perches on the spidery green apple tree near my window has darker spots than I originally thought it did.
- If you squint from the porch, you can see the couple that lives directly across from us in the squat blue house with the wide windows painting their walls blank white.
- People are very striking to watch in their cars: there's something strange and otherworldly about it, and the glass of a windshield of a car cannot protect you from it. The most difficult view of a person in their car, for me, is when they do not notice you watching them. They fight with their parent, they text and drive, they bob their head to

phantom music, and for a moment, I cannot reconcile whether we share the same world or it is entirely theirs.

MAY 20TH, 2016 - 6:21 PM
I walked to the gate today, to see a ladybug on the white picket fence starting a long journey home.

MAY 20TH, 2016 - 6:30 PM
Dr. March comes less and less these days.

MAY 21ST, 2016 - 5:42 PM
One-half of the couple that lives across the street came down the sidewalk to pick up the newspaper at the end of their driveway, dried white handprints pressed upon her smock and red-red hair that lit up like a Christmas tree bulb in the daytime. She waved at me slowly, and I waved back. What a strange thought that I am here.

MAY 23RD, 2016 - 2:01 PM
Today, when Stella showed up, there was a flock of teenagers flanking our front yard, all assembled behind her, hovering over bike seats and craning their necks to see me. I stopped in my tracks, hanging onto the door frame with one hand. I had a very bad feeling.

"Hey," Stella greeted, grinning entirely normally. "Wanna come ride with us?"

Us. A skinny boy with floppy hair and a Star of David necklace glinting in the sun peered at me from below his eyebrows, gaze darting between Stella and I, and my neck went hot. He probably doesn't like me. I bet they all don't like me. I shouldn't have done this. I shouldn't have done any of this. I try to blink away the clump of facelessness like tears.

"Just for, like, an hour."

There was nothing else I would rather do in the world. There was no way I could do it.

"I can't ride a bike," I say. Somewhere in the recesses of my mind, my parents carried me back inside.

Her grin vanished, and something pushed at the back of my eyes hotly. We didn't break eye contact for a terrible, terrible moment, and I don't remember either of us saying goodbye, only the feeling that lasted for hours after.

MAY 25TH, 2016 - 11:01 PM
Other kids my age *whir* just above my head like a mobile. I think I am a planet fallen out of orbit.

MAY 25TH, 2016 - 11:01 PM
I don't think there's a single person in the world who feels like me.

MAY 26TH, 2016 - 4:13 PM
I decided that Stella did not know when the apocalypse was to begin, but I do, and I have written down the details here for you:

- It will feel like deja vu.
- Her earbuds will be blasting 80s hip hop in her ears so loudly that she is oblivious to the glow of a cell phone cast on Davey's ducked face as his car prowls blindly up behind her.
- It will be like when you encounter someone and you both duck left and right in sync in an attempt in vain to pass each other, except it will be you and the universe.
- You will have to be the one to move first.
- You will run into that endless street, which is eerily still, like the last beat before you scream back something irreversible in a fight.
- You will feel the wind on your arms and in your hair and in your heart, breathe in the soft May air and

hear the unfamiliar hymn of lawn mowers and bugs and sunshine.

- You will take the apocalypse from her back and carry it on your own shoulders because you shouldn't have burdened her with that knowledge in the first place.
- You will wave your hands, galloping like a startled deer to glance off the side of wide-eyed Davey's Ford Focus, just before he nearly hits the sun with his car.
- You will have saved her.
- And yourself.
- And everyone.
- And every growing thing, repaying your imaginary debt for all of the years they sat outside and waited for you to find yourself again.

MAY 27TH, 2016 - 12:45 PM

I look out of my bedroom window to see Stella's window with a piece of paper pasted to the glass. There is a drawing of two girls standing on planets, but they aren't lonely out there in the dark universe. They are individual, separate, entirely their own, but they are on the same level.

Earth to Nia,
Do you prefer your "thank yous" in cash or cherry Popsicles?

An answer, in purple block letters.

In bike rides.

JUNE 1ST, 2016 - UNKNOWN

I feel the sun on my arms, hear the murmur of trees for miles. Everything I used to fear is caught between my teeth, and I am standing at the intersection of shadow and light with my own decision about where to go.

My bedroom longs for me to return rather than my longing for it. We have our arms outstretched like a pair of birds restless from the cage, my fingertips just barely brushing Stella's as we ride with no hands. Her laugh is halfway lost to the cold wind, but there's no way I wouldn't hear it. I think I'm half girl and half goosebumps, the world a smear of color all around me. The month starts with me. Nia means purpose.

The sky cracks open like a girl opening her bedroom window for the first time, and we spread our wings to mirror the sky.

I am something that saved itself. I am a ladybug on a fence post and a handprint of white paint and a hurricane and a bin of grocery store peaches and a girl. It is not important that I am still afraid in the corners of me that don't see any light. It is important that I am here despite that.

But before any of these things I am alive. I am alive. I am alive.

22.
Serendipity: A Subatomic Story
Nicholas Kroetsch; Senior

In the beginning, there was only the singularity, a point of infinite density that contained everything in the universe. I didn't exist back then, none of us did. But suddenly, one day 13.7 billion years ago, that all changed. Expanding at unimaginably high speeds, the singularity transformed into the infant stages of the universe as we know it. Quadrillions upon quadrillions of particles emerged into this brave new world, heating everything to temperatures on the order of millions of degrees. And amid all the chaos, I was born. I emerged from that cosmic soup as a new particle, an electron. We electrons aren't exactly the largest of particles, weighing in at a measly 9×10^{-31} kilograms. But hey, size doesn't mean everything. After all, look at the proton, which weighs over a thousand times as much as I do. But they take so much more energy to do anything, while I can just zip around on even the slightest amounts of energy. Oh, and speaking of protons, you should meet Penelope. She formed right next to me, and she says that whatever happens, we will always stick together. I guess she's correct in that regard, after all, as they say, opposites attract. Her positive charge is absolutely irresistible to me, I just can't stop orbiting around her.

Now, we particles obviously can't talk to each other like you humans can. After all, we don't have mouths or ears, and sounds don't travel well on a subatomic level. But don't take that to mean we can't talk to each other at all. We have our ways of communicating, much like your morse code. But for purposes of simplicity in this story, I'll format any of our communications much like your talking.

There we were, Penelope and I, two peas in a pod, or more accurately two subatomic particles in a hydrogen atom. Drifting through deep space for eons, ecstatic the whole time about just being together. Light-years away, we could see the genesis of entire galaxies, vast spirals of billions of newly formed white stars spinning away in the blackness. Out here, millions of miles from the nearest star, it was eerily quiet. With no nearby particles to transmit vibrations and nothing nearby to make a sound even if there were, it was like I only had one of my senses: vision. But there was a lot to see. If you've ever looked up and seen a night sky from the wilderness on a planet, with no light other than that of the stars, multiply that by a hundred. No, multiply it by a thousand. Deep blue nebulae thousands of light-years across, massive pillar-shaped gas clouds larger than solar systems, and rapidly spinning neutron stars pulsing their beams of light signaling their presence to the rest of the universe, were just some of the things visible from my vantage point so far away from it all. "Isn't it absolutely beautiful out here?" muttered Penelope. And it was. Floating out here, even traveling millions of miles an hour, everything was visible clearly and unblurred all the way across the universe. The two of us spun through space, happy as ever for thousands of years. We passed by blue-green gas giant planets, bright red stars as big as smaller solar systems, clouds of asteroids no bigger than a few yards across, and much, much more. It really was idyllic, sort of, with nothing to do other than sit and watch the stars pass by.

But suddenly, that tranquility all came crashing down on us. At first, we could only feel a faint rumble in the gravity of a nearby red supergiant star. The shaking continued, increasing and increasing until we could hardly think. The screams of a trillion particles writhing in agony pierced my ears. "WHAT'S GOING ON??" I yelled to Penelope over the massive vibrations of the star. "I HAVE NO IDEA! WHATEVER IT IS, IT CAN'T BE GOOD. HOLD ON TIGHT AND DON'T LET GO OF—" she shouted back, being cut off by a massive explosion that shot us, and the trillions of other atoms in the vicinity of the star, out of its star system at near relativistic velocities. The intensity of the shockwave was enough to strip many electrons away from their atoms, forming a massive ring of superheated plasma and gamma radiation flying out from the star. I just barely managed to hold on to Penelope, and we rode out the shockwave without too much harm. Turning around to look back at the star, the only thing visible was a brilliant white flash as intense as the light of a million stars. As the flash gradually dissipated, all that was left was a ring of pure blackness, so dark that not even light could escape.

"Oh, my Higgs Boson... All those particles... Trapped in there, with no way to get out. At least you held on tight and made it out, but the others... Dilated in time, spending eternity feeling their descent into blackness, knowing that there is no hope left for them." wailed Penelope.

"Hey, at least it's not us. But we've got bigger things to worry about than them. Mainly us. Because we're getting sucked in too, I can feel it," I replied, feeling the immense gravitational pull of the black hole accelerating us faster and faster towards the event horizon: the point of no return.

What in the world am I going to do? I thought to myself, knowing that there was no way for us to break free of the pull of the now-dead star. Faster and faster we plummeted down towards the blackness, each second pulling us miles closer to the point of no return. But there was still a glimmer of hope: the accretion disk containing all the material about to descend into the darkness and the massive jets of gas ejected from it as it nears the black hole. Only through those jets, spewing particles out into deep space at near the speed of light, could we escape the pull.

"Penelope, you see that column of gas shooting up and away from the black hole? That's how we get out of here, and it's the only way we can get out of here. Listen to me, if you don't want to be trapped down there, we've got to get over there," I told her, maintaining a soft tone to avoid frightening her too much. "Now, they're going to be accelerating really fast, but as long as we can stick together and hold on again like we did before, we'll be fine."

"Alright… If that's our only chance, I'll take it. It looks like we'll pass into the jets in a few minutes,. Hopefully, you don't lose me, but if you do, I just want you to know how much I love you," replied Penelope.

"We're going to make it, and we're going to stay together. Don't you worry, I'll make sure of it." And so we plunged into the accretion disk and made our way to the huge geysers of gas, spiraling away from the center of the disk. Immediately, as I approached the disk, I could feel the immense pressure from the jets and was overwhelmed by the noise of particles accelerating to nearly the speed of light in barely a second. In a matter of seconds, Penelope and I were two of those particles, ejected from the black hole, traveling thousands of miles in just a single second.

"HOOLLDDDDD TIGHT!!!!" she shouted as we were being yanked apart, tugged at by immense forces attempting to accelerate us in different directions. All around us, we could hear the wails of protons being stripped of their electrons, forming a beam of superheated plasma emanating from the center of the black hole. The faster we went, the harder it was to hold on. And eventually, I couldn't maintain my hold any longer.

"NOOOOO!!!!!!" I wailed, hopelessly grasping for her, drifting away further into the plasma jet.

"DON'T LEAVE ME!!!" she cried in reply, but it was too late.

Before I could even work up a reply, she was gone, blasted off into space in an entirely different direction. Gone. I didn't even know what to do with myself anymore. Since literally the beginning of time, we were together, inseparable, journeying together through the vast expanses of space. But those times were over. I would have to get to grips with being alone or find another proton to replace her. But nothing could ever really replace Penelope, my pair, my other half, from the very start.

After a while, trapped in the gas jet, traveling further and further from Penelope the whole time, I finally began to slow down. Before long, I was once again floating throughout the vastness of space. While it was as silent as always, there was something missing. Without Penelope's warm, comforting electrostatic pull, I was just free-floating. There was nothing to orbit around, no meaning to my life as an electron. I was just another particle, left out alone in deep space. This wouldn't do. I couldn't spend all of eternity like this, or even as short as a few million more years. But what could I do? She was far across the galaxy by now, traveling past completely different planets, different stars. Her sky was very different from the one I saw, and there was no way for me to know which one it was, or even which direction she had gone. I had nothing, not a single shred of evidence to find out where she had ended up, or if she had even made it out without being annihilated by some cosmic phenomena.

I spent thousands of years just contemplating where to start looking for her. But on a cosmic timescale, that's nothing. I had a lot longer to find her than just that. After many thousands of conversations that looked something like this, Me: "Have you seen a proton named Penelope, no electron with her, possibly looking for an electron named Eric?" Them: Some variation of "Nope." It got very disheartening. It seemed like it would be impossible to ever find her. Then it hit me, literally. I was asking too big of particles, and small neutrinos like the one that just hit me would be much better to ask. Now, neutrinos are some of the smallest particles, having almost no mass and no charge, and they travel very fast throughout space. After all, they travel the galaxy much further and faster than everyone else, so if I asked around, eventually one of them would probably know something regarding the whereabouts of Penelope.

As it turns out, my hunch was right. After quite a long search, I eventually bumped into a neutrino named Nil. Nil had passed by me on the way from a planet far off in the Orion arm of the galaxy, and I had reached out and asked if Nil had ever encountered Penelope. As it turns out, Nil had actually seen Penelope, a few thousand years ago, on that planet, the third from the star with a single large moon, lush, green land, and deep blue oceans.

"That planet, it's like nothing you've ever seen. The particles there, they've managed to organize themselves into amazing creations, capable of thinking for themselves and even manipulating the particles around them! What a wonderful planet to end up on! I would have stayed there myself if I could, but alas, I'm just a neutrino, and I just passed straight through that world," Nil told me.

"But how in the world can I get there? Even if I know where she is, it doesn't help me much if I can't get there," I questioned Nil.

"I'm not entirely sure, you could always make your way back to the black hole and try to shoot to the same place that she ended up, but that's risky. Very risky. I would not advise that because you could end up even farther away than you started. You could also just make your way there normally, but that would take forever. Like millions of years, and I don't think you want to wait that long. Hmm... I guess you could maybe ride a cosmic ray, but then again, that isn't going to help much. I know! There's another nearby star about to go supernova. Yeah, it's going to be a lot like the first one, but hey, at least you can try and position yourself in the right place to end up where you've got to go. It'll be quick, and reasonably accurate if you just ride the shockwave in the right direction."

"Thanks a lot, Nil. If you ever need something, you'll know where to find me. Anyways, I'll be off to go find Penelope," I replied.

I set off for the nearby star that was about to go supernova, and I positioned myself around the blazing ball of fire in such a way that the massive shockwave would push me towards Penelope. Like earlier, I could feel the rumbling beneath me on the star and see the brilliant white flash of light, followed by the shockwave that gripped me and thrust me out into the darkness beyond. I traveled for a few years, watching the stars and planets fly past at immense velocities until I finally had the planet in my sights in front of me. It was such a beautiful sight, covered in brilliant blue oceans, wispy white clouds, and lush green forests. As the planet rotated around the star, I could see one side of the planet become enveloped in darkness, but I could make out a faint glow radiating from the surface of the planet. Speeding ever closer, I began to be able to make out patterns in the lights, with thin veins of light connecting the clusters of lights to each other. The lights were only on land, the oceans were completely pitch-black at night.

As I neared the planet, a chunk of something whizzed by my head. It was a white metal cylinder of some kind, bearing the markings "USA" in black lettering down the side. I wondered what in the world it could possibly be, but then I began to see thousands more such objects fly by. These objects appeared to be orbiting the planet, and none of them seemed natural. Some of them contained black panels, capturing the sunlight and turning it into electricity that they then used to send out signals to other objects and down to the surface of the planet. Others seemed useless, hunks of metal with no signals being sent out at all. It was all very overwhelming, but it was nothing compared to what lay on the surface of the planet.

Entering through the thick atmosphere of the planet, I could immediately feel a change from the lack of material in space. It was so suffocatingly dense, other particles were constantly jostling me for position throughout the air. It was also much hotter than the frigid emptiness of space, although it was still cooler than both the supernova and black hole. Falling through the clouds and into the pouring rain, I was overwhelmed by the sudden abundance of noise. Raindrops falling to the ground, the howling of the wind, the crackling of thunder as massive lightning bolts penetrated the sky and arced towards the ground, all contributed to a feeling of helplessness compared to all the stuff that was in this new world. I would have to get used to this if I was ever to find Penelope on this planet, one proton out of many quadrillions.

As I finally landed on the surface of this strange planet, I was already starting to adjust to this over stimulus. I could finally begin to properly see where I was: an expansive valley surrounded by sharp, jagged peaks on all sides. Just below me, there was a still, crisp, blue lake fed by the mountain streams that trickled down around the lake. Scattered around the lake and through the valley, there were small clusters of structures, but on the lakeshore there lay a vast collection of structures. In it, millions of organisms with four limbs and a head scrambled around on their lower two limbs, doing whatever they do with their short lives. All around, I could hear the honking of horns and whooshing of four-wheeled vehicles transporting the dominant organisms around wherever they wished to go. Above there were loud shrieks of the metal tubes that they thrust through the sky to carry them across the surface of the planet, and the shrill chirping of smaller, winged organisms that seem to be far less intelligent than the dominant ones. But most of those organisms were irrelevant to the objective at hand: finding Penelope on this planet wherever she may be. This planet matched Nil's description word for word, so she had to be here. With so many particles everywhere on this planet, I once again had no idea where to start. Nil knew what planet she would be on, but had no idea where in the world she would be when I got here. After all, it had been a thousand years since I rode the supernova here, so she could be anywhere by now.

I knew that If Penelope was here for the past few thousand years, she would have been thinking about how to get me to notice her when I got here. She's smart, she definitely would have stayed on the planet, because she knew that eventually, I would find the planet. So where's the place on this planet where a particle could draw the most attention to herself? Somewhere where the dominant organisms would focus on her and study her. After asking around a bit, I lucked out. The nearest particle physics laboratory was only a few miles away, and they were definitely conducting experiments there on protons. I hopped into an electrical outlet on a wall and began to make my way towards the laboratory. Navigating through the thick strands of copper wire, I made left after right after left through various junctions and switches until I finally reached the laboratory. Exiting through an outlet on the inside of the laboratory, I could hear the faint hum of laboratory machinery, some of the organisms, which by this time I heard were called "people," clicking away at their keyboards, and the sound of air blowing through ventilation ducts laid throughout the ceiling. Everything was very white, clean, and sterile, and all the surfaces were smooth and cold. I could make out a sign at the door to another laboratory: CERN-Large Hadron Collider Division. This was definitely it, Penelope had to be here at the premier particle physics facility on this entire planet. Now I only had to find where within this sprawling complex of concrete and brick buildings she was. I searched around the laboratory for hours, looking through every nook and cranny, trying to find where she might be.

Climbing into a small exposed port on a computer tower, I entered into the labyrinth of small copper and gold traces on the circuit boards inside the tower. If I could find the data storage area, I could maybe use it to find out where they might be keeping Penelope. Speeding through the computer chips, left after right after left, over and over and over again, I eventually arrived at the hard disk, deposited onto a spinning magnetic platter along with thousands of other particles. I knew that if I searched around this enough, she would be there. Looking through the data, I found a section titled "Active Experiments." The things contained within this data were shocking. They were running horrific experiments on millions of particles, creating and destroying them at will, colliding them into each other to form strange new particles, and shooting at them with lasers. After examining hundreds of records, each as terrifying as the last, I found a subsection titled "Muon-Proton Experiments," which contained within strange information about unknown particles and apparatus. But, from the description of the proton involved, this had to be her, at the core of the active experiment here at the collider. Exiting the computer the way I came, still trying to shake the images of the heinous experiments, I eventually made my way to the collider ring where Penelope was residing.

I turned a corner near the end of the miles long, underground, metal-flanked tunnel, and there she was! My Penelope was sitting there in a magnetic field, waiting presumably for me to find her. But something was very off about her.

"Penelope! What have they done to you?" I asked her apprehensively, hoping for an answer. "Penelope!"

She didn't reply. As I inched closer, I could see what exactly was wrong with her. She appeared frozen in the magnetic field, unable to move or react to anything. Suddenly, the tunnel began to shake, and the magnets at the side of the tunnel began to activate in sequence. Electricity crackled through the tunnel, and I turned around to see a strange particle accelerating towards Penelope and me at near light speed. It impacted Penelope head-on, the resulting collision releasing enormous amounts of energy and knocking me into the walls of the tunnel. After regaining my senses, I turned around to see this strange new particle orbiting Penelope like I had long ago when we were together. He appeared to be much larger than I was, but still negatively charged like me. I had never seen a particle like this in my entire life in the natural world, so whatever he was, he had to be artificial.

"Who are you? What are you? And what are you doing with Penelope?" I shouted at the strange particle.

"Nice to meet you too! Hahahahaha! I'm Marvin the muon," he cackled, instability evident in his voice. "As for what I'm doing with Penelope, well, the scientists created me for this purpose. I appear at the other end of this tunnel, get shot at Penelope, get a little time with her, and then poof, I'm gone. And then I'm back at the other end of this tunnel, and do it all again! Hehehehe!"

"Well, I've come to get her out of here, to leave this infernal place together and get off of this planet for good."

"I'm sorry, I can't let you do that. She's mine now, the researchers said so. I get to do whatever I want with her until I decay away, and then they measure it to find out about both of us. She's mine! Mine I tell you!"

"Well that's too bad, tell the researchers that they have no right to torture Penelope like this or any of the other particles in this facility. I'm getting her out of this facility, whether you like it or not!"

"You can't. She's MINE! MINE I TELL Y—" Marvin cried, his voice raising with every word as he decayed away into nothingness. Far down the tunnel, the magnets began to fire again, glowing with heat and accelerating Marvin once again towards us. I only had a few minutes until Marvin would be back here, torturing Penelope with his muonic ways. Searching around the tunnel, I had to find something that I could do to cancel the experiment, shut down the magnets, and release Penelope. *What could I do to do this?* If I was bigger, it would be easy, I could just stand in front of Marvin and deflect him the other way. But since I'm just a tiny electron, what can I even do? He would just plow through me and barely notice anything.

What do I do? What do I do? That thought ran through my head, just thinking about how I could make this happen. Then I realized, if I orbited Penelope before Marvin even got here, the researcher's instruments would register that something was wrong, and the experiment would have to be shut down. So I did just that. At first, nothing happened, Penelope remained perfectly still in the field, as Marvin hurtled down the tunnel at hypersonic velocities. Then, I could hear a series of clicks echoing down the tunnel, and floodlights turned on bathing the gloomy tunnel in bright white light. The low hum of the magnets died down into silence, and the magnetic field holding Penelope de-energized. She dropped down to the floor and remained still and unresponsive as Marvin passed overhead with a scream of anger as he decayed into nothing.

"Where... am I?" mumbled Penelope, finally stirring after staying motionless for a few minutes.

"You're in a lab remember? On a planet where four-limbed organisms called 'people' run experiments on particles like us. I just got them to shut down the experiment, but we've still got to get out of here before the people figure out what happened and put you back in there. If you can move, come with me and let's go," I replied, motioning to the tunnel exit.

"Alright... Let's get out of here, the sooner, the better," she said, pain evident in her voice. But she was still able to move, and we rushed out of the tunnel as quickly as we could. We could hear the dull hum of the magnets powering on just as we exited the tunnel, barely missing being trapped again by only a few seconds. Making our way through the labyrinth of hallways and laboratories trying to find the exit, Penelope said to me, "Thank you so much back there, I knew the moment I woke back up and saw your face, that we were still meant to be together. After all those years apart, I began to lose hope that I would ever see you again."

"Hey, it's no problem. After all, we were together from the beginning, and now we're back together again. But I say that we get off this planet as soon as we can, I'm not a fan of this place so far," I replied. "Maybe we could go up on one of those machines that they use to send things up to space, like the ones that we passed on the way down to the surface."

"That sounds like a plan. While I had a lot of fun for the first few thousand years down here, I also want to get out of here. Especially because of what just happened to me, I definitely don't want to repeat that."

A few days passed as we made our way out of the lab, and hitched rides all throughout the air, land, and sea, to the coast of a peninsula where there were large pads, containing the rockets used to launch satellites into space. Towering over twenty floors into the sky, these rockets were massive. White in color, and bearing the initials "USA" on them, they were very similar to the debris I saw when I first arrived on this world. We hopped into the vent of a fuel pump, which chilled us down to temperatures far below the freezing point of water, and pumped us into a large, white cylindrical tank in the body of the craft.

After waiting in the tank for a few minutes, we could hear a loud rumble, and the entire craft began to shake. The fuel began to drain and ignite in the nozzle far below, and white-hot flames gushed out of the bottom of the rocket, propelling us upwards towards space. Up and up we accelerated, leaving the planet that had treated Penelope so poorly far behind us. We climbed higher and higher, piercing through layers of atmosphere and finally all the way to outer space. Continuing to accelerate, the rocket entered orbit and kept firing its engines, ejecting us out the back of the rocket into the vastness of space once again, propelling it away from us even higher, up and away from the planet. Finally, we were back where we belonged once again, together high above any planet or star, drifting through space like we had done for millennia before.

23.
Seven Years
Emma Latessa; Junior

It was six forty-three and Isabella was putting the finishing touches on her makeup. She was in a long, silk, pink strapless dress. Her dark and thick hair was flowing down her back with faint curls. It was just before the start of her freshman year in high school, and her new school was having their first pre- school dance. Isabella and her family had originally lived in Rome, but her father's job transferred them to Venice. Isabella was completely overwhelmed with the thought of starting a brand new school but, previously that summer she met some girls at freshman orientation who she planned to meet up with at the dance.

Isabella arrived at the dance alone after getting dropped off by her father. The minute she entered through the doors, she made eye contact with the most handsome guy she has ever seen. His silky hair glistened under the lights of the gym, and his bright, kind smile was the first thing that caught her eye. Leo is his name. Leo noticed Isabella too as she was walking in. He was staring at her beautiful, hazel eyes as long as she let him. Isabella was then approached by the girls she met at orientation. They were smiling and hugging Isabella, trying to make her feel as welcome as they could. Leo watched Isabella as the girls bum-rushed her to the dance floor.

About an hour passed and Isabella was walking alone to the drink table. Leo knew that this was his shot to go talk to her. He was determined to walk up to her and began to introduce himself. As Leo approached her he could not get the right words out of his mouth, Leo was never nervous to talk to girls. Leo was starting his sophomore year at the same school. He was popular, athletic, smart and very well-liked by his peers. Leo and Isabella began to talk at the dance for hours. Their conversation was mostly revolved around constantly flirting, laughing and making fun of Leo's stupid jokes. There was not a point in time within those hours where their eyes were drawn away from each other. They've been sitting and talking for so long that they were asked to leave because it was nearly midnight. Leo escorted Isabella out of the dance and walked her out to her father's car. The two said goodnight to each other and Isabella smiled at Leo as her dad drove the car away. As Isabella was on her way home, so many emotions were flowing through her. She was happy, anxious and excited to have met Leo.

Two weeks passed, and it was the first day of school. Isabella became good friends with the girls from the dance who she found out had lunch and some of the same classes as her. That made her feel a bit more comfortable with starting a new school. Although, she was very nervous to see Leo. Since the dance, she had not stopped thinking about him. Isabella wanted to know more about him, spend more time with him, and little did she know, Leo wanted the same. As Isabella pulled up in front of school Leo was there waiting for her.

The ache in her stomach was growing larger and larger by the minute, but it was a good ache. When she looked at him it wasn't butterflies in her stomach, but rather a flock of birds relentlessly fluttering their wings. Both their smiles grew as they saw each other. At school, Isabella and Leo would spend time together most days at lunch since they didn't have the same classes. They talk on the phone whenever they aren't together so, that was hardly ever. About a month into the school year Leo and Isabella started dating. Leo was not the standard cocky, rude, know-it-all type boyfriend, he was more of the old fashioned romantic, different from every other guy. Leo and Isabella went to a different Italian style restaurant each weekend, took long walks throughout the city, went to movies and went to the beaches to watch the sunsets.

Leo and Isabella have multiple common interests and hobbies. They both have a love for animals so, once a month they volunteer together helping with adoptions at the local pet shop. Leo helps in the cat section, and Isabella helps in the dog section. Both of them spend countless hours playing with the animals and introducing them to families. Their personalities were similar as well, charismatic, intelligent and they both have a good sense of humor which made them like each other even more. Leo and Isabella both excel in athletics as well. Leo was a first-string starter on a men's level soccer team. He plays with men who were all twenty-three or older. Every game is loud and filled with high intensity from the crowd and players. Isabella always takes Leo's dad to his games, and they cheer him on together. Isabella, though, has a talent of her own. Isabella is a star tennis player and has been playing for as long as she can remember. Isabella plays at an advanced tournament level with kids who are as old as eighteen, and she is only fourteen. Leo does not know much about the rules of tennis, he is still very supportive of Isabella and makes it to every match of hers that he can. Even though they both have very busy schedules, they always make time for each other, their friends, and family.

Leo's family dynamic is quite different from Isabella's. He has a sister much older than him, and no longer lives in Italy so, Leo only sees her on holidays. When Leo was nine years old, his mother died from severe breast cancer and his father has slight autism. His father is able to do things on his own, like make dinner but, Leo always worries about him.

Every Sunday Leo's father makes the same pasta dish for dinner. He makes it, so it is promptly ready at five-thirty and sets the table with three plates, one for himself, one for Leo and one for Leo's mother. Leo never takes away the third plate setting because he doesn't want it to upset his father. Most weeks Isabella will come over and fill the third seat. With all this, Leo still always manages to keep up with his grades and excels greatly in soccer because it makes his dad happy and Leo enjoys it.

Isabella comes from a bigger family than Leo. Her mother is a successful children's short story author. She writes children's stories and reads them to kids who are in the hospital battling leukemia. Her father works for a large corporate computer software company, and she has three younger sisters, all under the age of ten. Isabella's family is the kindest group of people Leo has ever met. Every night they have family dinner at seven, they all help out with chores around the house and support one another. The first day Isabella's family met Leo, they made him feel like he was a part of their family. A feeling Leo hasn't remembered in a long time was the feeling of being a part of a family. Leo has never met a family as close as Isabella's. Leo fell in love with Isabella that much more seeing her with her family.

The school year was coming to a close and summer was approaching. Isabella was busy with tennis tournaments and working at her family bakery. Leo was busy with soccer, his academics, and spending time with his dad. However, Isabella and Leo always found a way to make time for each other.

That summer, there may have been three days that passed without them seeing each other. Yes, they're young but, everybody knows their love is passionate and that it was real, their friends, family and especially them. When they lay together, they laugh and talk about how they're going to spend their days when they are married. They love to make up names for their kids, pets, and locations for a home where they are going to spend their summers.

Summer sadly can't always last forever and a new school year was right around the corner. Isabella was entering into her sophomore year and felt less nervous about going to school. Having Leo and her friends made her feel much more comfortable. This year, however, was crucial for Leo. It was his junior year, which meant he has to look at colleges, take the ACT and be on top of his game for soccer because American scouts and coaches were coming to watch him play. Isabella knew how much pressure he was under so, she was doing all she could to support him.

The school year flew by, Isabella was already a junior and Leo was a senior. Since Leo was a senior, Leo leaving for college was the main conversation topic between them. Leo's father cannot afford to send him to college so, his only hope of being able to go is if he gets a scholarship for soccer. Leo has received multiple offers from different schools, the only issue is that they are schools in the U.S., meaning he was going to have to leave Isabella behind since she still has one more year of school left. Isabella has an offer, though, for herself. She has been offered to go on a European tennis tour next year, during her senior year, instead of attending school. She would travel the cities of Europe playing other skilled athletes in tennis matches.

Leo and Isabella have very bright futures ahead for the two of them. They are both such athletic and bright people. They are good for each other. Leo and Isabella have never fought or disagreed on anything until the end of the school year. In the spring, Leo was asked to play for the Men's U.S. Soccer team. It was a two-year contract with a two million dollar payment offer. This was an opportunity Leo could not pass up but, Isabella was making him have second thoughts. Personally, Isabella would never tell Leo what to do, she always wanted him to make decisions for himself, and he knew that. Leo wants to spend the rest of his life with Isabella, he was not even able to imagine being without her. Isabella knew this tennis tournament was a once in a lifetime chance and she would be a fool not to go. The stress and pressure that each of them were under was eating out their insides. Leo went on long runs to clear his frustrations, and Isabella sat on the beach watching the sunset, thinking for hours. Leo and Isabella didn't know where their futures would be taking them so, they went their separate ways. It wasn't fair to either of them to stay together with the distance, and it was going to be so difficult for them finding time to see each other. Leo's flight to New York was leaving one week after school ended. Leo and Isabella cherished every last second of their final days together.

The day Leo was leaving was dark and gloomy, tears ran down each of their faces as they gave each other their last hug goodbye. For Leo to have to say goodbye to Isabella was one of the hardest things he has ever done. They unlocked arms, gave each other one final kiss and Leo boarded his plane.

When Leo was gone, Isabella knew she couldn't keep herself in her room all day. Throughout the rest of the summer, Isabella continued working at the bakery, training long and hard for tennis and spending endless amounts of time with her family. When August came around it was time for Isabella to leave for France. She never left Italy or her family before. This was a drastic change that was about to happen in Isabella's life. She was extremely excited to tour Europe playing tennis but, saddened that she didn't have Leo with her to share her excitement. Isabella said her final goodbyes to her family, friends, and took off on her plane.

Seven years have passed. Three months after Isabella left for Europe she came home because she developed tendinitis in her rotator cuff and her knee. The pain occurred when she was playing in her semi-final match that determined whether or not she made the top eight of the tournament. When she arrived back in Italy, she was distraught and completely devastated for months. This tournament was her one shot to make it as a pro. Isabella was forced to leave the tour and fly back to Italy to recover. Once Isabella returned home, she decided she was never going to play tennis again. She ended up spending her days working at her dad's company learning about technology, the complete opposite of her dreams.

Today Isabella is sitting on the beach in Venice, watching the sunset in her lonesome. She now owns her parent's bakery and lives alone in the apartment above the bakery. Isabella was on her way home when she got a call from her mother saying they need to discuss a family matter. When Isabella was arriving at her parents' house, she sat down next to her sisters and across from her mother and father. Her father told her that his job was transferring him to the United States, California to be exact. Isabella was shocked and unaware of how to react. She was unsure if her parents were going to leave her in Italy or have her come with them, considering Isabella is now twenty-three and has somewhat of her own life. However, her family wants Isabella to come with them and interview for a job at the company where her father was working. Isabella wasn't really hesitant whether or not she wanted to go to California because nothing was really left for her in Italy. When she returned back to Italy after her injury, she was too upset to go out most nights so, she has lost touch with a lot of her friends. Also, Isabella still has not found love again. Since the day Leo left, and to this day today, Isabella and Leo have both not seen or spoken to each other. Of course, though, she still loves him.

Isabella told her family she was going with them to California. She thought this change was going to be good for her to experience new adventures and scenery. Isabella and her family were both excited about the new chapter that was about to begin in their lives! They packed up their bags and boarded the plane to California within the next two weeks.

The smell of salt water and palm trees was running through Isabella's nose as she walked off the plane. Her family got their luggage and took a cab to their brand new home. Isabella's father's new job had given their family a lot more benefits. Their house is in a local, safe area with a walking distance to most restaurants and shops. Isabella was going to live with her family for a while until she was able to put up enough money to buy herself her own apartment. In order for Isabella to make any money, she was going to have to get a job. Isabella's father previously set up an interview for her at his new company the day after tomorrow. The company is technology based but, Isabella was going to be working with basic computer software information.

After Isabella settled in that night, she sat next to her mom on the couch, watched movies and they were talking for hours. Leo somehow came up in conversation. Isabella's mom asked her if she ever misses, or thinks about him. Isabella knew it was pretty pathetic, but she did admit that she thinks about Leo every day. She misses his big smile, kind heart and just being with him. Leo was Isabella's first love, and you can never forget your first love.

****

Isabella brewed her hot, hazelnut coffee, and headed off to her interview. She was extremely nervous because if she didn't get the job she'd be on a path to nowhere. Isabella was refusing to play tennis again, and technology was something she was familiar with from watching her dad all these years. Isabella never pursued any interests after her tennis injury. Technology is the one thing left that Isabella somewhat enjoys so, thinking about what she was going to say in her interview made her very tense.

Isabella arrived at the building and parked in the furthest spot from the entrance. She turned her car off and sat there thinking. After about fifteen minutes she gained enough courage to walk inside. She knew that when she was going to walk into the building she had to do it with confidence. Nobody is impressed when they first see someone, and they have poor body language. Isabella's head is held high as she walks into the office building, looking as if she owns it.

Her interview is with the department head of computer software, his name is Harold. Harold is the most muscular man Isabella has ever seen. He is bald, has an extremely deep voice, and even has two different eye colors which is very intimidating, to say the least. Isabella was not phased, nothing during this moment was going to distract her. Her answers to each of his questions are all well thought out and detailed. Every topic Harold brought up, he asked Isabella to analyze and show how the program would work on the computer. Isabella was having no problems with that task because she was familiar with all the topics Harold was talking about, and he was impressed. The company wanted and needed somebody like Isabella.

By the end of the interview, she got the job! Isabella was thanking Harold and his incredibly frightening appearance as she was heading for the exit. Isabella had just gained an inch of happiness. This was one of the first good things that happened to Isabella in a while but, she spoke too soon.

From across the hall, she saw a tall, handsome man with piercing blue eyes. Isabella knew right from that moment that it was Leo. When Leo turned around, he saw the beautiful woman looking his way and knew it was Isabella. When their eyes locked, it felt as if a million sparks went off in every direction. They walked toward each other and could not even find words to say because they were in shock of being reunited. Eventually, though they got to talking, and Isabella found out Leo was there visiting his sister who works in the same office building.

To this day, Leo still plays for the men's U.S. Soccer team and loves every minute of it. Leo has been single all these years, as well. He told Isabella that it was because he was always so busy with soccer training that he never has time to date, he was lying to her and himself. Leo never wanted to date again because his love with Isabella was too real to ever allow him to move on. Isabella and Leo's personalities have both changed a lot during these seven years, but their feelings, however, did not.

That night, they went out on a date, and every week after that for a few months. About four months into being together again Leo was going to do what they'd both dreamed of, he was proposing. They both have a love for beaches so, Leo took Isabella to their favorite beach in Malibu and proposed as the sun went down. The moment was the definition perfect. This was the happiest that Leo and Isabella have both been in a long time and they could not wait to start planning their wedding together.

Isabella wants the wedding back in their hometown of Venice, and so Leo's dad can be with them.

Two years later, Isabella and Leo gave birth to their first child. She was a beautiful baby girl, and her name was Margaux. Leo and Isabella decided to stay living in California because there are nice areas for them to raise their family. Just a year after Margaux was born, their son Antonio was born. They now finally have their perfect family. Leo continues playing professional soccer, and Isabella quit her job to spend more time with the kids. Each weekend Leo and Isabella went with Antonio and Margaux to a restaurant in a different city of California. Sometimes they made them little weekend getaways but, the two of them wanted to start making family traditions and memories.

When Margaux turned seven, and Antonio turned six, they purchased a summer home in Venice. It was beautiful during that time of year, and they also wanted their kids to see where they grew up and experience Italian culture. It was also a great way for Leo to get to see his dad for longer periods of time. Leo and Isabella work so well together because they balance each other out. They fight, yell, make sacrifices and love each other. Every relationship needs a bit of everything. A love story like Leo and Isabella's goes along with a saying, "If you love someone, set them free. If they come back to you, they're yours."

24.
Stinted Poetry
Nicole Stover; Junior

I wish I could write you lines that could mean something
Words that had actual depth
I wish I could write something that wasn't cliqued and tired
Less filled with intentional hyperbole and mixed metaphor that in
the end
Leaves you wondering what the fuck the poem was about in the
first place
The complicated and pretentious vocabulary and mispronounced
vowels would be completely awash
I wish I could write you something that felt even a little real
Like you could actually relate to any of my lines that I spit
Instead of needing to boil everything down from the three layers of
symbolism I implant there to convince other people but mostly
myself that I hold up to the intelligence run in my family
Because I think that rawness in a poem is what makes it worth
reading in the first place
Because it's very rarely that we see each other's human
And I think rawness is humanness
And I wish for one moment I could capture that humanness
Even in a minuscule way
Like watching the Pope masturbate or a person picking at a pimple
It's in these completely intentional and unabashed yet wholly self-
conscious moments, we exist as truly completely faulted human
beings

25.
Strengthened Self, Strengthened Journey
Sophie; Senior

For Me

She who works the hardest seems to have the toughest battles.
For when she finally believed, her beliefs got broken down,
As if her dreams were built only to be crushed,
Her heart was strengthened only to be broken;
For she was the girl who never gave up, but kept getting hit the
hardest.

I have always believed that everything happens for a reason,
Though sometimes those reasons are hidden,
Or ready to be built up to shine as large.
For I kept getting hurt as soon as I felt strong.
Maybe it wasn't meant to be, or maybe I'm just weak.

For she, that girl who hurt, was not ready to give up.
She shone, she fell, and she rose.
She rode the waves as if they never crashed;
She followed the path as if the cliff never came,
For she looked at the present, trying to forget her ugly past.

My past was evil.
Not evil in the sense of wrongdoings, but evil in the sense of dead
belief and lost hope.
I stopped believing, and troubles arose.
Troubles come to those who lose hope, those who moan, and those
who don't believe.
Those troubles came to me and never seemed to leave because I never
overcame them.

For she let those troubles eat her, take control.
She let those spirits arise inside of her, taking over her happiness and love.
A breakdown.
A horrific breakdown.
Something so special given, only to be taken away so abruptly.
She wanted it so badly.
And she would not stop until she had it.

I had the chance of my dreams to become more,
Only for it to be taken, a mistake, a devastation.
What was the reasoning for this?
For I could not see anything but a sign this was not meant to be.
To later be known that this was a sign of love, not hate, to be shown how badly I want it.
Sometimes it takes an overwhelming breakdown to have an undeniable breakthrough.
I am ready.

For she had always been ready.

But now I am undeniably ready to show the world what I am capable of,
To overcome my greatest fears,
And take over my toughest battles.
This is it, now,
And this is me.

26.
Tell Me A Lie
Gabriella Carvalho; Junior

September 1995

Every day he awakened in their king sized bed and looked to his right to see her lying next to him, silently sleeping. Today is a different day, he looked to his right and his beautiful wife is not there. She hasn't been there for forty-eight hours. Rebecca Wright has been missing, nobody knows what happened. The last time he saw her was Tuesday, they were eating breakfast together, without a single sound in the room except for each time he flips the page of his newspaper or each time her spoon would softly clink on the bowl. She stood up from the table and forcibly kissed him on the lips before she left for work. She picked up her briefcase and walked out the door. Gone. Just like that, she's gone.

She came home from work usually around seven o'clock every single night, Tuesday night she did not. It is now seven o'clock Thursday night, and she is still nowhere to be found. He called the police Wednesday morning, worried sick. "She could be at a family member's, or somewhere and forgot to tell you. We have to wait forty-eight hours to report a missing person" is all he got from the officers at the station. Although, her parents and siblings don't live in Illinois as they do. They live in Seattle, and her friends don't go out on Tuesday nights because they all have very important jobs to get to the next day. This didn't seem right from the second she didn't come home.

He looked at the clock, 7:09 AM. Over forty-eight hours, still missing.

Wilson and Rebecca Wright were a stunning couple. They seemed happy, carefree, and untroubled to everybody around them. Although, behind closed doors, she was not the perfect wife everyone expected her to be. She was brutally cruel to him in an emotional way that nobody should ever be able to handle or even put up with, at the least. He had stayed with her for ten years because neither of them believed in divorce. She didn't want to start a family with kids or move her relationship to the next step. She liked the way things are now, in spite of the fact that she was constantly screaming at him and torturing him without even noticing that it was killing him. A bad day at work made it an even worse night at home. She never hit him, slapped him or anything. But emotionally, she didn't realize that it is abuse. The day that she didn't come home seemed like almost a relief to him. The days had been easier, along with the nights of sleeping more comfortably. At the same time, he was devastated because, at the end of the day, she was still and will forever be his wife. The big house felt empty, and he somewhat missed the yelling and commotion because that was what he was used to. He can't remember the last time there was a night where he didn't have his head down on his hands, beyond stressed.

****

I opened my eyes for the last time to see the clock stand at 7:15 AM. I grabbed the phone and dialed the station. Thirty minutes later, Detective Beck was knocking at my front door. I opened it, and he barged in with two police officers behind him. They started to question me.

"Can I get your full name?"

"Wilson Wright"

"Age?"

"Thirty-two" *What the hell does my name and age have to do with anything, do your job right.*

"When was the last time you saw Rebecca Wright?"

"Tuesday."

"Did she call you anytime during the day?"

"No."

"Would she tell you if she wasn't coming home?"

"Yes."

All the wrong, stupid questions they're constantly asking and writing in their tiny little notepad. I guess it's their job and those are the first questions they have to start with but why couldn't they have been asking these questions forty-eight hours ago? *Oh wait, they did. Over the phone, and my answer each time is the exact same thing.*

Once all the idiotic questioning ended they went around the neighborhood questioning the neighbors, then to her work, then called her family, as if I hadn't already done. *Damn, maybe I should be a cop if it is this easy and all they're coming to is a bunch of dead ends.*

Detective Beck came back to my house, and I prayed it was only to be good news. It wasn't.

"We will find her, Mr. Wright."

"What do you mean? You haven't done much, and now you're clearly just going to go sit on your ass thinking about any suspects you could question next instead of actually doing so," I said.

"Listen, Wilson, I know you're frustrated, and you want your wife back, but I promise you, just let me do my job, and we are going to do everything we can to get her back to you," said Detective Beck.

"Okay." I began to show them out and Beck looked back at me with a strange, confused look on his face for a few seconds and then continued on his way. I shut the door and secretly stare at them getting into their cars. They sat in there for a few minutes talking and turning their heads towards my house every once in a while. They finally drove off, and now there was nothing I could do except try to relax, although it was a bit hard when the love of your life went missing and was possibly in danger.

I took a seat on the couch and turned on the TV to watch the news, *let's see what other awful things are occurring in this great big world.* "Great."

BREAKING NEWS: 24-YEAR-OLD MISSING GIRL FOUND DEAD

There is no way it can be Rebecca, she is not twenty-four years old. Unless there has been a mistake and it really is her? I ran to pick up the phone and called Beck holding my breath as hard as I could, He answered quickly and said, "It's not her."

I let go and finally breathed again. "Oh, thank God. Did you catch whoever did this? Maybe it is the same guy who took Rebecca." I say.

"I know, I know, we're doing everything to find this guy and try to connect him with the disappearance of your wife. I have to go now Wilson, I will see you tomorrow."

Beck hung up on me, and I walked over to the liquor cabinet and grabbed an entire bottle of vodka.

＊＊＊＊

At the station, everyone was going berserk. Two missing girls within the last two weeks is something that Killdeer hasn't experienced since 1945. I've been the head Detective here for twenty-five years now, I've seen all the good and all the bad of this city. But two missing girls... That is just odd. I heard a voice calling from a distance, I turned to see it was one of the police officers.

"Hey, Beck! We found the guy!" he said.

"Where is he?" I said.

"We're taking him in right now for questioning."

"Okay, good. I'll be in there as well."

I walked in the room to question the guy, and he seemed a little bit off from the second I got in there. "Hello, Robert? Is it?" he shook his head. "My name is Detective Beck, and I am probably about to ruin your life," I said with an evil smirk on my face. I set down two pictures in front of this guy, one of Rebecca and one of the other twenty-four-year-old. There was one thing about him, he only stared at the other girl's picture. Rebecca's did not even phase him, to say the least.

"I've never seen that girl in my life," The suspect said. *That*?

"So you have seen the other girl?" I pointed at the twenty-four-year-old.

"Maybe. Maybe not," he said.

"Don't try to play these games with me. Your fingerprints are all over her body, there is so much evidence, there is no way you can try to hide this." I leaned in closer to his face. "Just so you know, for a murderer, you're really bad at covering your trails buddy. You're going to jail anyways." He spit on my face. Angrier than ever I said, "Get him the hell out of here," pointing at the door. "Enjoy lifetime in prison smartass."

He was connected to the first girl in every way, but, it didn't match with Rebecca Wright. He didn't take her, and whoever did, I guessed, was keeping her alive. I had to keep researching and call the Bureau to see if they could help. Meanwhile, I grabbed the phone to call Wilson Wright.

"Hello?" Wilson said.

"Hey, it's Detective Beck. We found the guy, but I don't think he's the one who took Rebecca," I said.

"What? So who did?"

"I don't know, I'm still trying to figure that out. I'm getting close."
Wilson is speechless, the phone went quiet for a few seconds. "Uhh, okay." And he hung up. *That was strange.*

****

KNOCK KNOCK KNOCK

I was grabbing all my clothes and putting them in a suitcase. Grabbing everything that I needed to get away. *Who the hell is at my door?* I walked over and opened it. *Oh, my God. It's my brother David, who I have not seen in years.*

"As soon as I heard Rebecca was missing, I came here as fast as I could," said David.

"Thanks, man, it's been tough, but we'll find whoever did this, and hopefully her," I said.

"Damn, you're positive," he laughs. "Can I crash here tonight?"

"Yeah, of course, make yourself at home." I closed the door slowly after he walked in and stared at him softly. I was very tired from that long day, I walked over to grab another bottle from the liquor cabinet and told my brother good night.

****

David woke up the next morning in the guest room and walked downstairs to grab a cup of water. The house was silent, more than it would be with two people in it. He walked into his brother's room, and no one was there. *He's gone.* After seeing David for the first time in years, it was odd that they did not even catch up, Wilson grabbed a bottle and headed straight to bed. That was not like Wilson at all, him and his brother and have been close all their lives. The doorbell rang. He walked over to open the door, and it was Detective Beck. They had not met yet.

"Who are you?" said Beck.

"I'm David, Wilson's brother. I'm guessing you're the Detective?"

"Yeah, Detective Beck." They shook hands and moved on quickly. "Where is Wilson?" Beck said.

"Wilson? I don't know, I just woke up, and I don't think he's here."

"He's not picking up his phone either." *Weird*. Detective Beck walked in the house. "It's him," Beck said.

David had a very confused yet concerned look on his face.

"He took Rebecca, and I'm thinking murdered her," Beck says.

David is even more confused now. "What are you talking about?" David says.

"Everything comes back to him, and his mood. It's strange. You can see this through elements of psychology. He's on edge. Do you know where we can find him?"

"I know of one place he's been going to since we were kids. It's the dock on the lake at the corner of Main and Court Road."

Beck and David got in the car and got five police cars to follow them to the dock. When they got out of the car, they ran out and there he was; Wilson Wright stood at the end of the dock. It was a dark cloudy day, the air was thin and cold. The wind was light, but the waves were a bit stronger when hitting the shore. There was a smell of something rotting when the men reached the end of the dock.

"WILSON! WHERE IS SHE!?" Beck shouted at him.

He didn't say a word, he only stood there without any motion. They finally got directly behind him, and Beck got very close to his face and aggressively said, "Where. Is. She?"

Wilson looked straight down at the water, and David's jaw dropped. The cops came running up behind him and threw him in cuffs and put him in the car. Still not a single emotion from him.

When they got to the station, they went into the interrogation room. Beck barged in and threw papers down on the table. "You coward. Your own damn wife? How can one do that?" Nothing. "Now you won't speak eh?" Still nothing. "Wow." He slammed the table with his hands and got way up in his face. "Did you do it?" Nothing. "Wilson, did you kill her?"

"Yes."

27.
The Flower That Faced His Fear
Paige W; Junior

Fred was quite a lonely flower. He liked to stay in the garden where it was warm, sunny, smelled like fresh cut grass, and sounded like the laughter of children. He was also very beautiful. He had light blue petals and a crooked but charming smile.

Fred's best friend Lilah was very different. She liked to be outgoing and talk to different people.

Once a week, a little girl would come to the garden to pick the prettiest flowers. Fred was very pretty, but he chose to fit in with the garden because he did not want to be picked.

Fred was afraid that if he were picked he would have to leave his home, which was a familiar and comfortable place.

The garden was full of vibrant, pastel-colored friends and the air was filled with sweet nectar. Fred liked to feel his feet under the cool dirt and listen to the bees buzz all around him.

One day, a long time ago, Lilah and Fred made a promise. They promised each other that they would never show their beauty to the little girl so that they wouldn't be picked from the garden and they could stay together forever.

What Lilah never told Fred was that she really wanted to leave the garden. She was curious about what her future was like outside of the garden.

But Fred really hated the idea of leaving. He liked the garden because he already knew that he was safe there. If he left, he would have to start a new life, and he was scared.

The rest of the week seemed normal. Lilah and Fred played garden games with each other, having fun with each other. The girl who picked the flowers soon came, and Fred noticed something about Lilah: she was acting weird.

She was making sure her petals looked perfect and that her colors were bright. When the girl approached the garden, Lilah stood up straight and stood out from the crowd, whilst Fred was crouched over in the corner looking worn out.

The little girl bent down and plucked Lilah from the ground along with a handful of others.

Fred felt sad. His best friend left the garden, and he didn't know what he was missing.

Fred spent a week reflecting about the flower picking. He felt left out because he wasn't picked and betrayed because she broke their promise. He thought about it hard and made a decision. Fred wanted to be picked at the next flower picking.

When the girl came the next time, Fred was very scared. He wondered what being out of the garden would be like. Would it be scary? Would it be fun?

The girl trotted up to the garden and looked around. Fred stood tall and extended his sky blue petals making sure they looked as pretty as possible.

The little girl's deep brown eyes scanned the many flowers in the garden, after picking a few clean and nice-looking flowers, she placed her hands on Fred's stem and pulled his roots from the cool dirt.

He was brought back to a house, lying on the cold kitchen table along with the other flowers that were picked. The little girl was in the kitchen, running around looking for craft supplies

She grabbed scissors and a long, pretty ribbon that was white with pink and blue polka dots. Then she walked over to where he lay on the table.

She gathered the flowers in her hands making sure they all looked beautiful, stems together and their petals long. She took the ribbon and wrapped it gently around the healthy green stems. She tied the ribbon and finished it off with a perfectly tied bow. They were now part of a bouquet.

Fred was confused. What would happen next? Why were they grouped together? Would they stay on the table forever?

The girl picked up the bouquet and began walking into another room of the house. There was another girl that was sweeping the floor. She looked older and more tired. The little girl ran up to the women with the bouquet in her hand.

"Mommy" the little girl screamed with excitement. She ran up to the lady and handed her the collection of flowers, including Fred.

Mommy took the bouquet in her hands and looked right at Fred. She smiled a big smile and looked down at the little girl with happiness in her eyes.

They joined together in a hug and smiled. Fred smiled back at the lady and the little girl.

Fred had never made somebody so happy before. In that moment, he wondered why he was scared of what might happen. Why didn't he ever leave the garden before? How come nobody told him it was that amazing?

Fred realized that when he was in the garden, he was scared of what might happen. He was comfortable in the garden, and it didn't scare him.

But when Fred stepped out of his comfort zone, he could find happiness, and others would find him beautiful when he was himself.

28.
The Hole
Marlene Mamia; Senior

Chapter One

I know they exist. I know I'm not the only human. I can hear them, above me, walking over my house, over the Hole. If only I could scream, if only I could just speak, maybe they would help me get out of here. Now, all I can do is dream about how the life is over there. People are running, laughing, I also sometimes hear them crying. I always try to guess when they are smiling. Sometimes, depending on the sound of their steps, I know their mood. If steps are calm and quiet, people are relaxed and in a good mood. If steps are fast and noisy, people had a bad day, they are angry... Or sometimes they are just children running and having fun together.

I'm just a child too. I wish I could run with them, instead of staying here alone. I'm not really alone. I live with Slider, my earthworm, and Rambler, my caterpillar. I named my earthworm Slider because he doesn't have any feet. He just slides. It's annoying when Slider tries to escape through the soil, but I'll never let him go, he is my friend. My best friend is Rambler because he never tries to escape. He just walks around for hours, but it's because we don't really have anything else to do here.

The Hole is not that big, just enough for me to dance. I love dancing. I used to dance with the sound of human's noises above me. The best thing ever is to dance when it's raining! Rain days are the best. When it's raining, I get water coming through the soil so I can drink. And if I get enough water, I build small pools for my two pets.

Soil is also better when it's raining. It's less dry. I often think that if I only ate wet soil instead of dry soil, maybe I could speak. Dry soil may be the reason why I can't speak, why I can't escape. I'm so excited about autumn coming soon. I heard, from people above me, that autumn is the rain season. But it's also getting colder every day; I'm so scared about that.

I remember my last winter in the Hole. I spent most of my time sleeping, trying to forget how cold it was around me. Those winter days were the worst ever. I kept crying, trying to make a sound so people could hear me, but nothing came.

If I should introduce myself, I would absolutely not know what to say. How old am I? I have no idea. I can just say I've been living here for a very long time. Enough to know a language just by hearing people talking to each other, even if I know I still have to improve it. Enough to know there is a world around me. I feel like many things are happening every day, but I can't see farther than my Hole's soil.

My hair is very long and brown. When I get bored, I try to braid it, but I can't see the result. I guess I'm not bad. I have a tanned-looking skin. I think I'm tall and skinny, but I can't say for sure because I have never compared with someone else. Are the other humans fat? Do they only eat soil and drink rain's water too? One day I heard someone chewing very loud, like if this person was eating something really hard to chew: something that is not soil. There is this other day where I smelled something, an unusual smell, so I guess it was food. Finally, to be honest, I'm really dirty. It's hard to be clean when you live in a hole.

But I like my Hole, it's my own house, and I can do whatever I want. Dancing, sleeping, eating, and playing with Slider and Rambler. Our favorite game is when I'm doing a bowl with my hands, and they try to escape. The winner is the first who gets out my hands. Rambler always lost because it's harder for him, he's smaller, and so I often help him. But Slider should not know that, or he would get mad.

Telling my story, it sounds like living in the Hole is not that a good thing. I think that the main reason I like it is I'm scared of what the world is. What would I be if I was outside the Hole? I don't know anybody. I don't even know what my face looks like; maybe I would just scare them. I may look like a monster compared to them. What if they don't have any hair or any hands? I love my hair; I will never ever cut it.

And the same time, I feel curious. I have so many questions. I'm wondering if there are colors in the landscape, or if everything is brown like in the Hole. I want to know how big it is, and what people are doing over there. Are the animals bigger too? Is it just a bigger version of my life here?

But above all, the questions I would do anything to get an answer for, "Why am I here? Why me? And how did it happen? Did I do something bad when I was younger, and so I deserve it? Or am I just a kind of flower, who grew into the soil thanks to the power of nature?" I guess I should just stop wondering about that, because, anyway, my life is here, and it will be here for the rest of my days. I always keep a very small hope, the hope that maybe someone will find me and help me to escape, and to discover everything I haven't seen before.

Chapter Two

Today is a happy day. It's raining. I'm lying on the floor, collecting drops of water in my hands. I'm getting enough water to drink, and then I'm just enjoying the freshness of water falling on me. I'm feeling good and falling asleep.

It's cold now, and the noise of rain is waking me up. When I open my eyes, I'm surprised to see that the Hole is flooded; I could almost swim if I were smaller, like my pets. My pets! Where are they?? I'm not sure if they can swim and breathe underwater! I have to find them; they are my only friends. First I'm just watching all around me.

I almost have a heart attack when I see Slider floating on the water. He didn't survive. I'm starting to cry. I remember many adventures that I've had with Slider. One day I was eating, and he made me a joke. He was here hiding in the soil I was going to eat. It was so funny; I could not stop laughing after that. Now I'm just feeling decomposed, but I keep looking for Rambler.

Then I have the idea to watch above my head, but what I see is not Rambler. It's Rambler in a cocoon. What is he doing inside of this weird and white thing? I'm hesitating to rescue him, but then I see him moving a little bit. I'm reassured; he's alive. I think Rambler was just cold, so he built this blanket.

It doesn't stop raining. In my entire life, I had never seen that. The Hole keeps filling up, but it's not that bad because the floor's soil absorbs the water. I'm looking one more time above me to check if everything is fine with Rambler. He is fine, but something unusual is happening in the Hole.

I'm seeing a very bright light, coming through the soil. A hole is appearing in the Hole. I've never felt that happy, this hole is maybe the sign that I'm going to escape, I have the hope that someone is going to notice me. The hole in the soil is still very small. It's the size of my eyes. But I'm sure it's going to get bigger, thanks to the rain. And people may walk on this hole, and so make it bigger.

I'm waiting, minutes are running away, and nothing happens. It's sunny now; I can see it thanks to the little hole. But no more rain, no more hope.

Days passed, and I'm still in the Hole. I heard that now winter is coming, and I can feel it because it's getting really cold here. Moreover, I'm still alone, because Slider died and Rambler is still sleeping in his cocoon. Rambler is lucky; he has a blanket for winter. I wish I was a caterpillar too; it looks so comfortable. Being a caterpillar, I would try to escape, by climbing the walls of the Hole. Rambler doesn't do that because he likes me, he is a real friend.

I'm looking one more time above me, cause I have nothing else to do, and I'm watching the most amazing scene ever. Rambler is moving, the cocoon is moving. It's just awesome; I'm seeing one wing, then two. And then this new thing is flying in the Hole: it's not Rambler. Or maybe it is, but I can't recognize. It is absolutely different from Rambler; it looks different and acts different. Rambler walked, was green, and had feet. Now, the new Rambler is flying all over the hole, and I can't see any feet. The new Rambler is not green anymore. It has orange and red wings, it looks really pretty. I have to find him a new name; I can't call him Rambler anymore. I think Butterfly would be a good name; it corresponds well to what the new Rambler is doing. Let's call him Butterfly.

Now I'm almost sure winter is here. Some days it's raining, some others it's just cold and dry. During these winter days, I'm never hungry. I don't eat more than once a day.

I'm checking the little hole, and I think it's bigger, even if we don't really see the difference. Now, if I am to concentrate, I can see something through the hole. All I can notice is a blue color. It makes me feel so good to see this because now I'm sure that it's so much different over there. It's not only soil, I have no idea what it is, but it's blue and very attractive.

I'm lying on the floor. I can't move anymore, so I'm just lying on the floor. I can't move because it's too cold. If I move, I'll loosen the warmth of my body on the floor. I'm starting to feel bad. I'm feeling empty, I have not eaten since at least three days because I don't want to move, and I'm not hungry. I'm glad that I can now count days, thanks to the little hole in my Hole. I can see when it's dark outside, and I guess that means it's the end of a day.

I don't have any more strength; I think I'm just going to die, here in my Hole. If I move, maybe I will just die because I would be so frightened. All I can do now is wait, lying down, and staring at the small hole.

Butterfly is still flying all over the Hole, but then, when I'm looking at him approaching the small hole, I'm starting to die inside.

Chapter Three

It's gone. Butterfly is gone. He left me alone. I don't deserve that; I've done everything for him. I helped him when he fell, I played with him when he was a caterpillar, and now that he can fly, he just leaves me alone.

Crying and still staring at the hole, I'm jumping on my feet when I see something really unusual through the hole. It's still blue, but not the same blue that I used to see. Now, it looks just like an eye, staring at me without moving.

Then there are fingers, and then a hand, digging and making the hole bigger and bigger. I'm panicked, I can't speak, I can't scream, and I have no idea of what I'm supposed to do. I'm just standing here, paralyzed.

The moment I've been waiting for all my life is happening. I can see her; I'm seeing another human, this person who dug in the Hole to help me. She is so beautiful and so different than me. She has amazing blond and curly hair. She is wearing a pretty pink dress, with lace on the side. She is also wearing white opened shoes to protect her feet. I wish I had some too because I sometimes am so cold being completely nude all the time. But the most amazing part of her is definitely her blue and big eyes, still staring at me.

"What's your name?" she whispers. What's my name? I didn't even know that I was supposed to have a name. It seems like I'm going to have so many things to learn in this new world. Anyway, even if I had a name, I can't answer, so I just keep looking at her.

Then she says: "Don't move, I'm going to find something to help you getting out of this hole." Don't worry about this, I won't move. Actually, I can't, I have nowhere else to go, still being in the Hole.

Around a few minutes later, she is back with a ladder in her hands. She puts it into the Hole, but I'm still not moving, I'm not sure of what I'm supposed to do, I have never seen that before. So then she explains me, and I'm following the instructions. One hand and one foot after another, I'm climbing slowly and carefully the wood ladder. Here I am, finally, on the other side of the world.

Everything is so big, so beautiful; I can't even describe it because there are too many things that I have never seen before. The more I'm looking around, the more I can see people. They are everywhere. I knew they existed, but I couldn't imagine they were that numerous. They are all different. Different sizes, different hair colors, and different outfits.

I'm feeling observed by everybody when the little blond girl tells me: "Hey, I brought you some clothes, I thought maybe you want to wear something. What do you think about these sweatpants and this pullover?" I just nod; taking and threading on me the clothes she gave me. I'm feeling comfortable with her; she is really nice and patient with me.

I'm also reassured when she understands by herself that I'm mute, not stupid. So, she is speaking alone, and I'm glad to hear everything she is saying.

"My name is Chris Kavinsky. Chris is my first name given by my parents, and Kavinsky is my last name, the one in common with all my family. I guess you don't have any family here, so you should just have a first name. What do you think about Treasure? It would be perfect for you." I nod to answer that I agree.

"You look so lost. I'm going to explain to you about the world, I hope you'll feel better after that. I found you thanks to this beautiful butterfly, which was going out of the Hole. I guess I don't need to explain to you what a butterfly is because it was inside the Hole before going out. So this butterfly is nothing in this world. It's only one of all the kinds of animals. Nowadays, in 2016, we are more than seven billion people living on the Earth. By the way, the Earth is our planet, but there are many other planets. You and I are only children, and then we'll become an adult, and we'll die when we are very old, like in ninety years maybe. I'm an eight-year-old girl, and I live in a house with my mother, my father, and my little brother. We live in New-York City, in the United States. You're lucky to be here, there are many things to discover. Now, we are in Central Park, a famous part of New York. I don't know how long you have been here in the Hole, but you must be hungry. Let's go to buy something to eat."

So we're standing up. I don't even have the strength to think about all she said. I listened carefully, but I can't realize. I'm feeling stunned, just following her towards something, which seems to be a food store. She orders two "sandwiches," one for me, and one for her. Then, we sit on a bench and are eating our sandwiches.

It's the best thing I've ever had. It tastes like something indescribable, but it really is so good. I'm eating the entire sandwich, and I'm also finishing her sandwich because she wasn't hungry enough to finish it.

Then, she asks me if I want to live with her, in her house with her family. I nod, smiling. I'm still lost, but this girl's kindness makes me feel so much better. Now, I dare watching around me.

I suddenly stop thinking when she says: "You know, you're going to have to go to school. That's what people our age do. We're going to school every day to study and to be able to have a job later, in our adult life. You can come in my school, it's Jefferson Primary School, I'm sure you'll love it." I don't want to go to school; I can't confront the look of all these children. It's already so much for me to speak with Chris, to stay here without crying, or hiding somewhere.

Chapter Four
First day of school: I'm wearing jean pants and a black pullover that Chris' family bought for me. I also have shoes on my feet. Now I understand why humans are wearing shoes, there are too many dangerous things on the floor, such as water bottles. Moreover, most of the floor is made of tar; it's not only soil.

Passing the main school entrance, I'm walking next to Chris. If she was not here, I would probably hide somewhere until the end of the day. I have no idea where we are going; it's just too big. Everything is huge and every place looks the same, because there are long red lockers everywhere. All the classrooms also look the same, I mean, view from the outside.

We stopped in front of one of the classrooms, and Chris explains to me that here is my class, and that I just have to wait for the other people to come. I'm in first grade. She leaves me behind to go to her first class. My first class is contemporary life issues. Chris chose this class for me because she told me it's going to help me to understand how the world works. I'm going to learn what the other humans do to survive in this huge world.

At the end of this first school day, I'm feeling reassured, because it was not that bad. People were really nice with me, and I met someone who can understand me. His name is Hardin; He is eight years old, but he is in my grade because he moved here from India three months ago. He is also kind of new in this world. So his English is not perfect, like mine. But of course they'll never know it, because I can't speak.

Hardin is one of the rare persons with who I don't need words. I really get along well with him. I can't really say that we have any common point, because I don't know yet what I like to do and who I am in this new life, but I'm sure that we'll have many common points.

He is a musician; he plays piano. I think I'm going to take piano lessons too. I saw him playing, and it's really attractive. This sound in my ears was so unusual, it was the first time I heard what real music was.

Physically, Hardin is taller than me. He has brown hair and dark eyes, as me. He is like a boy version of me; I guess that's one of the reasons I feel really good with him.

I need to know him more; there is something intriguing in him. I love Chris too, she is the nicest person ever; but I can't feel with her what I feel with Hardin.

One week later, I'm still getting closer and closer to Hardin. Now, we can really understand each other just by a look. It's two-thirty in the afternoon, we just passed the entire day together, when he tells me, with a stressed and unusual tone: "Would you like to become my girlfriend?" I'm surprised, but I nod, smiling. I do want to be his girlfriend.

Then, he kisses me on the cheek and runs away to his father's car.

The night is coming, and I'm laying in my bed in Chris' house, thinking about him. I'm glad that he asked me to be his girlfriend because I really like him, but I have never had a boyfriend before. I don't know what is supposed to change since now. I don't know how to act with him anymore. Maybe he is going to kiss me on the mouth tomorrow, and I don't know how to do that either.

I guess the only thing I can do right now is sleeping, and trying to not think about it. Let's see what the future of this wonderful world is going to show me.

Chapter Five

Hardin hasn't kissed me, but I don't care, because now I'm stressed about something else. He invited me to meet his family! Maybe this love story is going a little bit too fast. I have to talk to Chris about it, to know if it's a good idea.

When I see her in the hallways, I run in her direction. I quickly give her the sheet of paper that I prepared, where I wrote: "Do you think I should meet Hardin's family tonight?" To answer, she starts speaking and speaking for long minutes, but the main idea of what she said is that I have to make my own decision and that Hardin's family is really nice.

So I think I'm going to do it. After all, nothing bad could happen to me; they are just a family going to meet his eight-year-old son's girlfriend.

End of school is coming, and I'm walking next to Hardin toward the entrance door. The atmosphere is weird because Hardin is not speaking with me either. Maybe he regrets his decision to introduce me to his family.

Here he is, his father, waiting for us in his big Volkswagen. Hardin and I go together in the back of the car.

His father is really nice; he instantly talks to me trying to know more about me. Hardin answers for me, he tells him my name, Treasure, and he explains where I lived before. I'm not scared anymore to hear or to think about my story. I'm kind of proud about it.

Then, his father tells me about himself. His name is Abhijit Ilesh, which means "the Victorious Earth Lord" in English. He is from India too, but Hardin's mother is American. Abhijit explains to me that he moved to America with his family because here, everything is easy and accessible. Everyone is always playful, it seems like we live more. He tells me that they already went to America seven years ago, in New York City, to visit. That's where they realized how life was better and easier here.

When we arrive at Hardin's house, her mother kindly hosts us. She introduces herself and hugs me like if we already knew each other. Then, she was asking where do I live when Abhijit suddenly catches her by the arm and brings her towards the kitchen. I'm looking at Hardin, confused. From the kitchen, Abhijit is yelling at us to go in Hardin's bedroom and to stay there for ten minutes.

But we don't. I don't know why, but Hardin is not moving, so I'm not either. Instead of obeying his father, he is walking in the opposite direction: towards the kitchen. Obviously, I'm just following him.

So here we are, listening to an intriguing dialogue I think we were not supposed to hear:

"Please don't ask me why, but don't ever try to understand where this girl comes from."

"Why? She looks lovely, and she seems to be a very interesting girl. She is my son's girlfriend, I need to know her more."

"About it, she can't be his girlfriend anymore. They have to be separated, since now. Please just trust me, I found out something about her, and if you knew you would agree."

"So just tell me! I'm your wife and his mother; please let me know. I promise I won't overreact. If you don't tell me, I won't separate them."

"Fine. She is your daughter, the one you buried at birth. She survived, and now here she is; in your house."

"Oh. My. God. Are you kidding me? How can you be so sure? And what are we supposed to do now?"

"I'm almost sure because of the story she told me. I don't think many other girls have been buried in Central Park a few years ago. And you are not going to do anything. If I asked you to do that, it was for a reason; you were not supposed to see this girl again. It didn't work, that's it."

I don't want to hear one more word. Before Hardin can do anything, I start running away from the kitchen, crying. Hardin screams my name to stop me. Now the entire family is running after me. I can't go anyway; so I just stop and listen, panicked.

Chapter Six
Hardin's mother, I mean… my mother takes me delicately by the hand. I'm too choked to react, so I just follow her. She brings me to her bedroom, and we sit on her bed.

"Don't be afraid sweetheart, I want the best for you. I'm going to explain you everything, so maybe you'll be less confused. I'm going to start with a history point. You know we lived in India, right? We were in the Rajasthan. This state is particularly rude about a rule: we are not allowed to make girls born. Boys are considered as superior. I wanted you to live, but you would have had a miserable life in India; girls are not welcome there. So seven years ago, I was pregnant with you went we went on holidays in

New York City with your father and your brother. After two days visiting, I started having contractions. I gave birth to you the same night. I was so happy that you were born in the United States, because I thought you were going to have a chance to survive. I thought I could have given you to an American host family. But Abhijit refused. He really wanted to respect his religion. So he ordered me to kill you before we came back in India. I took care of you as long as I could. I fed you and kept you during our four last weeks of holidays in New-York City. However, the moment that I dreaded arrived. We had to leave the next day; I had to separate myself to you. I went by night with you in Central Park, and I did it. I dug a hole, the biggest that I could. It took me three hours. I had this very little hope inside of me that maybe you would survive, even if it was almost impossible. But apparently, you are a strong person. I can't believe that you did it, I'm so proud of you. So now you know: you're seven years old, and your last name is Ilesh. Concerning your first name, I guess. Treasure is perfect for you. Whoever found it; this person had an amazing idea. Welcome to our family, Treasure."

29.
The Least Suspected
Alexandra Eick; Senior

Victoria's black suede heels clicked against the concrete as she leaped into the cab. "1333 Pennsylvania Avenue, and step on it." She sipped on her black coffee while watching all the people commute to work. Looking down at the thirty text messages blowing up her phone, while taking a deep breath, she had a moment of serenity before the chaos began.

The minute Victoria stepped out of her cab she saw the paparazzi and writers swarming her building. She knew that there was a big client inside, but who could lead hundreds of cameras to her firm?

Victoria's job was different from many. She worked to protect people, but not like a police officer. Victoria helped the high-profile residents of D.C. with private matters that could not be trusted with the FBI. Victoria worked on cases from extortion to murder. If you wanted your case to be kept quiet, Hunt Agencies is the place for you.

"Victoria you're needed in the conference room immediately. The blinds are closed, you know why."

Blinds closed only meant one thing. Celebrities. Victoria swiftly slides into the conference door turning toward the couple weeping in the corner. She couldn't quite make out their faces til they turned her way. She softly said, "Hello I'm Victoria Hunt, I guess all those cameras outside are for you."

The couple turned her way, suddenly realizing it was Congressman Price and his socialite wife, Camilla.

Camilla let out a long wail and finally said, "Help me find my baby. I need him home."

Congressman Price did not seem as upset, so he began to explain the situation at hand. "We have two sons, Jake and Benjamin, Jake is our older son. About two nights ago he didn't come home from his lacrosse practice. We weren't that worried because sometimes he forgets to call us if he stays the night at his best friend's or girlfriend's house. When it had been twenty-four hours, we still never got a call. We have a tracking device on his cell phone, and it traced back to Rock Creek Park, which is almost forty minutes from our townhouse. His phone was abandoned and cracked. Early this morning we received a miniature package on our front porch. It was a video of Jake tied up with large purple swollen bruises all over his skin. I have never seen my son that terrified. The note on his chest read: *You have forty-eight hours to deliver $300,000 to P.O box 2000 at American University or for the next three months you'll be delivered pieces of your beloved Jake.* Our poor Jake's eyes became so wide; the tears came running down like a flash flood. We came to you because we heard you're the best. We want to keep this out of the news. Please, they know we have a lot of money. We will pay it, we just want our son home."

Victoria sat in shock. Confused why anyone would want to hurt the so-called 'royal family of D.C.' She knew she had to push every power she had in D.C. to help this family find their son. The wheels began to turn in her head, and the case was open.

"I have a certain process in solving my cases that is far different from any other agency. I begin with a timeline of events. I need to know every single detail from a week before he was kidnapped, to minutes before the crime. Building off the timeline, I interview the people that were around Jake in those final days. I want to know how everyone saw Jake. Was he angry, nervous, or jittery?"

Victoria began her interviews in the glass-walled interrogation room. You could see the sweat drip off the suspect's foreheads. Why would they be nervous if they were so called "innocent"? The same set of basic questions would be asked unless a suspect seemed guilty, and then the questions became detailed.

****

The Prices strolled into the office hoping for good news; they realized that Benji was about to be one of the interrogation suspects. Benji and Mr. and Mrs. Price were suddenly torn apart and thrown into separate interrogation centers. Victoria locked the door into Benji's interrogation room. Slipped down into the chair, she began her questioning of Benji

"So Benji, you must be horrified at how long your brother has been missing? You both seem pretty close." Victoria slides a picture of Jake and Benji with their arms wrapped around each other.

"I really do miss having my brother by my side. The house is so lonely, and the press won't leave me alone. At least his friends are out of our house."

Victoria confused says, "What do you mean at least his friends are out of the house? Did you have issues with his friends?"

Benji hesitated for a moment and then leaned in towards the table. "Jake's friends were mixed in with some sketchy groups. For the past few weeks, Jake has been short on money. He spent a lot on a gold charm bracelet for his one-year anniversary with Nicole. Our parents were pretty mad at his ridiculous spending habits and cut him off for a few weeks. He had to pay to party with his elite friends. Late at night, he would make hour long phone calls to unknown numbers and then sneak out returning around two o'clock in the morning. I found a huge bag of cash under his bed with ropes, wires, duct tape, and cameras inside. When I checked the under his bed after his teammates left, all evidence of the bag was gone."

Victoria released Benji back to his family. Victoria threw her arm up to check the time. 4:52 P.M rolled across the watch. She had about thirty-six hours to find Jake, or he was done for. The case seemed so strange. Why couldn't he just wait the two weeks to get his trust fund reimbursed? What organization was Jake involved in, and how dangerous is it? It was time to bring Jake's so-called "friends" in for some questioning.

The interviews began with Jake's best friend, Chase. "So Chase, it seems as if you and Jake go out quite a bit. For high school seniors, you do like to party."

"Hey, it's my lifestyle. It's how Jake and I always party. We have the status and the connections so why not make the most out of it?"

"Connections you say. A source has told me that you and Jake have been involved with some late night phone calls and a secret organization? I won't rat you out, but every detail counts to save Jake."

Chase became very pale and fidgety. Victoria knew she had struck a nerve.

"It honestly is nothing too serious. We are part of a real-life fantasy draft. We meet with real NFL players and place bets on them. The players earn a thirty percent cut of the bets. They don't want their agents to find out about the game, so we meet late at night to place our bets. Jake got really into the game. He was so good at the draft that the owners of the organization put him in charge of the money."

Victoria realized why the sack of money was under Jake's bed. It all made sense except why the owners would want to get rid of Jake.

Victoria became intrigued and leaned into Chase and stated, "This all can be put together except the question of why would the owners or anyone involved in the organization want Jake to disappear."

Chase scoffed as if he was laughing at Victoria. "Everyone in the organization went to the top private schools Trinity, Bishop, St. Mary's, and Dalton. We were so close, and everyone loved Jake. If you were a lower ranked player in the draft, Jake would make sure that each player got some type of profit."

Victoria started to piece Jake's life together, and nothing seemed too out place. Jake had it all. He had the perfect girlfriend, he was an excellent student, star athlete, and even a successful businessman. The only event out of place is the night Jake disappeared. It was time to get a step-by-step run through of the night. The real interrogation began.

"Chase it seems the last time partied things go pretty intense for Jake. This was the night he disappeared. Can you explain to me the details of your night out on the town?"

"Jake and I, and about twelve other guys from the lacrosse team went out to party after our win over Bishop Boarding School. We haven't beaten them in over six years. It was a pretty monumental night. Jake decided to get a little too drunk and wasn't speaking or seeing clearly."

"As his friend maybe you should have cut him off or never let him drink. You do know you're underage?"

"Listen boss lady, the way I have been raised, drinking and partying are typical events. Congressman children go to galas and premieres twice a week. I have a beer or two to take the edge off. Jake just took it to far. He seemed as if he was being watched or hunted. The only way to calm him down was through the shots of tequila. He could only see blurred figures, and his words sounded as if a preschooler was learning how to read a picture book. It had been pretty, to say the least."

"Let's stay on topic Chase. When did this start getting out of control"?

"Around two o'clock in the morning Jake claims he saw his girlfriend Nicole lip locking with one of the Bishop players. He started aggressively knocking over chairs and tables. Nichole was pretty terrified, so Jake was escorted out the back, so no paparazzi saw him. I took Nicole home because she was so worked up. Some driver said that he was sent to take Jake home. I figured Mr. Price sent the car since he prefers the family stays out of the paper ever since the Benji incident."

Victoria remembered an article in the newspaper about Benji.

"Chase, thank you for the details, but I think interview needs to come to an end."

She sprinted out of the interrogation room and slid into her chair. Her fingers were moving a mile a minute on the keyboard. That's when the article popped up. *Congressman's Son Held For Harassment.* Victoria was in complete shock, and her draw dropped. Her eyes were scrolling the page trying to catch every detail in the article, she stopped in a deep gasp. The article told the story how about three years ago, Benji Price was harassing a boy for not paying for his technology help. Benji got carried away and broke the windows in the boy's house and set his car on fire. The aggression resulted in Benji being held in custody till he could pay off his bail. Victoria flicked her wrist realizing the time on her wristwatch read 10:30 P.M she snatched her phone and dialed Mr. Price's number as fast as she could.

"Hello, Mr. Price, I know it's late, but I have some very important questions to run by you. Do Benji and Jake usually get along? Can Benji be trusted alone? Lastly, does your son have a history of excessive violence?"

"Ms. Hunt, it's never too late for help on this case. Unfortunately, our sons haven't always been the closest of brothers. Benji is a little awkward and shy compared to Jake. Jake is the star of his high school, while some people don't even know Benji exists. Benji expects his brother to make him popular, so when Jake doesn't follow through, Benji can get very aggressive. We usually don't like to leave Benji alone for too long, but if he needs peace a quiet, he goes to his research lab right by Central Park. If you need to check on him, he won't be leaving the townhouse."

****

Victoria needed to know if Chase and Benji were telling the honest truth about their last encounters with Jake. She hopped into her slick royal blue Mercedes and drove to Dalton.

Chase was just getting out of lacrosse practice when she pulled up to the school. A young woman was walking towards his car. Victoria squinted realizing it was Nicole! They began talking for a few brief second until Chase grabbed Nicole and kissed her. It made sense. That night at the bar, Jake didn't see Nicole making out with a random Bishop boy; it was his best friend, Chase. Nicole and Chase may have not committed the crime of kidnapping, but they did commit the crime of being terrible friends.

The suspect pool was growing smaller, and so was Victoria's window of opportunity to save Jake. She sped over to the Price's townhouse where Benji was sneaking out of the house. His black hoodie covering his face, Victoria knew that he seemed pretty suspicious sneaking out of the house past his curfew, especially when a case this large was surrounding his family.

Victoria walked up to the door and was let in by the maid. She slowly walked up the stairs heading for Benji's room. For a townhouse, Benji's room was about the size of Victoria's whole apartment. Plastered across the walls, Benji had maps with different arrows and symbols leading a path from the club that Jake was spotted at, to a random location by Central Park. Tip-toeing around the room, Victoria picked around Benji's binders, and computer software until she came across a software box named *Winner Takes All.* Hoping that no one would notice, Victoria slid the software into her purse pocket. A few minutes left to find the incriminating evidence, a duffel bag strap was hiding behind a dresser. Pulling the bag out of the corner, Victoria threw her hands over her mouth in shock. The duffel bag contained duct tape, wires, thousands of dollars, and video surveillance of Jake sitting in a warehouse. She found Jake!

She began to make her call to the police to send them to Jake's location, but a figure slowly begins to creep up behind Victoria. Benji grabs her neck and starts to strangle Victoria. Gasping for air, she couldn't escape his steel trap of a grip. Victoria was being pinned to the ground, the Prices rushed upstairs hearing all the commotion. The Prices, in shock of what they were witnessing, their son strangling Victoria. The Prices pulled Benji off Victoria. The police heard all the commotion from the other side of the phone and rushed over to arrest Benji. The Prices were heartbroken to know their son would be capable of such terrible things.

At the same moment in time, Jake was being rescued from Benji's research lab right by Central Park. Jake finally returned home and ran into his parents his arms. The Prices never wanted to let go of their handsome son who was finally safe.

Victoria tapped on Jake's shoulder and began to speak. "Hi Jake, my name is Victoria Hunt I was in charge of your case. I just have a few brief questions for you. What was the software in your brother's room named *Winner Takes All?* Also, what was the motivation for your brother deciding to kidnap you?"

Jake looked at the ground feeling a wave of despair topple over him. "My brother has some serious anger issues and hates when people cross him. I made that mistake. The software helped the guys in the organization of NFL draft picks cheat their way through the game, and ultimately have the greatest players. I took credit for the software and didn't give Benji an in into the draft. He became so angry, he hired men to follow me, and when I eventually had no protection, the men kidnapped me. The ransom was for how much the software was worth. Ms. Hunt, I truly thought my brother would forget about the draft. I guess sometimes the least suspected commit the crime."

30.
The Mysterious Grand Hotel
Charlie Appleford; Junior

I just finished my last final for my 5th-hour class, Math. I'm not sure how well I did because I guessed on the whole back page but I'm hoping for the best. I and all my friends Luke, Connor, Tommy, Victoria, Cate, and Kendall are all going to Kendall's to party and swim because today was the last day of junior year. We all arrived at Kendall which is about fifteen minutes from school. Kendall's house is beautiful. It is an old mansion with four floors and seven bedrooms with a very long gravel driveway, with a big square pool in the backyard. Kendall went into her house to get lemonade and ice water. Victoria and my parents are both leaving today to go on business trips, so she is staying at my house. The party goes on until eleven-thirty, and Victoria and I get in the car to go to bed.

The next day we sleep in until noon. We are both so tired, and it feels so good to be done with school and not having to stress about anything or wake up at six-thirty in the morning. Victoria and I throw on a sweatshirt and shorts and go to brunch at Toast which is downtown. This is by far my favorite place to eat in town. I get chicken and waffle every time, and Victoria gets a Greek salad with chicken.

Victoria goes on a website called makeamove.com. It's about traveling all over your state and visiting certain places. Victoria is looking at this website the whole time we are eating, and I soon come annoyed with her, so I look. I look on the website, and it seems very sketchy. There are many places that are run down and are private property and have no trespassing signs. "Louis looks at this beautiful hotel! It's super old and run-down, but it must look amazing on the inside!" says Victoria. It is a five-star hotel that is on an island about thirty-five minutes down to the coast from us. "Let's visit Louis!" says Victoria.

"Definitely not," I said.

We leave breakfast, and outside it is pouring. I'm on the way home to drop off Victoria to shower and then take her to lacrosse practice. "Louis my practice is canceled because of the rain!" says Victoria. I do not want to have to drive her all the way to practice, but I'm afraid that she is going to force me to go the abandoned n hotel.

Victoria cannot stop talking about the hotel so we finally decided that we will go there but no get out of our car just visit. The drive there is very rainy and lonely evening. It almost feels like you are the only person for tens of thousands of miles. We arrive at a very long driveway with a huge gate. Everything was super worn down and rusted. You could see in the distance a very large hotel that looked like a castle, but you could only make out the outline and windows of the hotel. It looks very creepy. Victoria runs out of the car like a dog. I yell after her, and she is very far. She stops running. She yelled out my name and wanted me to follow her. I did because I didn't want her to go in by herself.

The door is about twenty feet tall and looks insanely heavy. We walked in, and the door was unlocked and opened right up which was kind of unsettling. It was about four o'clock, but it felt like eleven because it was so foggy and rainy. The grand lobby is beautiful, and all the furniture is still there. It almost looks like someone just did all of the work to make this beautiful and then on opening day just left it to rot and die. Victoria is loving it's and running all around the lobby. I don't want to go much farther than I am because definitely more people than just us have thought of checking this out. I sit down to check my phone to see if I even get cell signal here. Of course, I don't. I stand up, and Victoria is out of sight. I start panicking, but I cannot find her anywhere. This is exactly why I didn't want to come here. I am looking all over, and it is pitch black upstairs. I look for hours and cannot find her. I don't want to call the cops because we are not supposed to be here, so I leave.

I wake up in the middle of the night and I hear knocking on my door. I run downstairs and see Victoria crying. I open the door and hug her. She was in shock and wasn't able to talk for about five minutes. "I got grabbed, and something with a man's voice told me not to return," says Victoria. I am so struck right now I don't know what to say to her. This hotel is for sure haunted and is not a place to go and explore.

The next morning me and Victoria go to the library in the morning and see if we can find anything about the hotel. We find a lot of interesting articles about the hotel. The owner of the hotel was named Luke Knox who was a very intelligent man. He went to Pepperdine University and majored in business. He died on June 24, 2006, unfortunately. The hotel has been shut down since then because no has the time to take care of it or put money into it. We later find videos that are very creepy saying the place on haunted. We study all night and finally go to bed.

The next morning we wake up and keep studying. We find out that the reason that it is so heavily guarded it that there lots of gold that Luke put in the hotel because he was doing a lot of illegal things with money, and had nowhere to keep it. He wasn't able to put that amount into a bank.

Many people try to find the treasure and gold, but many get lost in the hotel, or the police come before they do. The gold is very safe though because people have been trying for many years to find it and no one has even come close. Victoria and are deprived of sleep, so we go to bed at eight o'clock.

The next morning I wake up and walk my dog and get all my chores done before I start the day. Today is the day that Victoria and I are going back to the hotel. We are going back prepared and ready for what's going to happen. Victoria and I are going to be tied to each other with a rope so if we can't find each other or try and get separated we will be connected. The drive out to the island is foggy and drizzly. It feels that the weather stays the same on the way to the island no matter what. We arrive at the hotel and it looks the same as before. You can only see the outline of the hotel which makes it look humungous. We walk in, and we step right into the lobby. My heart drops every time I walk in, and my legs feel like they are going to collapse. I walked and ran all over trying to find Victoria, so I know my way around the hotel a little better than Victoria.

We walk towards the back of the lobby, and there are three elevators. Victoria and I step in the first one. Unusually the elevator light is still on which I very creepy because this place has been closed for eighty years. We step in to go down a floor to the basement. The elevator plummets and drops thirteen feet to the ground and slams us on the ground. Victoria thinks that she broke her ankle, but after sitting for a while, she feels okay to walk. The basement is very wide open, but at the end of the wall, it almost looks like a book shelf. "Hey, Louis! I remember reading this; this room was Luke's personal room when building the hotel." There are only two books on the self. The Bible and a book about the architecture of the building.

I grab the book that tells about the architecture, and a big screeching noise comes from the shelf. We both step back, and the book self slowly spins around showing a secret room. All that I can see in there is a briefcase. I look inside, and there are about thirty-five blocks of pure gold. Victoria and I cannot believe our eyes. We grab the case, sprint up the stairs, and run out the hotel as fast as we can and get into the car and start driving.

Victoria and I were reading an article saying that this gold is sacred. We look at each other and stop the car. "It feels wrong to take all of this money," I said. "I know what we are going to do with all of this." We turn the car around and go back and put the money back in the hotel. When we walk out, the wind picks up and makes all the trees dump water on us. When Victoria and I picked up and put back that treasure, it felt that so many people and spirits were present in that room. Victoria and I both agreed that we should put the treasure back.

The next morning Victoria and I and went to the beach.

31.
The Necessary Hero
Mr. Fletcher; Junior

The day restarts and I am reminded why I exist
Sweat is dripping down my furrowed brow
As my heart beats to the drum in my mind
A steady rhythm that reminds me to keep fighting

It took the force that could destroy my city to ignite my powers
I was once considered average to most,
Through fighting the monsters that have taken over my city, I have
more than proven otherwise

I am strong
I am fearless
I am the necessary hero that the world needs
It is up to me to stop the evil that is flooding my surroundings

32.
The Not So Great Life
Madison T.; Junior

"Go to your room this instant, Jeremy Mayfield and don't plan on coming out until you're ready to apologize!" Jeremy's parents aggressively screamed at him.

"I hate you guys!" Jeremy yelled back as he dragged his angry little body up the staircase.

Jeremy slammed his bedroom door out of anger and fury.

"I don't need them; I would be just fine on my own." Jeremy confidently murmured to his dog, Benji. As his rage dialed down, his brain started to become jam-packed imagining how perfect life would be if he didn't have his parents. "I could eat whatever I want, never go to school, never do homework, play outside all day, and never, ever have to clean up. It could be perfect," Jeremy said to Benji.

Jeremy woke up the next morning to a horrible smell that stretched across the entire house. As he investigated the house, he found the rotten smell was dog poop on the kitchen floor.

Jeremy called for his parents to clean up the mess because there was no way he was going to. Jeremy screeched for his parent's numerous times. However, he never got a response. He soon realized his parents weren't home which was extremely peculiar.

Seconds, minutes, and hours passed by with no sign of Jeremy's Mom or Dad.

Although most kids would be very worried that their parents had suddenly gone missing, Jeremy was thrilled.

First things first, Jeremy sprints over to the freezer and pulls out a huge quart of Vanilla bean ice cream. He then whips out Hersey's chocolate syrup and drizzles it all over the ice cream. Next, he snatches the huge can of whipped cream and rainbow  sprinkles from the cabinet and makes himself an Ice Cream Sundae.

Jeremy was ecstatic that he had no one yelling at him or telling him what to do. Within just an hour of no parents, Jeremy was in paradise.

"Benji what should we do next?" Jeremy frantically asked his dog as if they were in a race against time.

 "Wait! I got an idea!" Jeremy shouted to Benji with a disturbing smirk on his face.

Jeremy decides to acquire different color paints, markers, and crayons so that he can draw all over the house.

He first paints on the kitchen walls a picture of a great big dinosaur that he names after himself. He then draws pictures of Benji and himself on the living room furniture, then the bathroom ceiling, and then all over his parent's bedroom windows.

Once he is done, Jeremy makes his way to the TV room for a little break.

His little break then turned into five hours of TV and popcorn.

"Isn't this great?" Jeremy asked Benji. "We would never be able to do this with Mom and Dad home," he explained.

The next morning, when Jeremy awoke, he didn't feel too good. His stomach was hurting and had a pounding headache. Jeremy was bursting out in tears from the agonizing pain. But still, no matter what, Jeremy did not want his parents coming back home.

As Jeremy lays in pain on his bed, Benji is barking up a storm at the back door for a potty break. Despite the loud, obnoxious bark, Jeremy cannot gain the strength to stand up.

And what do you know? Benji went to the bathroom inside the house again!

On top of Benji having another accident, Jeremy realized that there is no more food in the house and he has no money.

Jeremy was starting to realize how many responsibilities he has without his parents being home. Jeremy was now unable to take care of himself and Benji.

It was going on a few days now without his parents, and he finally was realizing he couldn't go on without them much longer.

Jeremy went to bed that night and prayed that his parents would come back. However, he wasn't sincere, his prayers were selfish and greedy.

He woke up the next morning and his parents still weren't home.

On top of being sick, no money, and no food, it was a hot summer day, and the air conditioning broke down. With no idea how to fix it, Jeremy sat all day sweating, hungry, and miserable.

Jeremy couldn't handle it any longer.

"Mom! Dad! Please, I need you. I love you, I miss you, and I'm sorry" Jeremy yelled with all his might.

This time, his prayers were sincere and meaningful.

KNOCK, KNOCK came from the front door. With no clue who it might be Jeremy slowly, carefully, and squeamishly walked to the door.

He couldn't believe what he was seeing. It was his Mom and Dad! Jeremy and Benji jumped in glee and gave their parents a warm hug.

"Did you miss us?" Jeremy's parents questioned him.

"More than you'll ever know!" he responded.

33.
The Struggle Of War
Izaak Gerkis; Senior

Private Tony Blackwell, along with thousands of other Marines, was awaiting his time to disembark the landing craft and step foot onto the volcanic island of Iwo Jima. The landing craft was thirty seconds away from the beach, and Blackwell could feel the butterflies beating their wings in his stomach—he had never been so nervous.

He turned to his friend, Private Frank Bianchi, who he went through basic training with. Blackwell met Bianchi's eyes, and he could see that Bianchi was struggling with nerves as well.

Their sergeant had assured them that there would be little to no enemy resistance on the island, but Blackwell had heard stories about the Japanese and knew that they were smart. Taking Iwo Jima was not going to be a walk in the park like many were anticipating.

The landing craft touched the black volcanic ash on the island, and the Marines began to disembark. Blackwell closed his eyes, took a deep breath, and stepped off the landing craft onto the island. He joined his squad on the embankment as planned and awaited further orders. He was a part of the first wave of soldiers ordered to make an initial sweep on the beach.

The first wave got their order to advance and Blackwell, with Bianchi right beside him, climbed over the embankment and saw the vast nothingness that was ahead of them.

They slowly tiptoed forward, rifles pointed, watching for any Japanese soldiers that may be lurking on the beach. There was an eery silence as the Marines moved forward. Blackwell turned to Bianchi and questioned without speaking. They were given strict orders not to communicate, but Bianchi knew exactly what Blackwell was asking.

Blackwell and the first wave of Marines landed at their objective without any resistance, and the order was given to the next wave of Marines on the embankment to push forward. Blackwell could see Sergeant Thomas peering back at the other Marines pushing forward and was not reassured that everything was going to be okay by the look on his face. Thomas was confused, he didn't know why there was no resistance and he clearly did not like what was going on.

Sergeant Thomas had been in the Pacific since Guadalcanal. For three years, he had been fighting the Japanese, and he knew their tactics like the back of his hand. However, he had never seen anything like this.

"Sarge, what's going on?" questioned Blackwell.

"I don't know, but I don't like it," replied Thomas.

Thomas turned and ran towards the lieutenant in charge to try and convince him that the Marines were walking into a trap. Blackwell followed him with his eyes and saw that he and the lieutenant seemed to be arguing about something. Thomas returned, red-faced with anger, and sat down on the black ash. Blackwell did not dare to ask what was going on.

Only minutes had passed since Thomas returned from talking with the lieutenant, but things had taken a turn for the worst. Artillery was raining down on the advancing Marines, gunfire was erupting from the ground, and every Marine was in a panic to find cover that wasn't there. Sergeant Thomas knew that something was wrong and no one had listened.

Private Blackwell was with Private Bianchi, and they were frantically searching for somewhere to take cover. This was their first taste of battle, this is what they had been waiting for, but it was nothing like they had expected. They were scared, and they didn't know what to do.

Blackwell stopped and began to break down. He looked across the beach and saw the volcanic black ash rise up from the ground. Artillery shells bombarded the beach, tossing bodies like rag dolls.

He couldn't fathom the hell he had been put into.

In Blackwell's moment of absence, Bianchi found a nice area that would shield the two from gunfire, but from artillery shells, well, that would be determined by a higher power.

"What the hell were you doing?" Bianchi exclaimed.

"I don't know what I'm doing here, man," replied Blackwell. His hands were shaking, and the color was absent from his face.

Blackwell dropped his weapon by his side and curled up into a ball in the soft ash. He ran his fingers through the ash and watched the individual granules as they trickled down, finding their home again where they would be safe. Home is where Blackwell wanted to be right now.

Bianchi looked at Blackwell with disgust, grabbed him by the scruff of his uniform and yelled, "What are you doing? Stop crying like a baby, pick up your rifle, and shoot!"

Blackwell picked up his rifle with trembling hands and pointed it out of the crater where they were taking cover. What he saw ahead of him was total chaos. He couldn't find where the Japanese were shooting from.

"Bianchi, where are they?"

"Where are who?" replied Bianchi.

"The Japanese, where are they shooting from?"

"Shoot at the ground, I think they've tunneled."

Blackwell placed his index finger on the trigger and squeezed. The muzzle flashed, there was a loud bang, and the rifle recoiled into his shoulder. He didn't want to know if he had hit someone or not. Blackwell fired off a few more rounds and began to feel reenergized. The adrenaline was coursing through his body now, and he felt more alive than ever. He began to scream and ran from the crater toward the enemy gunfire.

"Blackwell! What the hell are you doing?" Bianchi exclaimed from the cover of the crater.

Blackwell had no idea what he was doing, but somehow he knew it was the right thing to do. He sprinted in between the bodies of the dead, he looked at their faces, some with their eyes wide open, and he felt sorry for them—they would never experience anything like this ever again.

He ran about fifty yards before he heard the faint whistling of an artillery shell in the air. He didn't stop running, but he looked up and at that moment, the shell landed fifteen feet from his position. Blackwell was swept off his feet and thrown into the air like a stick. He landed on his side and could hear nothing but a loud ringing in both ears. He saw a blurry Bianchi running toward him, yelling things that he could not understand. Bianchi reached him and called for a medic.

The medic and Sergeant Thomas, who had seen the entire ordeal, ran to his side to see if he was okay. The medic did a full body search and saw that Blackwell had suffered no serious injuries and was going to be okay. Nonetheless, he was still escorted from the beach to the embankment by the coastline where the wounded were being held for observation.

Blackwell was stuck on the coastline with hundreds of other injured Marines because he had suffered mild trauma to the head when being struck by the artillery shell during the initial landing. He had missed many patrols, but Bianchi would always relay back to him what happened.

Since being stranded on the coastline, Blackwell had time to think about his actions and how lucky he was to have only suffered a mild head trauma. He didn't know what was going through his mind at that moment. He hadn't been trained to run into enemy gunfire and artillery barrage, shouting obscenities, firing blindly, and hoping for the best. Blackwell realized that he needed to control himself and his emotions because it was putting himself and his fellow Marines in harm's way.

"Blackwell!" Private Blackwell turned to see Bianchi running toward him.

"Are you good to go today?" asked Bianchi.

"Yeah, I think so. My head hasn't been throbbing like it was the past couple of days, so yeah, I should be good to go," replied Blackwell.

"Okay, good. You're gonna love the mission Sarge has us doing. Tunnels. We're going into the Japanese tunnels and clearing them out! I can't wait to see one of those bastards face-to-face and blow his head clean off!" Bianchi exclaimed.

"Yeah, sounds like fun."

Blackwell turned to pack his bag and grab his rifle. He began to wonder if he had gotten too lucky on landing day. What if this mission was going to be his last?

He remembered what he had thought when he ran between the lifeless bodies of fallen Marines—that they would never be able to experience this thrill ever again. Now that he was going to experience it again, he realized how stupid he was to think that. Those soldiers had lost their lives, but they were free from this hell on Earth. They would never have to experience anything like that ever again and yet, he was about to go face-to-face with the enemy.

Blackwell and his squad had been walking for almost an hour before they reached their intended target. A Marine with a flamethrower accompanied them on the journey; Blackwell suspected that he would be the one clearing out the tunnels.

The plan was simple: Blackwell and his fellow squad members would be surrounding the entrance of the tunnel, guns pointed, as the Marine with the flamethrower would burn them out. As the Japanese came out of the tunnel, they were going to shoot them one-by-one.

Blackwell aimed his rifle at the entrance of the tunnel, and the flamethrower specialist walked toward the entrance. The Marine squeezed the trigger, and a jet of flame erupted from the barrel, engulfing everything in its path. Blackwell turned to Bianchi who looked stunned, they had never seen anything like it.

The screams of Japanese soldiers could be heard from a mile away. The noise echoed through Blackwell's head as he stood waiting for them to run out of the tunnel.

"Bianchi, I don't know if I can do this," Blackwell said.

"Don't worry about it, just aim and squeeze the trigger," Bianchi replied.

Bianchi looked fierce. His brow was furrowed, eyes staring directly into the entrance of the tunnel, the muscles on his forearm rippled from the tight grip on his rifle—Blackwell had never seen him like that before.

Soon, the sounds of screaming became louder and louder as the fiery Japanese soldiers came closer.

"Get ready men!" yelled Sergeant Thomas.

How could anyone be ready? Blackwell thought.

Within an instant, the soldiers were running from the tunnel. Gunfire rang out, and the enemy soldiers dropped like flies. The continuous barrage of gunfire didn't cease for a few minutes as more and more Japanese soldiers came pouring out of the tunnel. By the end of it, all but one soldier was cheering.

Blackwell hadn't fired a single shot, he just watched the horrors of war unfold right in front of him. He looked around and saw the charred bodies of the enemy. Faces which were once husbands, fathers, sons, or brothers, now melted away and lying face down in the ash of a volcanic hell.

"What's the matter with you?" questioned Bianchi who had a smile from ear to ear.

"What's the matter with me? Did you not just witness that?" Blackwell said shockingly.

"Yeah, I did, but that's the nature of the job."

Blackwell couldn't believe what his friend had become. He promised himself that he would defend his fellow Marines, but shooting burning Japanese soldiers like chickens in a coup was not his idea of defending his brothers.

Bianchi was walking toward one of the fallen soldiers in hopes of finding something special to take home with him. Blackwell watched as he pushed the soldier by his charred shoulder and watched as the black skin fell off the bone. Bianchi was searching every pocket, every nook, and cranny. He moved from body to body in search of a special treasure.

"Bianchi, is that really necessary?" called out Blackwell from the distance.

"You just shut your mouth and mind your own damn business," he snapped back.

Blackwell turned away and sat down on a rock. He continued to watch his friend rummage through the dead. Bianchi seemed to be searching one body for a particularly long time, and Blackwell thought he might have found something. Then, a loud bang.

"Bianchi!" screamed Blackwell.

He sprinted over to his friend and knelt beside him. Bianchi's ribcage was gaping open, exposing his vital organs—there was so much blood. Blackwell's blood soaked hands were trembling, and his vision became blurry as tears began to pour from their ducts. A medic sprinted over, but it was too late; Private Frank Bianchi was dead.

March 26, 1945
Blackwell had witnessed a lifetime of atrocities in one month. After the passing of his friend, Private Frank Bianchi, things

had only gotten worse. He could never get a decent night's sleep because of the nightmares. Once, while out on a mission, Blackwell woke up in the middle of the night in a fit and had to be sent back to the main beach where he would not be a liability. A liability, that's all Blackwell was. He promised himself after the first incident that he'd change, but he never did, especially not after the horrible tragedy at the tunnel.

His only remaining friend, who was more so a mentor than anything, Sergeant Thomas, had been transferred to a different unit. For the remaining days of the battle, Blackwell had to go with no one that he knew or felt comfortable with—he never made any friends.

However, despite all the bad that happened, there was some good. Blackwell had been able to witness the flag-raising on Mt. Suribachi.

He was busy cleaning oil drums—he had been taken off patrols—when all the Marines on the beach started cheering. He looked up at the ominous mountain to see a tiny American flag fluttering in the wind. Blackwell remembered that at that moment, he felt hope that he would get through the battle and that everything would soon be over.

****

Now, he was ready to head home. He sat on the embankment, watching the surviving Marines step onto the landing craft that had once deployed them into hell.

"10th Squad, up on the craft!"

Blackwell slowly got to his feet and approached the landing craft. Before stepping onto it, he turned to face the island one last time. He saluted in remembrance of his dear friend, then turned toward the landing craft and placed his boot on the solid steel floor of the vehicle. Blackwell was finally on firm ground.

The engine roared, and the vehicle began to move away from Iwo Jima. It became smaller and smaller as Blackwell got closer and closer to safety. Blackwell was the first to step on the island and the last to leave.

34.
The Unexpected Killer
Gabby; Junior

As my dad made his way out the door, and said, "Guys, I am leaving. I will be back soon."

I shrugged and replied, "Fine. Leave once again out of the blue, have a fu—" by the time I finished my sentence, the door was already closed, and he drove off. I knew something was suspicious about his scheduled leavings, always around five o'clock on Tuesdays, and on the weekends he would be gone for hours and hours, and he would say that he was at his 'friend's house'. However, everyone in the family knew that it was not a friend that he was visiting. I knew I had to get to the bottom of whatever this was, so I made my way upstairs to the nearest door on the right, to his office, where his computer is. I realized I have never even been in his office, it seemed like I was never welcomed to go in there. Nevertheless, I did not have a lot of time to look because I knew that if my mom caught me in here, I would have gotten in a lot of trouble.

I quickly rummaged through the drawers and found the computer under his work papers in the dark oak drawer connected to his desk. The computer was not locked, luckily. I first noticed his background; it was a picture of my dad, my mom's best friend Sarah, and my mom. Sarah would often come over, and talk to my mom about their lives, children, and husbands. They always try to see who can do the most bragging about their family. Sarah has long golden blonde hair, with bright blue eyes that blind you when you're outside. She is one of the most beautiful people I have seen.

I went through his files, trying to find anything remotely related to something suspicious, but nothing came across that could help me. Until I found the folder named 'phone records'. Though this folder still could not help me, something hit me at that moment, He is no phone expert, and has no clue I could track his phone from my phone. I quickly snatched my phone from my jeans and opened my tracking app to find his locations. I see that he is at my mom's friend, Sarah's house. But, he was making his way to the convenient store, right across from the park I used to go to when I was younger.

The park brought back many cheerful memories for me. The swings, the slides, the naive and innocent children, those were the days where you did not have to worry about what you wore, your grades, and all the bad things that were going on around the world. All of that was just blocked from you by everyone else. I was kind of relieved to know nothing was wrong.

As I put the computer back down under the piles of paper, I came back up with blonde strands of hair stuck to my hand. "Oh... my... God..." I thought shockingly to myself. I came to the conclusion that he is cheating on my mom with Sarah; I was so angry and frustrated. I had to somehow catch them cheating because I knew my mom would never believe the horrible idea that my dad is cheating on her with her best friend. So I decided that the next time he went out, I would follow him and prove what a horrible man he is to her.

After a few hours, I heard the doorknob get unlocked by a key, and my dad had returned with a bag in his hand.

"What's this Dad?" I questioned.

"It's a present for you and your mom, I know I leave a lot, but I just like to still live my own life and do what I want."

"What present did you get me?"

"Check for yourself."

I reached for the bag in his hand and quickly ran to the table to see what he had gotten me. Presents are my weakness, it just brings memories of all the wonderful times I have had during my birthday and other holidays. I lurked through the bag and found a necklace, which I figured was my mother's gift. I looked again and found two front row tickets to my favorite band ever. I excitingly shouted, "You got me tickets to Jerry Stone & The Band! Thank you so much Dad", I rushed in to give him a hug as if I never found out all the information in the office. I decided to choose the present over instincts, but I promised myself I would still look into what was happening with him no matter what.

He then showed my mom her present, and I saw the sparkle in her eyes; she had a lust for materialistic things. I, on the other hand, am quite the polar opposite. I view money as something that should not be spent on something like a thousand dollar jewelry, but memorable experiences like a concert or a journey with friends.

With mom and I both happy, my dad was glad everything was back to okay: In his eyes, but I would not give it a rest. A few days later, he mentioned he was leaving for a work trip, which I thought was weird because he said he had to drive there. So my plan was to follow him for a bit to see what was really happening. With that, I hoped his whole lie would unravel right in front of me.

I woke up Thursday morning ready and prepared for this potentially life-changing journey. In my gut, I knew I should do this, but at the same time, my gut was telling me it was going to be worse than I thought it was. But I live by justice, so I took the risk of the possibility of something happening. I flipped over my silk pillow to grab my secret box cutter and inserted it in my rain boot, just in case. I grabbed my black parka, black beanie, and black earmuffs to blend in with the cold weather, and the dark sky that would appear around dinnertime. I left my room and made my way down the stairs, and I noticed the suitcase next to the door, I knew my dad was ready to leave on his 'trip'. I said my goodbyes to him, and he made his way to the car and proceeded to leave.

As soon as he left the house, I told my mom I had to go retrieve some items from the convenience store, so she permitted me to go. I traveled down the doorsteps and followed the sidewalk directly to my car, I then opened the driver's door, and got into my car. The car was a gift from my dad after he got extremely mad at me and bashed my computer into pieces. So he apologized with a gift of a new car, which I thought was a little melodramatic, he could've just given me a new computer, but I was not going to complain about that. I quickly started the engine, ready to follow my dad, but I realized he was going to notice me in the car. I knew my plan would be impossible to complete, even if I was disguised and went unnoticed. I just proceeded to the convenience store near the park so my mom wouldn't be suspicious why I suddenly changed my mind about going.

I reached the convenience store parking lot and parked right next to the door. I quickly grabbed a few sweets from the candy aisle, and a root beer, just so I had something to bring back.

I then walked out with my newly purchased items and put them inside my coat, but then I noticed something suspicious. There was a black truck with tinted windows parked in the empty parking lot at the park. It looked just like my dad's car, this led me to question everything. I was feeling not only scared but really confused. *Why would my dad be there?* I started to try and draw conclusions, *was he meeting Sarah, and was she his secret lover?* I quickly looked around to make sure no one was watching, and quickly stomped on the half-melted snow towards an old oak tree. I squatted down and moved my head just enough so I could see the car, but still not enough to get caught. Luckily, I was wearing all black, which blended perfectly with the winter evening.

He got out of the car, and slowly proceeded to walk to the swing sets where this twelve-year-old was seated. Her name was Ashley; she lived two doors down from us. She had this beautiful blonde curly hair that glowed so much, you could have spotted her anywhere. She was known as the girl with the bubbly personality, who was going to leave this small town, move to California, and start an acting career. She had starred in every play she has auditioned for. She was born to be a star.

My dad started to talk to her, while gesturing at the car, proposing that she should go to the car. I felt a sigh of relief knowing he was not cheating with anyone and was just helping out a fellow neighbor. Soon enough, they were both walking towards the car, and I got out of my spot to go talk to him. When I reached the halfway point towards my car and his car, I noticed my dad reaching over into the trunk of his truck. He then grabbed a metal frying pan and forcefully plunged it upon Ashley's head, which knocked her out. I mistakenly screamed, which caught his attention in an instant. I was paralyzed for a second, I had just witnessed my dad trying to kidnap a little girl, of who was now laying there unconscious, as the snow absorbed her blood from the aftermath of the frying pan. I quickly snatched out of my frozen state as I saw my dad sprinting towards me with the pan, I bolted towards my car, whilst crying and screaming for help. As I passed the oak tree I was just hiding behind before, I tripped over a stump that was hidden underneath the snow. I knew then my idea of what my dad has been doing all along was better than what was really occurring.

Next thing I knew, I woke up to someone shaking me to wake up. At first, I could not see who it was due to my initial blurry vision, but it soon became apparent that it was Ashley, the girl who was hit with the pan. Ashley questioned, "What are we doing here? Why did your father take us?"

I slowly mumbled back, "I have no clue. But I am going to find out." I then got up from the sleeping bag that rested next to Ashley's on the concrete floor. It was extremely cold, the walls were dirty with cobwebs, and made out of concrete. However, there was a window located on the ceiling, too high for my reaching. It was covered with snow, which in turn blocked out the sun. There was a metal door in the room, which I ran to in an attempt to open it, but it would not open. I banged on the door while shouting, "Let us out of here!" After ten seconds of that, I accepted my defeat and fell to the floor.

Ashley then said, "I have tried it all. Opening the door with my bobby pin, breaking the glass, but nothing has worked. Look what I noticed over there too," she then pointed to the corner near her sleeping bag, and mentioned how there was a bloodstain in the corner. "Looks like we weren't the first visitors," she added.

I was completely shocked, all this time I thought my dad was cheating, but instead he was doing this? It didn't add up. *Why he was going to Sarah's house?*

Hours went by, and all I did was stare at the window, confused and scared, until I heard the door unlock, and Ashley and I both moved next to each other. I felt her left hand reach for my hand. I could feel the fear through the shaking of her palm. My dad did not even acknowledge I was in the room; he just quickly picked up Ashley, whilst she screamed and cried, protesting to be released. I tried to snatch her back, and my dad kicked me in the face, and hurried out, shutting the door behind him. I felt my face beginning to swell up from the kick. I busted out crying as I thought of the horror my father had done.

Never in a million years could I have pictured my dad to turn from an absent father who I thought was cheating on my mom, to a crazy psycho who lures children into his truck. I knew I had to think of a plan to escape quickly, or I would be dead, along with Ashley. So I started to conspire, I thought I could somehow choke him with the sleeping bag, but he would have over-powered me. I knew I couldn't unlock the door, especially since I didn't even know what was behind it. I then reached for the sweets that I still had in my jacket for comfort, it was the only thing that could help me through such a traumatic experience at the time. As I reached for my second candy bar, I felt the root beer and immediately realized my next plan. But I had to wait for Ashley to be here to escape because I knew I would never live with myself knowing she would be here, and I would be safe.

I quickly woke up to the noise of the door again after I took a short nap to regenerate my energy. My hazy vision saw my dad fling Ashley on the floor, and quickly scurry back to the door to lock it and leave. When my vision cleared, I examined Ashley's new hairstyle. Her hair looked like someone put it in a ponytail, then chopped it where the elastic band would be. I questioned, "What happened to your hair?" She just kept crying and crying. Thankfully, it did not look like he did anything else but chop her hair off. Since she was not responding, I told her, "I know a way to get out of here," because I knew that would make her speak up.

"H... how?" she mumbled.

"First, you tell me what he did to you. Then I will tell you my plan," I responded.

She then explained, "Well, after I left this room, he injected something in me. So I don't remember anything that happened for a while until I woke up, and I saw him holding my hair in his hand. He took it to this wig head holder, and he kept mumbling something like, 'This is all for you, Sarah.' I couldn't really hear everything he was saying because I was still lightheaded from the injection. It looked like he already had a few blonde wigs on other wig head holders. Now tell me how to get out of here."

"Just give me a second," I commented.

I was so curious about why he mumbled, "This is all for you, Sarah." *Was he trying to make the wig for Sarah? Did she ask for the wig?* It just did not make sense to me.

Ashley shouted, "Come on! Tell me! I need to leave this place!" She started crying again. I reached over and comforted her until she stopped crying. I knew I could not show weakness or else she would be even more scared.

I whispered to her, "Okay. You are going to use your acting skills and pretend you are really sick. Coughing, sneezing, stomach problems, you figure it out. When he goes to go get the medicine from the pharmacy, we break the window, and I am gonna try with all my power to get you on my shoulders to push you up to the ceiling to escape. Then you are then going to find help nearby, and get them to call the police". Her facial expression went from tears of sadness to a smirk and brightening eyes. It made me feel like I had a purpose when she smiled like that. I knew I was accomplishing something.

We waited for hours, we were both super thirsty. My dad came back with two small pixie cups filled with tap water. I knew if I tried to confront him, he would hurt me again. As he was about to close the door, I nudged Ashley's shoulders, and she started our plant to escape. "Wait!" She coughed at my dad, "I don't feel good at all. I think it's the needle you gave me." She itched her arms really fast to give the look of rashes. "Can you please run up to the pharmacy for some allergy medicine?"she requested.

"Fine, I will be right back," he sternly said while he rushed out the door.

"I can't believe he believed it."

"Well, we've got to act quick. How are we gonna break the window?"she replied.

"Well, we have to give it time, so he leaves, but, look at this," I reached into my coach pocket to get my glass bottle of root beer. "We are going to use this to hit the window. Then we are going to do the plan we said we would." We counted five times to sixty, so we knew he would be gone.

"Are you ready?" I gladly whispered.

"Let's get out of here," she said.

I gestured her to move back to the corner and duck her head, I moved to the other corner and thrust the root beer bottle at the ceiling window. The window shattered into pieces, and the snow came fell to the concrete floor. I went on my knees so Ashley could put her feet on my shoulders. When she was steady enough, I gradually stood up while still holding her, "Can you get it?" I asked.

Yes, yes, I can get it," she confirmed as she jumped at the shattered window. She held onto the edge of the window for a second, then screamed, and collapsed onto me.

"What happened?" I remarked. She pointed to her left hand, which had a small piece of glass in it.

"We have to try this again or else he is going to kill the both of us right now. You are going to get back on my shoulders, then you are going to put one foot on my hand, and I will push you out the window." I bent back down, and she got back on my shoulders, leaving a trail of blood on my shirt. She took her right and placed it on the palm of my right hand. She then quickly placed her left foot on my left hand, and I immediately pushed her as hard as I could out the window. I was so relieved to not see her when I looked up at the window, I knew she made it out.

"Are you okay?" I questioned.

"Yes! I made it out." Ashley confirmed.

"Okay, go run to a neighbor or the closest telephone."

Before I knew it, I heard the police sirens which confirmed this was all over. I heard the police dogs barked, and the voices of many gradually getting closer to me. "She's in there!" I faintly hear. I then catch my eye on a police officer, then two, then three.

"We will get you out of here. Don't worry, you are safe," he told me. All my worries were washed away in that second. I have never felt happier to be alive. A stranger lowered a ladder down for me to climb to escape the room. I reached the top, and finally smelled the fresh winter air, I never knew I would be so happy to see the dead trees of winter time, the memorable ivory snow piled up, hiding the dirt. They proceeded to give me a blanket to wrap around my shoulders, and a cup of hot water to keep my hands warm. They took me to the the cop car to take me to the police station for questioning.

****

Five months later, the investigation on my dad closed. He is locked up for the kidnappings of fifteen children, and the death of thirteen. It's crazy how you can live under the same roof as someone, and not see that they were doing this all along. I found out that my dad never cheated on my mom, though I wish that were the case instead of what he was actually doing. He would actually go to her house, and watch her from the window; he was obsessed with her, and her beautiful blonde hair. He knew he couldn't have her, so he would kidnap girls with the same looks, and was trying to make wigs to remind him of Sarah. I'm just happy, that in the end, justice was served.

35.
Their Eyes Are Watching
Alexis G.; Senior

The Creator looks and searches
The hearts of all men,
And to his disdain he finds:
In the hearts of those who lord
Over His Creation, there is sin
That binds the deeds and actions
Of humankind.

Such was the case of the young man
Who lorded over the oppressed.
In the eyes of those who were like him,
He was a man of great virtue
And reverence.

But in the eyes of those from whom
He was made in likeness,
He was a foolish man;
One of great iniquity.
So much so that the darkness
enslaved within his spirit
Drowned any peak of light.

In his selfish nature, he became
A predator of the night,
Hunting the one he abused and
Wounded for his own desires,
Convincing himself that his desires
Were of noble kind, but

In a haze, guilt lies awake
Pondering the deeds of his actions.
Rising in the madness of his slave,
It stands up and walks into the darkness,
Where he journeys every night.

To that lone house he goes,
Where he commits the horrendous
Acts of his heart,
And leaves the remnants
Of sin dripping from the bedside
Of that Nubian woman.

And if you listen closely, above
The croaking of the creeping creatures,
You can hear her muffled cries,
And the bellowing of her soul,
Agonized by the traps set forth to
Diminish her

Thinking of the glories that were:
To become men and women of honor,
Where the children laugh, play,
And run freely to and fro
In that precious land
flowing with milk and honey;

A land that was once hers.
But in this land of oppression,
She now stands at freedom's gate, knocking.
In which she is met with the horrors of her reality:

Feelings of great death;
A death of her spirit, the
Elusiveness of love, a pure and
True love that had somehow
Been replaced by the infiltrating
Lusts of the man of the night.

So now she stands, becoming
The spirit of freedom
of which she sought,
Running out in the World,
never looking back toward the
Darkness that had clouded her
To the relief of those
who had come before her.

Their eyes are watching as they
Spin uncontrollably in the night.
Swaying against the darkness;
They, dead forms of life,
Stricken by the hands of death
And tormented by the shackles of their skin.

Their restless souls escape to that
Distant land, where they find
Rest in the palms of the Creator.

Then the earth now at peace opens,
Causing rivers of his sin to circle into the day,
Where the dripping blood cannot be hidden,
And the hands of the master cannot be cleansed
Of his wrongdoing.

36.
To Be A Student Athlete For A Day
Ava Suchara; Senior

It begins; that terrible, horrible, ear-piercing noise. You roll over; eyes still closed, and fling your arm across your body in an aim to hit the snooze button on the first try. You miss. You open only your left eye, and all that can be seen is the bright illuminated numbers on your alarm clock; 5:15 AM piercing through the darkness of your bedroom. You awake once again to an even louder noise, this one more startling than the last. You open both eyes now and make out the numbers 5:24 AM. Your heart drops at the same time that you are flinging your bed sheets off of you and swinging your legs from the bed to the floor, standing up but having to sit back down because all the blood just rushed straight to your head. After stumbling into the bathroom, you manage to get both contacts into your eyes and then and quickly slip your too-tight swimsuit over your body. You slip on a pair of sweats and fling your school bag over your left shoulder and your swim bag over your right. After flying down the stairs and jamming your feet into a pair of shoes that may or may not be yours, your head still kind of thumping, you grab a banana in one hand and your car keys in another and continue to fly out the garage door, slamming it shut behind you.

Whipping into the parking lot on two wheels, you choose the parking spot closest to the doors and struggle to yet again get both heavy bags over each shoulder and shut the car door without one or both of them falling to the ground.

5:45 AM: an electric shock suddenly fires through every vein in your body as your plunge yourself into the cold, deep water. The only thing in your path of vision is the color blue, and that one black line that your eyes are forced to follow for the next mile or so. You're flailing every muscle in your body, trying to stay afloat. Your brain feels like its spinning and your eyes are seeing double.

Approaching the wall once again, you sigh out bubbles as it comes the time to fling your legs up and around over your head, place them on the wall, and use all the strength in your legs to push you in the opposite direction. While holding your breath. Flip after flip after flip and your stomach begins to feel a little nauseous.

It's 6:44 AM and you've done more flip-turns than imaginable for this hour of the day. You're on your last lap, approaching the wall and watching tirelessly as your right arm extends as far as it can stretch in aim grab the tiny ledge on the gutter to pull your body into the wall. Your arm reaches toward the wall as if trying to reach for something to hold on to that will save you from drowning, because that's exactly what it feels like.

"Time check!" you yell while you stand in the humid, crowded locker room trying to run a brush through your wet tangled hair.

"7:12!" a voice yells back from around the corner.

Great, you're behind schedule, so today you'll have to settle with your hair in a bun. You quickly slip on your tennis shoes and pull a hoodie over your head, and once again, swing your heavy backpack over your right shoulder, off to class.

"Thanks," you mumble as you're shoving spoonful after spoonful of cheesy potatoes into your mouth while trying to balance your full plate of food that's sitting atop your AP Government textbook that you're struggling to hold with only one hand. Two moms provide breakfast for the team after morning practice, and it's hard not to snatch the entire pan of banana bread and run.

With your head huddled into your folded arms, you drift asleep to the sensation of cold water dripping down the back of your neck. What feels like three minutes later, you awake to yet another startling, ear piercing noise; the bell. You slept through your first hour, again. You glance down at your notebook to see a blank page staring back at you, your eyes drift to the notebook of the person next to you and notice your classmate is three pages deep in notes about Civil Liberties. You roll your eyes both at their tendencies overachieve and your own tendencies to be lazy. Then you fall back asleep.

Dragging your feet as you walk, you scratch your head as you try to figure out what class you are headed to next. Once you remember your next class is on the second floor, you sigh to yourself as your brain tells your feet to take you up the flight of stairs; your sore legs throbbing with each step.

When you're sitting in your third class of the day, you hear that one girl who always gets on your nerves complain about how tired she is. You want to swing around and say something back about how tired *you* are, but you actually are too tired to care about one-upping her.

Running down the science hallway with a coffee in one hand and a half-eaten bagel in the other with your car keys dangling from your pinky finger, you fly into your classroom after lunch, late, again. You suddenly start overheating, then remember that this is the classroom that lacks air conditioning, and it doesn't make it any better than you just ran as fast as you could from the parking lot to your desk by the window. There is a PowerPoint being projected on the promethium board about how to detect different kinds of blood splatter. This is forensic science. You didn't actually learn what the study of forensic science was until the first day of class; it would have been nice to know what it was before signing up for it. And it would be even nicer if you didn't have a class about murder right after lunch.

The end of the day is always conflicting for you. Because on the one hand, it means that your endless day is, actually, reaching closer to the end. But on the other hand, every class that passes by is one hour closer to having to plunge yourself back into the pool.

When the final bell rings at 2:50 PM, you slowly get up from your desk and start headed towards the natatorium; a place where you are convinced you spend an unhealthy amount of time. Your feet are dragging even more so than they were earlier today, and your eyelids feel so heavy that you can actually feel your eyes shutting, opening, shutting, as you make your way down the crowded hallways.

3:05 PM: An electric shock suddenly fires through every vein in your body as your plunge yourself into the cold, deep water.

37.
Trapped
Alexis W.; Senior

It was a regular day in New York on June 5th, 1987. Faith started her morning the way she did every day. She took her shower, put on the clothes she had laid out the night before and ate the breakfast that her mother, Lisa, had prepared before she went to work. She was always on time to school and never missed a day, she had in her mind that if she missed school, she was missing an opportunity to be successful. As Faith leaves home, she notices her neighbor, Mrs. Miller, who works at her school as a counselor. She asked Faith if she needed a ride to school, but Faith wanted to get fresh air, so she politely declined and proceeded to walk.

As time goes on, she checks her watch, realizes she got out the house later than usual and immediately regrets not taking the ride to school. She then comes across a shortcut, a dark, dusty alley that her mom had told her many times never to go through. She stood there for five minutes contemplating her decision until she finally realized she was wasting more and more time. "If I went through the alley how would my mom know?" she thought, trying to convince herself that the choice she was about to make was okay. It wasn't okay. Faith, a thirteen-year-old girl in a rush to get to school, didn't know that her whole life would change for the worse by making one wrong turn. When she walks down the alley she sees a man who looks like he's in need of help, he's on the ground holding his leg as though it was broken. She stops in concern and tries to help the man, as she bends down to see if he's okay he jumps up, tackles her to the ground and covers her mouth with a cloth covered with chloroform. After inhaling the chemical, Faith becomes unconscious.

She wakes up an hour later from a tight pain she feels on her wrist, she looks down and sees she has on handcuffs which are attached to a pole in the basement of a home she is unfamiliar with. Faith is in a panic and doesn't remember when or how she got there. Her mind is roaming free about who could have done this to her, this felt like something that only happened in movies, she tried to convince herself it's a bad dream and pinches her skin until she turns red.

She then realizes that this is real and nothing was going to wake her up. She apprehensively observes her surroundings trying to see if there was a possible way to escape the house, there was nothing. As Faith is looking around, she notices that there aren't any windows and see's what looks like blocks of foam on the walls. It doesn't take Faith long to figure out that she had seen that foam before. A few weeks back she watched a documentary about performing art schools, and they showed a studio where the students could record music. The walls of the studio were filled with this foam. The foam that was in the studio made it so that no one outside of the studio could hear them. That room was sound proof. Tears start to form, and Faith is inconsolable. She keeps asking herself how she even got into a situation like this. "will anyone ever find me? "is the question that crosses her mind the most. Stuck in a windowless and soundproof basement, she wonders how anyone will ever hear her cries for help and how she will get through the dark nights alone.

An hour after school started, Lisa received a very startling call from the principal. Faith never showed up to school. The principal suggests that maybe Faith has skipped school, but Lisa knew that it was something more than that. A mother knows when something is wrong and she was forced to put matters into her own hands.

Lisa left work in a rush. Instantly, the police were called, and a search party was started. She was determined to find her daughter and wasn't going to stop looking for her until she did.

"What happened to Faith?" was the talk around town. Some thought that she ran away from home and others thought that maybe she just got lost, both of these speculations were wrong. Faith had been kidnapped. Her whole life changed by making one wrong turn, and her will to care for others had been taken advantage of.

It is now 2016, and Faith who would now be twenty-nine years old is still missing, the police stopped looking a while ago but Lisa still desperately tries to find her daughter and won't stop looking until she does.

38.
Twenty-Three
Mallory Metikosh; Senior

Twenty-three, once a home,
but now a number
A number so unyielding,
a barrier so secure
Remnants of that night branded into me
like the linguistics of the alphabet

At the door, I ponder,
systematically debate my choices
For her vexation is waiting
and I am the cause

My buoyant mind,
young and optimistic,
wonders if this is the chance
The final encounter, the last blow
of ill-fated feelings
consuming my entirety

Hands lifted, wall up
A soft knock will suffice
I succumb to the terror,
autoscopic phenomena endures;
intently fixed, I lose myself

One abrupt swing of the door,
my childhood door
And I'm confronted by
the matron herself

Eye to eye, face to face
That is when I know,
the infrangible me is gone,
devoured by her

Psychedelic emotions arise,
flooding me with recollections
all too hard to bare
Swallowed by my resentment,
a burden I thought could be destroyed
Has just accumulated, multiplied in size

Head buried, moisture too meaningful
to wipe away
One last look at door twenty-three,
and a house with no place for me

39.
Vanished On Halloween
Gabby Kurschat; Senior

Thud. Abby stumbled backwards recovering from her collision, startled by the impact. "Watch where you're going, or you'll ruin someone's Halloween," remarks a snappy mother as she yanks her son from the sidewalk where he had toppled due to Abby's carelessness.

"Sorry," she muttered. She had no time to be concerned about bumping into children today, though. She strode with a brisk pace to match the biting October air, walking with purpose, but not enough to draw attention to herself. The dusk had settled in the air, and Abby checked behind her shoulder to make sure there wasn't someone following her, shadowing her every move as if the sun were still out.

She could see it just up the block, her sanctuary. The house of her old middle school friend, Jackie, with whom she had been planning to stay until she felt safe enough to return home. She had one year left before she graduated, that is if she made it to the house. Her pace quickened as she approached. Her heavy and unsupportive boots offered no relief from the pain of a stress fracture in her toned runner's leg. Her legs felt heavy from walking so quickly and her lungs stung from the cold air and fast breathing.

She had made it. Her thick rimmed black boots plodded up the large oak steps to the front door. Suddenly, Abby felt her heart beating in her throat and the sense of panic took hold of her body. A large black van with tinted windows was moving remarkably quickly towards her from down the street. Abby pounded on the thick wood of the front door and called out "Jackie! Jackie! It's me Abby," trying to hide the twinge of panic in her voice. The door opened just as the car pulled up to the cozy looking home. Abby quickly pleaded for Jackie to let her in, but the anxiety was so much that she could hardly muster a single full sentence. Jackie looked puzzled and nodded in agreement, but before Abby could choke out a thank you, she was being dragged towards the van by a man dressed in black.

Abby awoke, her bare legs sprawled over a cold floor speckled with dirt and debris. Her wrists were bound together tightly by a pair of dingy handcuffs that attached her to a water pipeline. Her almond shaped fingernails, festively polished in glitter for Halloween, scratched around looking for freedom. She tossed her head to send a stray black curl from her face back into place and peered around the room. She was in what looked like a dimly lit basement, with stray furniture pieces collecting dust and scattered knickknacks sprawled about the shelving units. Her eyes, still adjusting to being conscious, could just make out the figures of what looked like two men across the room. "Hello?" her shrill voice pierced the silent air.

The first man clutched a small backpack to his muscular shoulders. He was a tall black man, relatively young looking but the anxiety on his face aged him a few years. His brown eyes looked into Abby's own as if staring into her soul. His dark brown hair was messily swept under a forest green hat to match his army jacket. Abby watched his hands as he unzipped the backpack, the neatly trimmed fingernails almost looked as if they were shaking from Abby's eyes. His hunched over posture displayed his discomfort in the environment.

The second man stood at the base of the stairs as if guarding the exit. His shifty eyes peered at Abby from across the room, inspecting Abby through a pair of blue eyes with thick black circles beneath them.

Abby broke the quiet stillness with her abrupt attempt to bring herself to the same standing level as her captors, but she quickly stumbled over back onto the floor. She winced and yanked her ankle out from beneath her. The searing pain of a stress fracture had been built upon by her tumble, to create a whole new world of physical pain that helped distract her momentarily from her peril. She looked up to see the taller man gawking at her ankle that was now bent at an angle that no human ankle should. He looked away quickly, embarrassed at being caught staring. "It's a stress fracture," Abby softly said. "I'm on the cross country team at my school." He nodded in response and went back to fiddling with whatever was in the small backpack.

"Hurdles," he said without looking up from his work "I used to run track in high school. My event was the six hundred hurdles."

"I've never done track before. I've always been more of a distance kind of girl." Abby' voice seemed to ring in the quiet air. "You know, gotta outrun the kidnappers" she added with a chuckle. Daniel let the corners of his mouth rise into a half smile. A hush fell over the two of them. It was an uncomfortable feeling to have two opposing forces coming together with similarities. They weren't here to be friends, he was here to kill her. But judging by his shaking hands, she would live to see the sun once more.

"You're pretty chipper despite being tied up in some basement," he mused.

Abby nodded "I like to make the most of every minute. Gotta make it count because you never know when it might all end."

"Daniel, are you almost done? Let's go, we don't have a lot of time; they will be here soon," said the blue-eyed captor by the door. He fidgeted with his feet and checked his watch impatiently. When he angled his body to look up the stairs, Abby caught a glimpse of something that made her heart go cold. The man had a knife, a bit bigger than a kitchen carving knife, tucked into his pants. She felt a tremor run through her body as she remembered her own knife in her shaking hands, covered in sticky blood. She turned back to Daniel who was pouring a clear liquid into a syringe, the look of despair filling his eyes.

"Yeah just give me a minute John I need to do this right. If she escapes, the boss will fire me."

He rubbed the sweat from his palms onto his jeans as he asked "Are we sure this is the right girl?" he inspected Abby skeptically, not believing that the girl he had just joked around with could be the girl he was being paid to kill.

Abby's voice wavered as she pleaded "Please you have the wrong girl! I can prove it! Please just don't kill me I haven't done anything wrong."

Daniel raised his brow with suspicion and took a step closer. "How can you prove you don't work for the corporation?"

Abby slowly untucked her chunky boot from beneath her petite frame "You're going to have to trust me. My driver's license is beneath the sole of my shoe. My name is Olivia Loveland, and I'm eighteen years old." Suddenly Daniel froze and his gaze turned icy with rage. His powerful legs propelled him to the table on which the syringe was resting. "Please, you didn't even look! Why don't you believe me I just want to live!" she pleaded, her shrill voice nervous for her future.

"You killed her." Abby stopped cold.

The sound of Olivia's screaming echoed through her mind, sending a chill down her spine. The hot blood had stuck to her hands, under her nails, staining her once pure and innocent fingers. Death had seized her body almost immediately after the knife struck her chest, leaving her body limp and cold. The emotions of shame and guilt would never leave her. She could feel the boss's hot breath in her ear once more, telling her to kill Olivia or suffer a slow and painful death herself. Olivia had severely compromised the corporation Abby worked for by threatening to give information to the public that would smear the company's squeaky clean reputation. It was never Abby's intention to do the company's dirty work when she took the highest paying job she could find to help pay off her medical bills from her stress fracture. Her parents were already working two low-income jobs a piece, just trying to make ends meet to send Abby to college. With her season over due to injury, she had lost the scholarship that she was relying on to cover the cost of her education. Not only would she have to pay for college, but she would have to pay off the excessive medical bills that come with having a stress fracture. Olivia had simply been a civil rights activist who had found out about under the table jobs such as Abby's and wanted to make a change in the treatment of the workers. Taking the life from Olivia was the hardest thing she had ever willed herself to do. Abby shook off the memories, reminding herself that it was either Olivia or her. There was no way of denying her guilt, so she accepted her fate.

"How did you know?" she whispered.

"She was my sister. My little sister," he said, his face twisted with grief. "She was the kindest person I've ever met. Maybe the kindest I will meet." Daniel approached Abby with the syringe and unlocked the handcuffs. Her thin arm looked weak and frail in the basement lighting, but Daniel knew that he had found the right girl, the killer of his passionate and youthful sister, Olivia.

"What will be the difference between you and me after that goes into my arm?" she said nodding to the syringe that was incredibly close to puncturing her youthful skin. "You don't know anything about me or why I killed Olivia. It wasn't my own choice. I had to do it to survive. You're taking away the life of a teenaged girl who never got to live out the rest of her youth, just as I did with your sister. You and I, we're the same now."

Daniel gripped her arm with an alarming force and through a set of tightly clenched teeth, he choked out the gritty word

"Revenge." With that, Abby watched the long needle tip submerge itself into her arm, letting the toxic liquid soak into her blood. Almost instantly the lights began to fade. Her heartbeat slowed to a mellow pace, its pulse weak for the amount of adrenaline pumping through her veins. As she slipped further and further away from reality, she heard pounding at the front door.

"Perfect," she thought; "Just in time to watch me die." Abby was vaguely aware that her leader was here to retrieve her. She smiled at Daniel, letting out a drug induced laugh. Her slurred words managed to form a sentence "We're the same now," before her body became limp and the life fled her limbs.

Daniel and John fled as quickly as they could, using the adrenaline from taking another human life to fuel their escape. They managed to get to their car, which had been parked through the neighbor's yard one street across from the murder house. Daniel looked out the passenger seat window, watching the houses roll by, but couldn't help but think that maybe he was the same as the young girl he had killed. They had both ended a life, a cruel and cold-blooded act, *but was revenge really a justification to inject Abby with a lethal fluid?* His mind flooded with guilt just as the drug had flooded Abby's healthy pink skin. She was right, they were the same. Daniel always thought of himself as the good guy, his team fought to do the right thing, to keep killers like Abby away from the public. *If Abby hadn't been lying about killing Olivia to save her own life, was she really a cold blooded killer? Is protecting your own life justification for taking another?* He had become a different person, an evil killer, a heartless murderer. If this was true, then why did he feel the same as he always had? *Could it be that evil and good are not as different as we thought? Could they even be the same thing?*

www.ingramcontent.com/pod-product-compliance
Lightning Source LLC
Chambersburg PA
CBHW070843250626
47159CB00003B/903